My heels grew wings like the sandals of Mercury.

My pursuers poured into the street, screaming and cursing. I caught a glitter from something metallic; they had their daggers out. I flew, not daring to look behind me.

But a scream from above made me pause and look up. Something large was descending upon me from an overhead balcony. I had a quick impression of a face that was a mask of blood, a mouth twisted into a grimace of fury and demented eyes.

He landed on me like a stone from a catapult, driving me to the ground and forcing the breath from my lungs. He stood over me, screaming a victory cry. He had won, and I was lost.

*Other Roman Mysteries Featuring
Decius Caecilius Metellus the Younger*
by **John Maddox Roberts**
from Avon Books

SPQR

SPQR II
THE CATILINE CONSPIRACY

JOHN MADDOX ROBERTS

AVON BOOKS ◆ NEW YORK

SPQR II: THE CATILINE CONSPIRACY is an original publication of
Avon Books. This work has never before appeared in book form. This is a
work of fiction, and while some portions of this novel deal with historic
occurrences, actual events, and real people, it should in no way be con-
strued as being factual.

AVON BOOKS
A division of
The Hearst Corporation
105 Madison Avenue
New York, New York 10016

Copyright © 1991 by John Maddox Roberts
Maps by Loston Wallace
Published by arrangement with the author
Library of Congress Catalog Card Number: 90-93563
ISBN: 0-380-75995-0

First Avon Books Printing: April 1991

AVON TRADEMARK REG. U.S. PAT. OFF. AND IN OTHER COUNTRIES, MARCA
REGISTRADA, HECHO EN U.S.A.

Printed in the U.S.A.

RA 10 9 8 7 6 5 4 3 2 1

For
Gerald Page—
Who knows all about mysteries, history,
and, of course, about armadillos.

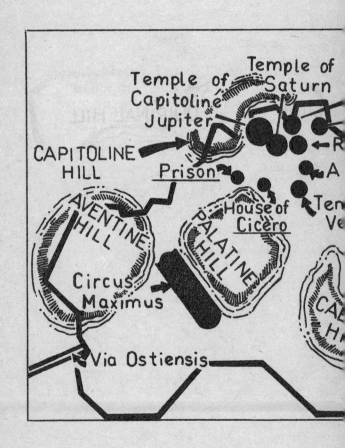

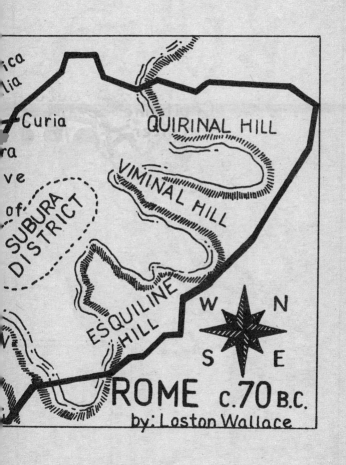

ica
lia

Curia

ra

ve

of.

SUBURA
DISTRICT

QUIRINAL HILL

VIMINAL HILL

ESQUILINE
HILL

W
N
S
E

ROME c.70 B.C.
by: Loston Wallace

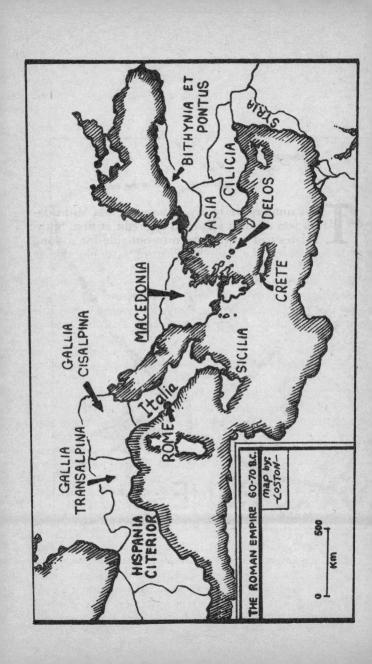

I

That summer we received the news that Mithridates was dead. It was hard to credit at first. Mithridates had been a thorn in our side for so long that he seemed like a force of nature, as immutable as sunrise. Only the oldest citizens could remember a time when Mithridates had not been there to plague us. He died old and friendless, somewhere in the Cimmerian Bosphorus, plotting yet another sally against Rome, this time an invasion of Italy by way of the Danube. He was the most consistent of enemies and we would miss him.

The news came in the midst of a splendid summer, one of the finest in living memory. It was a time of peace and prosperity. The civil wars of Marius and Sulla were fast fading from memory, the horrors of their murders and proscriptions seeming to belong to another age. Everywhere, Rome was victorious. In the East, Pompey was the overwhelming victor. He had smashed the Mediterranean pirates and then he had gone on to subdue Asia, Pontus and Armenia, robbing Lucullus of the final glory for which he had fought so long and so honorably. Crete had been subdued after a long and desultory campaign. Who was left to threaten Rome? Carthage had been exterminated generations before, its ruins plowed under and sown with salt so that nothing would grow there. The East, from Cilicia to Palestine, was under the Roman heel, only remote Parthia remaining independent. To the south, Egypt was a joke, fat and indolent as an overfed crocodile. Africa and Numidia were muzzled. In the west, Spain was a taxpaying province. To the north were some Gallic tribes that had not yet been civilized, wearing long hair and trousers and providing the comic playwrights with good material for laughs.

The answer, of course, was that we Romans would ourselves provide the enemy. We were poised on the brink of yet another series of civil wars, convulsions so vast that they would be fought all over the world. The wars were still years in the future, but as I look back upon it, that was the last summer of the old Republic. It died in the fall.

None of that was apparent at the time, though. There are those who would argue that it never truly died, that our esteemed First Citizen actually restored the Republic. That is the talk of fools and toadies. I am now too old to care what the First Citizen thinks of me, so I will describe these events as I lived them. If his ancestor, the Divine Julius, comes out looking less than godlike, it is because I knew Caius Julius back then and the First Citizen didn't. Hardly surprising, considering that the First Citizen was born that year. Fitting, in a way.

None of these weighty matters troubled us that summer. The most serious political controversy of the day was the action of the *Praetor* Otho. Four years before, as Tribune of the People, he had introduced a law reserving fourteen rows of seats in the theater for the *equites*, the moneyed-but-not-noble class. Now, as *praetor*, he upheld it. There were no riots, but he was hissed every time he went to the theater.

The great event of the season was the triumph of Lucullus. He had returned to Italy almost four years earlier and had petitioned the senate for permission to celebrate a triumph in recognition of his victories over Mithridates and Tigranes. Pompey had manipulated the Tribunes to block this, but Lucullus had finally been granted permission. Until that time, he had been compelled, by ancient custom, to dwell outside the walls of Rome, where he had company. Quintus Marcius Rex, the victor of Cilicia, and a kinsman of mine, Quintus Caecilius Metellus Creticus, victor of Crete, were likewise blocked by Pompey's adherents from celebrating their hard-earned triumphs. Pompey had a simple interpretation of natural law: all the glory in the world belonged to him, and anybody else who got any was guilty of thieving.

The triumphal procession was a splendid one, for Lucullus had smashed some great armies and had taken immense booty at Tigranocerta and Artaxata and Nisibis. I watched this triumph wind its way into the Forum, from my place atop the *Rostra,* so I had a good view. First came the trumpeters, sounding shrill, snarling blasts on their instruments. Behind them came the standard-bearers of Lucullus's legions. These, like all soldiers in the procession, wore only their military boots and belts in token of their status. Armed soldiers were forbidden to enter the city by ancient law. After the standard-bearers came a float bearing a colossal reclining image of Jupiter with white sacrificial bulls in tow. Then there were more floats carried by soldiers, bearing great paintings of the battles. Then came more soldiers, all in snowy new tunics, gilded wreaths on their heads, palms of victory in their hands, draped with flower wreaths, showered with flower petals by pretty slave girls, accompanied by drummers and flute-players who kept up a shattering din.

Then there were trophy floats bearing the captured arms of the defeated enemy. These were artfully constructed to resemble the impromptu trophies set up on the battlefields in the old days, when the soldiers lopped the limbs from a nearby tree and hung it with captured weapons. Each of these floats bore such a tree, glittering with swords and spear-points, brilliant with polished armor and colorful with painted shields. Plumed helmets were scattered about among sheaves of arrows. Seated all around the bases of the trophies were dejected prisoners, bound and haltered. Considering the lapse in time between the victories and the triumph, these prisoners may have been hired stand-ins. After the trophies came yet more prisoners, more sacrificial animals, a whole train of musicians, and then the spectacle everyone was waiting for: the loot.

The gasps and cheers that greeted the plunder of Tigranocerta drowned out even the racket of the musicians. There were platters of solid gold, jeweled cups, chains of silver, carvings of ivory, chests decorated with amber, precious vases, crowns, scepters, fabulous works of art taken by the eastern monarchs from the Greek colonies. There were even signs painted on white wood giving the figures for ransoms and the sale of prisoners as slaves. There were bolts and heaps of brightly dyed silk, a fabric worth far more than its weight in gold. There were plain gold and silver bars, as large as building bricks and enough of them to build a medium-sized temple. All this was greeted with ecstatic outcries of Bacchic intensity. Say what you will about Romans as conquerors, we have always taken an honest delight in plunder, theft and rapine. It is one part of our souls that hypocrisy has never touched.

Finally, almost last in line, came the man of the hour, Lucius Licinius Lucullus Ponticus himself. The soldiers had already marched out of the city and had the gates shut behind them, because by yet another ancient law, a general and his soldiers could not be in the city at the same time. He looked like an Etruscan statue, dressed in a triumphal robe of Tyrian purple. Below his wreath of gilded laurel, his face was painted red, as were his hands which held a scepter and an olive branch. He rode in a gilded chariot drawn by four white horses and behind him stood a slave who, from time to time, whispered in his ear: "Remember, thou art mortal."

Last of all came one man, the most distinguished of the prisoners. Since Lucullus had not captured Mithridates, and Tigranes had made a deal with Pompey, this honor fell to one of the generals of Tigranocerta. The chariot rounded the *Rostra* and began its climb to the Capitol. At that time, the final prisoner was led away to the prison below the Capitol, where he was strangled. I could feel some sympathy for the man. I was clapped in the prison once, and it was an unpleasant place to occupy, much less to die in.

Only one thing marred the proceedings, and that was the condition of the Temple of Jupiter Capitolinus, where Lucullus was to sacrifice a bull upon being told of the prisoner's death. Two years before, lightning had struck the temple, and the *haruspices* had been consulted concerning the omen. They had pondered and duly proclaimed that the old statue of Jupiter must be replaced by a new, larger statue, this one facing east, toward the Forum. Once in place, this would aid the Senate and People in detecting plots against the state. On the day of Lucullus's triumph, the statue still stood outside the temple, where a huge hole had been made in the wall. Carefully and painfully, an inch at a time, it was being moved toward the hole.

The reason for my privileged position atop the *Rostra* was my office. I was *quaestor* that year, the lowest of the elected officials. Other *quaestores* acted as personal assistants to the Consuls, or traveled about Italy and even the overseas Roman holdings conducting inquiries and investigations, or at least got to go to Ostia to oversee the grain shipments. Not I. I, Decius Caecilius Metellus the Younger, was assigned to the treasury. This meant that I spent my days in the Temple of Saturn overseeing the public slaves and freedmen who did the actual work. They would have a lot of work to do, after the triumph. Lucullus was to donate a handsome proportion of the plunder to the treasury and the military standards would be returned to their place of honor in the temple, until such time as those legions should be reactivated.

As I descended from the *Rostra* to the pavement, I had only pleasant prospects before me, always excepting my dismal duties in the treasury. As a public official, I was invited to the great banquet Lucullus would host that evening, following which he would sponsor several days of games in gratitude to the gods and in honor of his ancestors. There would be plays and races and combats and feasting, with an extra dole of grain, oil and wine to the public. Lucullus would dedicate a new temple to Minerva, which was his gift to the city.

And, it was a beautiful day. Rome was not a beautiful city, but the Forum with its magnificent public buildings and temples was the most majestic setting in the world, and that day it was draped in huge wreaths of flowers and was carpeted with the petals that had been strewn by the slaves and cast down upon the procession by people standing on balconies and rooftops. Everywhere, the city

smelled of flowers, of incense rising from the temples,
of the perfumes lavishly splashed on everyone at these
celebrations.

It was with a light heart that I crossed the Forum to
see to the storing of the gold and the standards. Official
business was forbidden on a day of triumph, but an exception was naturally made in this case. I passed the
Temple of Janus, that most Roman of deities whose two
faces gazed out through the open front and back doors
of his temple. The doors were shut only when no Roman soldiers were at war anywhere in the world. I did
not know what the temple looked like with its doors
shut, since they had never been closed in my lifetime.
They had not been closed, in fact, since the reign of
King Numa Pompilius, who had built the temple more
than six hundred years before. There was a legend that
the doors were closed for a few days during his reign.
With a history like that, it is no wonder that we grew so
adept at warfare.

At the Temple of Saturn I pretended to supervise
while an old state freedman named Minicius, who had
spent most of his life in the temple, performed the actual task. My own contribution had been to unlock the
doors, since I was the *quaestor* entrusted with the keys
that day. While the endless, sweating procession of slaves
carried the loot into the treasury chambers below the
temple, I watched the soldiers carefully and reverently
place the standards in their holders, to be watched over
by the age-blackened image of Saturn.

One of the soldiers, satisfied that he had placed a
gleaming eagle properly, walked unsteadily over to me.
He was very young, slightly drunk, and flower petals
stuck to his sweaty arms.

"Excuse me, sir," he said, his voice thick with Gallic
accent. "Could you tell me why the old gentleman
there"—he jerked his chin toward the image of Saturn—"is wrapped up like an Egyptian mummy?"

I contemplated the statue. I had known it all my life,
and it had never occurred to me how strange it must
look to someone who had never before been to Rome,
wrapped as it was in woolen bands.

"They are supposed to prevent him from leaving Roman territory," I informed the youth. "They are only loosened during Saturnalia."

"Might as well," the boy said. "Everybody else gets pretty loose then."

Just then Minicius came up from the basement, a scandalized look on his face. "You men should be back in your camp!" he said. "Soldiers aren't supposed to be in the city while the *triumphator* is within the *pomerium!*"

"Easy, old fellow," said a hard-faced veteran. "These are the sacred emblems of the legions and we have to see them stored properly."

"We promise not to overthrow the state while we're here," said another.

"Let it go, Minicius," I said. "Our soldiers deserve a little license on their day of triumph." The men saluted and left, respecting my aristocratic grammar if nothing else.

"*Those* are soldiers of Rome?" Minicius said. "I didn't hear a City accent among the lot."

I shrugged. "Except for officers, the legions are all provincials now. They've been that way since Gaius Marius. What City man ever takes service with the eagles any longer?"

"You need to sign for this next load, *Quaestor*," he reminded me. As we walked back toward the basement stair, a group of slaves came in through the front portal and, confused by the sudden dimness, went to the right, toward a low doorway in the wall.

"Not that way, you idiots!" Minicius shouted. "The treasury's this way!" He pointed to the stair that lay almost beneath Saturn's wool-wrapped feet.

"What's through that door?" I asked. I was not terribly familiar with the temple, except for the parts open to the public during festivals.

"Just stairs leading down to some old storerooms," Minicius told me. "Probably haven't been used in a hundred years. We ought to brick it up."

We went down into the basement and I watched while the treasure was put away and then signed for it. When everyone was gone except for Minicius, I locked the iron doors and we went back up the stairs.

Outside, evening was coming on. But the days of summer are long, and it was still bright. The city was still rollicking with its holiday cheer. It was almost time for the banquet to begin, and my stomach was reminding me that I had not eaten all day in anticipation of the feast.

The banquet was to be held in the beautiful garden adjoining the new temple Lucullus was to dedicate the next day. I descended the steps and turned in the direction of the garden. I saw a man walking toward me through the rejoicing throng. He wore a purple-striped senator's tunic and his feet were bare. I groaned. A Senator's tunic coupled with bare feet meant one thing: Marcus Pórcius Cato, the most formidably boring man in Roman politics. He attributed all the ills of the day to our failure to live as simply as had our ancestors. He regarded himself as the exemplar and embodiment of antique virtue. The early Romans had not worn shoes, so he didn't either. He had just won election as Tribune for the next year, hinting all the way that it would be unpatriotic and an insult to our ancestors not to vote for him. He gave me a good old-Roman salute.

"Hail, *Quaestor!* It is good to see an official who is ready to look after his duties even on a holiday."

I jerked a thumb over my shoulder in the direction of the temple. "There are about fifty million *sesterces* in there with my name on them. When I'm out of office next year, some fool is sure to prosecute me for embezzlement if I can't account for every last copper *as.*"

"Most conscientious," Cato said, utterly immune to irony. "I am on my way to the banquet of Lucullus. Will you accompany me?"

With no graceful way out, I agreed, keeping pace with him in my decadent, degenerate sandals. He stepped out at the standard legionary pace, which was decidedly more vigorous than my customary urban amble.

"It was a splendid triumph, splendid!" Cato said. "I fought tirelessly in the Senate to obtain this honor for Lucullus."

"Your efforts have been an inspiration to us all," I assured him.

"Pompey's supporters have grown insufferable. Did you know that Balbus and Labienus are trying to push through a law that will allow Pompey the right to wear the garments and attributes of a *triumphator* at all public games?"

Hardened cynic that I was, I stumbled at this news. "Are you serious?"

"I am always serious," he said seriously.

"This is going a bit far," I admitted. "Of course, you can expect something like this from a man who named himself 'the Great' when he was barely in his twenties."

"A bit far? It is impious! An affront to the immortal gods! What next? A crown, perhaps?" Cato's face had gone quite red. It looked as if apoplexy might snatch him from our midst, a prospect I was prepared to accept with philosophical resignation.

"Now Lucullus," he said, calming, "is a general of the old Roman type. I cannot condone his taste for luxury, but the way he disciplines his legions is exemplary. His administration of the Asian cities was a model of honesty and efficiency."

I had to agree with that. It was also merciful, but that was not something Cato would have perceived as virtuous. We were walking downhill, toward the river. While Lucullus had waited in his villa outside the city, his agents had purchased a piece of unused, marshy ground that had never produced anything but mosquitoes. They had drained it, laid out and planted the lovely garden, and erected the fine temple to the goddess of wisdom and patroness of craftsmen. At that date, she had not yet fully taken on the attributes of the Greek Athena, to become a patroness of war.

Images of all the state gods had been set up at the entrance to the garden, along with an altar to the unknown god. Cato insisted on stopping before each to toss a pinch of incense onto the coals glowing in braziers beneath them. As we walked into the grove, a leather-lunged herald announced us.

"Senator Marcus Porcius Cato and the *Quaestor* Decius

Caecilius Metellus the Younger!" he bellowed. I tipped
him and complimented him on his splendid volume.

"You're the second Decius Metellus I've announced,
sir," he said.

"Oh, my father is here?"

"Yes, sir, and several of the Quintuses."

Perhaps I should explain here. I come of a pestilen-
tially numerous family, distinguished beyond words, one
of the most important families in politics, but dreadfully
unimaginative in the way of names. For generations,
most of the males have been named Quintus. In that
particular year, there were no fewer than five in public
life, all named Quintus. Of Quintus Caecilius Metellus
Creticus, waiting outside the walls for his triumph, I have
already made mention. He was not granted permission
until the next May. There was the *Praetor* Quintus Caecilius Metellus Celer. The *Pontifex Maximus* Quintus
Caecilius Metellus Pius, under whom I had served in
Spain, lay on his deathbed; and his adopted son, Quintus Caecilius Metellus Pius Scipio Nasica, was also a *pontifex*. Rounding out the lot was Pompey's legate, Quintus
Caecilius Metellus Nepos, who had that year returned
from Asia and, like Cato, had won election to the next
year's Tribunate. For purposes of clarity, I shall hence-
forth refer to them as Creticus, Celer, Pius, Scipio and
Nepos.

I took my leave of Cato and made my way into the
crowd. All the most distinguished men in Rome were
there, even Lucullus's enemies. A triumph was, after all,
a gesture of gratitude to the gods of the state, so it was
not considered hypocritical to have a good time at your
enemy's victory banquet. Long tables had been set up
between the rows of fragrant trees, some of them almost
full-grown, that had been brought up the Tiber in
barges, their roots balled in great masses of dirt. The
planting of this garden had been a logistical feat on a
par with building a pyramid.

A large number of women were there as well, many
of them as important in the affairs of the city as their
husbands, some merely infamous. It was a great time for

infamous women. A troop of stately Vestals lent dignity to the occasion, one of them my aunt.

I made no attempt to greet the guests in any orderly fashion, as would have been expected at an ordinary gathering. I did seek out the Consuls. A junior official was expected to be able to find them in any size of crowd. The Consuls for that famous year were, as everyone remembers, even now, Marcus Tullius Cicero and Caius Antonius Hibrida. I found them with Lucullus, greeting some of the throng of foreign ambassadors who always were honored guests at this sort of affair. It was thought a good idea to impress upon foreigners how inevitably preeminent we Romans were in war, and how magnanimous we could be. Some of the guests were former enemies who had surrendered on good terms, rather than prolonging their foolish resistance.

Cicero had achieved the height of his dignity. He was a man who had come from nowhere (that is to say, he was not from Rome but from Arpinum, a town that had enjoyed Roman citizenship for a mere 125 years), and had risen through the world of Roman politics with the speed and force of a stone hurled from a catapult. He was what we called *novus homo* in those days, a "new man" not belonging to one of the old political families. This did not sit well with a good many of his contemporaries, but few men win the consulship without acquiring enemies along the way.

His colleague, Hibrida, had been last among the candidates, but had won through Cicero's support. This was the sort of political deal that went by the wonderfully apt name of *coitio*. As an Antonine, Hibrida had all that family's famous combination of geniality and viciousness, of astuteness and childish impulsiveness. This dichotomy was even more pronounced in Caius Antonius than in most of his family. His odd *cognomen*, which refers to the offspring of a domestic sow and a wild boar, was bestowed in recognition of his half-savage nature.

He was in a good mood that evening and took my hand heartily. His face was flushed and he was well on his way to drunkenness, even at that early hour, another Antonine characteristic.

"Good to see you, Decius, my boy. Splendid triumph, today, eh?" I could see that the sight of all that gold had done him good. The Antonines were also famously greedy, although by way of compensation they spent as freely as they stole. They were fearsomely violent and rapacious, but nobody ever said they weren't generous.

"A glorious occasion," I agreed, "and well earned by the *triumphator*." I nodded toward where Lucullus stood, in a plain toga now and with the red paint washed off, amid a crowd of well-wishers.

"It makes me eager to accomplish something of the sort myself," Hibrida admitted. This, I thought, did not bode well for Macedonia, the proconsular province he would govern after his year in office.

Cicero greeted me as warmly, although with somewhat more formality. We had always got along well together, but at this time he had achieved the peak of public service and I was at the bottom. By this time he had acquired the vanity and self-importance that marred his otherwise admirable character. I had liked him better when he was younger.

The smells of the feast-in-preparation made my stomach grumble and I fought down the urge to grab one of the cups being passed so freely about. Brawny slaves strolled about with heavy amphorae balanced on their shoulders, making sure that the cups stayed full. If I were to start drinking too soon, I might not remember the banquet at all.

Standing beneath a lovely cypress was a very unlovely man. A great scar crossed his face, nearly halving his nose. This was my father, Decius Caecilius Metellus the Elder, but known to all and sundry as Cut-Nose, for obvious reasons. He was dressed in a snowy toga and immense dignity. He had recently returned from his proconsular province of transalpine Gaul, and had not yet recovered from the godlike status of that office. I went to speak to him and he greeted me in his usual fashion.

"Still sober, eh? Responsible office must have improved you. How goes it at the treasury?" He took it as a sign of my ineptitude and unpopularity that I hadn't been given one of the better quaestorial assignments. He was right.

"Lucullus should have built us a new temple to Saturn," I replied. "We'll be stacking the loot on the roof soon."

"You'll find out soon enough that it flows out as fast as it comes in. Faster, more often." His look was even more sour than usual, probably because he had never celebrated a triumph and now would probably never have the chance. His proconsulship had been without a decent war. He was scowling at a strange-looking group of men who stood by an ornamental pond, admiring the carp, drinking heavily and appearing uncomfortable. A few were decently shorn and togaed, but most had long hair and mustaches and wore tunics with trousers, vividly colored in patterns of stripes and checks.

"Who are those?" I asked Father.

"Allobroges. They're a pack of savages from the northern part of my former province. They've come to town to complain about extortion on the part of Roman officials. They'll probably get some ambitious lawyer to bring me up on charges."

"Complaining of Roman extortion has become a minor branch of philosophy," I noted. "Any justice on their side?"

"They're just born troublemakers who can't stand to pay their taxes," Father said. "Oh, I won't say the local publicans haven't turned the thumbscrews a bit too tight from time to time, but that's to be expected. It's nothing compared to what their old chiefs used to put them through. They're just sulking because we won't let them fight each other anymore."

"Well, Father, now that you're home," I said, bored with the subject, "what do you plan to do?"

"Do? Why my usual duties as patron and friend, what else?" he said innocently. He looked as innocent as a man with a bloody dagger in his fist.

"There will be an election of Censors next year," I reminded him, as if he needed it. "The office used to be a family tradition. No Metellan has held it in ages."

"And why should I not stand for Consul again?" he said. "I will be eligible in seven years."

"Father," I said, finally taking one of the winecups being offered by the servers, "in seven years, all of our generals will be fighting for that office. They'll have their armies camped outside the gates to remind the citizens how to vote. That's no time for a moderate like you to be standing for Consul. The censorship, now, is the capstone of a political career. How many men have ever held every office, including that one?"

Father nodded as if he hadn't been thinking the same thing for years. "True," he grumbled. "And it *is* a family tradition."

This set my mind at ease. He was not seriously considering a run for the consulship. The censorship, on the other hand, carried no *imperium* and thus was not coveted by generals. What it did carry was the power to purge the roll of Senators deemed unworthy. I was sure that Father was already at work on his list.

The wine, an excellent Caecuban, struck my senses with inspiration. "Father, why wasn't I named Quintus?"

"Eh? Why, because you were named after me, idiot!"

"It's just that it seems every other male in the family is named Quintus except for the odd Lucius."

"Your grandfather, whose mask you pass every time you enter my house, was visited by the Dioscuri in a dream. They promised him victory over the Samnites the next day if he would name his firstborn son Decius, a name never before used in *gens* Caecilii."

"Did he win?" I asked.

Father glared at me. It was something he did well. "This is a rather large banquet. I am sure there are many fools who would relish your company and conversation. And get a wreath."

I went in search of more congenial company. Heeding Father's warning, I took a wreath and a garland from a slave girl. Vine leaves, guaranteed to forestall drunkenness. In the center of the garden had been set up the paintings of Lucullus's battles that had been carried in the triumph. I went to examine them while the light held. Soon the torches would be lit, providing excellent illumination for intrigue or seduction, but not the best for appreciating art.

These huge panels had been commissioned from the best studios of Athens and Rhodes. They depicted, with wonderful liveliness and detail, the greatest battles of the campaigns against Mithridates and Tigranes. Lucullus was always shown slightly outsized, in the middle of the action. The foreign kings were likewise larger than life, but were always depicted in terrified flight. In their usual fashion, the Greek artists had depicted the Roman soldiers armed like the warriors of Alexander's day or even earlier, in muscled breastplate, high-plumed helmet and great, round shield and bearing a long pike. But the dead and dismembered barbarians littering the bottom of each panel were painted most realistically.

"Nicely executed, don't you think?" The man who spoke was an old friend, the physician Asklepiodes, who treated the gladiators of the Statilian school. He had become famous for his writings about the human body and how to treat its wounds.

"Beautiful," I said. "But the artists ought to take the trouble to find out what Roman soldiers look like before they try to paint them."

"It would make no difference," he said. "Greek artists are taught to revere the ideal and paint what is beautiful. Roman military equipment is ugly and functional, so they go back to the graceful designs of antiquity." He leaned forward and peered at a picture of Lucullus. "You see, the general is shown here as a handsome young man, which is not how he looked when I spoke to him a few minutes ago."

I leaned closer to see for myself. "You are right. He didn't look that good in red paint and a purple robe." I straightened and strolled down to another painting. "How goes your work?"

"I may remove to Capua for a while. The Statilian school in Rome will close down temporarily, until a new one is built."

"Closing down? Why?"

"Haven't you heard? General Pompey has bought the property. He plans to demolish the school and its an-

cillary buildings to erect a magnificent new theater with
an attached meetinghouse for the Senate. It will be a
permanent building of stone, in the Greek fashion."

"Leave it to Pompey to come up with something outrageous like that," I commented. About a century before
this time, somebody had begun a permanent, Greek-style
theater, but the Censors had ordered it demolished before it was completed in order to combat encroaching
Greek laxness of morals. We had only had temporary,
wooden theaters since that time, complete, now, with
their fourteen infamous rows reserved for the *equites*. As
it turned out, Pompey forestalled criticism by building
his tremendous theater with a little temple to Venus
Victrix atop it, so that he could say that the seats were
actually steps to a temple. He was not without a sense
of humor.

A bellow from the heralds announced the beginning
of the feast, and I sought my place eagerly. A servant
guided me to the central table, at the head of which
reclined Lucullus himself. A single, long couch ran the
length of the table, beyond which was a narrow space
for the servers, and then a lovely pool at one end of
which stood a statue of Juno with one of Venus at the
other. In the water, performers costumed as Tritons and
Nereids frolicked. This was the most distinguished table,
with the Consuls and *praetores*, along with proconsuls
and *pontifices*, further down the *aediles* and *quaestores*. As
the least of these, I was well down toward the foot of
the table, but it was nonetheless a great honor to lie at
his table on such a day. I could almost have hit his couch
with a javelin.

A slave took my sandals and I sprawled on the couch
just as the servers began to set platters before us. Lucullus had always been noted for his taste for luxury,
but this was the first of the banquets for which he became even more famed than for his victories. These were
noted not only for the excellence of the food, but for
their theatrical effects. The first platter set before me
and the diners near me, for instance, consisted of hard-
boiled and baked eggs of many species of birds in a
framework of pastry, ascending tier upon tier, forming

a model of the great Pharos lighthouse at Alexandria. Perfumed oil burned in a bowl at its crest.

The succeeding dishes continued the nautical theme. A trireme sailed by rowed by roast suckling pigs, which slaves dressed as sailors transferred to the table. Roast fowl were brought, with their feathers replaced so that they appeared to be alive, but they had been cunningly joined to the bodies and tails of mullets, so that they looked like mythical, hybrid sea creatures.

Lest we starve between these imaginative servings, the tables were heaped with more prosaic eatables: breads, cheeses, nuts, olives, tiny grilled sausages and so forth. All of this was washed down with excellent wines, any one of which would have been the showpiece of an ordinary banquet. Besides the noble Falernian, Lucullus served the finest wines of Gaul and Judea, the Greek islands, Africa and Spain. For the adventurous, there were novelties such as date wine from Egypt and berry wines from Armenia, taken at the siege of Tigranocerta. One of the best was from nearer home; an unusually fine vintage from the slopes of Vesuvius.

"I think our host is confused," said someone to my left. I twisted around so I could see who it was.

"Confused?" I said.

"Yes," said a red-haired, red-faced man who examined the beautiful embossed figures decorating the bottom of his cup. Instantly, a slave filled it. "I think he should have built that temple to Bacchus, not Minerva."

"Hello, Lucius," I said. "I've been so busy gorging myself I didn't notice who was near me."

"We can always socialize. How often do we get a chance to eat like this?" He reached out and seized a grilled rib of a wild German aurochs. The whole rack of ribs had been formed into the likeness of Neptune's crown.

This was Lucius Sergius Catilina, a man I knew slightly. He had sought the consulship more than once and the most recent time had come close to winning. There had been such hard feelings that Cicero had worn armor to the elections. Catilina could put up a jovial

front, but inwardly he was consumed with envy for all
who were richer and more successful.

"I never thought to see you at the same table as Cicero, even at such a distance." It was not the most diplomatic thing to say, but I had been loath to waste all
that splendid wine. Luckily, he took it with good humor.

"Even the sight of that face won't spoil my appetite
for a feast like this. Here, boy," he called, holding up
his cup, "more of that Judaean."

"Too bad Cato doesn't share your delight in this
bounty," I observed. Several places up from me, Cato
was restricting himself to bread, cheese, olives, and occasional bits of grilled meat or fish. He drank as much
as anyone else, though.

"Do you know why Cato drinks so much while he rails
against all other forms of indulgence?" Catilina asked.

"Why is that?" I tore into a roast kid that had been
part of the *Argo*'s crew just moments before. The ship
made its stately way along the table as the slaves reduced
its crew at each place.

"It's because it hurts so much the next morning." We
both found this extremely funny and laughed immoderately. Catilina could be good company when he put
himself out, and he was putting himself out that evening.

"Someday, Decius," he said, pouring a bit of wine on
the ground in token of a vow, "I'll be able to give a
banquet like this."

"The way Pompey's going," I said, "there won't be
anybody left to triumph over."

"There will always be plenty of enemies," he assured me.
"At least men like Pompey and Lucullus have earned their
places of honor. What is Rome coming to when a jumped-up lawyer reaches the highest position over men who have
given their lives in service to the state? Men who are of the
highest birth?" That was more like Catilina. He was a patrician and, like most such, thought his birth entitled him
to office. Then he changed direction again.

"Ah, don't listen to me. I can talk like that every day.
This is an occasion for rejoicing. Hard to believe, isn't
it, old Mithridates dead, I mean? He was causing us grief

back in the consulship of Claudius and Perperna, back when Sulla was still *propraetor* in Cilicia." He took on a nostalgic look as the next course was served; lark's tongues in caper sauce, as I recall. Catilina had been one of Sulla's more bloodthirsty supporters during the proscriptions and had done well out of them. He had good cause to be nostalgic, for the newer generation of politicians, men like Cato and Caesar, were pushing for prosecution of Sulla's executioners as his old supporters faded from power.

Thinking of this, I looked around to see where Caius Julius might be. He and his brother Lucius were not in office that year, but they had been given a praetorian appointment under a bill introduced by the Tribune Labienus to try the *eques* and financier Rabirius for the murder, almost forty years before, of the Tribune Saturninus. Considering what the times had been like, this was rather like prosecuting a gladiator for his victories, so the obsolete charge of *perduellio* had to be brought against the old man, relating to the semi-sacred status of the Tribunes of the Plebs. Oddly, his son later became a fervent supporter of Caesar, but then, sons and fathers often do not agree, I have noticed.

Finally, I spotted Caius Julius at another table, keeping company with that gaggle of Allobroges. This struck me as odd, because I never knew Caius Julius to socialize with anybody unless he had a political motive, and those long-haired barbarians certainly had no votes in the assemblies. All I could imagine was that he had arrived late and that was the only place left.

Trained slaves appeared, white-robed and carrying lyres, their brows wreathed with laurel leaves. These began to stroll among the tables, declaiming Homer and the odes of Pindar. This was a signal for the first break in the banquet. Most of us pushed heavily to our feet, put on our sandals and staggered off to let some of our intake settle. There was a public bathhouse next to the garden, and this was being kept open, manned and luxuriously equipped for the whole night.

The light of hundreds of lamps shimmered off the agitated water as I entered. I put off my admiration until later, for I had more urgent business to transact and made a straight line for the privy. That facility had more than a hundred seats, but there was still some jostling, as a few of the feasters had to be helped onto their seats by slaves. Elsewhere, others, even more overcome by their overindulgence, vomited in prolonged, roaring convulsions. I ignored these with a superior air. I was proud of my absorptive capacities in those days.

Intensely relieved, I reentered the main room, which in this house contained a swimming pool in which a number of the younger guests disported themselves. Respectable women did not mingle promiscuously with men at the public baths, but there were a few decidedly nonrespectable women circulating, some of them quite highborn. I recognized at least two senator's wives and the sister of a *pontifex*. As I made my way toward the steam bath, a feminine voice hailed me. I looked to see who it was but the crowd had grown dense.

"Down here, in the water." I walked to the lip of the pool and knelt by a damp, brown-locked head. It was my cousin Caecilia who, since all of my female cousins are named Caecilia, we called Felicia, not because she was happy but for her catlike looks and temperament. She was the daughter of that Creticus who waited outside the walls of Rome, and had recently wed Marcus Crassus, eldest son of the ex-Consul who had defeated Spartacus.

"This is naughty for a lady so recently married in so respectable a ceremony," I chided.

She rested her chin on crossed forearms and kicked her pretty feet in the water. "Don't be silly. I was married off because our family and the Crassi wanted to mend fences after being at odds for so long and with Pompey coming back soon. I am just a knucklebone on the great game board of politics."

"Knucklebones are hard and knobby, which scarcely describes you, cousin. Where is your fortunate husband, by the way?"

"Snoring on the couch, when I left him. I have no intention of missing any part of an occasion like this, so I came here to refresh myself. Why don't you join me?"

I stood. "Some other time, Felicia. Dignity of office, and so forth."

"Quaestor?" she snorted. "That's not an office, it's a sentence!"

I winced at her cruel but accurate assessment of my place in the scheme of things, and took my leave. In the exercise yard, a troupe of gladiators were going through a series of mock duels, using blunted weapons but wearing their most splendid armor. I passed their clash and clatter and found the steam room. There I gave my clothes and wreaths to an attendant, took a pile of towels and went into the muggy heat. In the dimness, I found a bench and sat. In moments, I was sweating like a legionary at the end of a long day.

Anyone seriously dedicated to the joys of feasting knows that it is essential to take an occasional break and purge oneself of the more heroic excesses. I fully intended to see the sun come up on this one. Even here, though, Lucullus had seen to our comfort. In the center of the steam room was a huge basin in which pitchers of wine sat packed in snow hauled down from the Alps in wagons.

An extraordinarily handsome young man came in, followed by a group of youths of similar age. He was about nineteen, with black, curly hair and a smile that would have shamed Apollo. He squinted through the steam, then walked up to me and held out his hand.

"The *Quaestor* Metellus?" he asked.

"The same. And you are . . . ?"

"Marcus Antonius." I had thought the family look was familiar.

"The Consul's son?" I asked. A companion handed him a cup of the chilled wine.

"His nephew. My father is the elder Marcus." He sat next to me, while his friends, whom he clearly dominated, found places for themselves. "Your father presided as *augur* at my manhood ceremony a few years ago."

"Then this must be your first triumphal banquet," I said. "There hasn't been one since Afranius and Calpurnianus celebrated theirs seven years ago."

"I've heard those were nothing like this one." His eyes

gleamed with youthful enthusiasm. "Lucullus knows how to throw a banquet."

I agreed that this was so. His father, the elder Marcus Antonius, had been an incompetent and a criminal even by Antonine standards. Sent out to destroy the Mediterranean pirates, he had instead gone plundering in the provinces. He attacked Crete on the pretext that they were allied with the pirates. On that island he had accomplished the truly extraordinary feat of being utterly defeated by the Cretans. He was nicknamed *Creticus* in derision and had died in Greece, unmourned, about ten years before this memorable banquet. One had to pity this splendid young man his paternity.

"Do you know what I love about the baths?" he said. "They're the only places in Rome where you can go and be sure of never running into any Gauls." His friends laughed loudly at this, although he laughed even louder. He had a fine, infectious laugh that made his weakest witticisms seem brilliant.

"Do you mean those Allobroges over there at the banquet?" I asked.

"Who else? They've been calling on my uncle nearly every morning. That means I have to endure them when I make *my* morning calls." Men that young think that all of life's vexations are aimed solely at them.

"It could have been Germans," I said consolingly. Then one of the youths challenged him to a wrestling match and they all ran out to the exercise yard. A plunge into the cold pool almost completely cleared my head. After being vigorously toweled and pummeled by the attendants, I felt ready to face the next few courses of the banquet.

On the street outside the bath, a great crowd of citizens had gathered. Facing the garden, they chanted praises and congratulations to the *triumphator*. Some of the chants were so ancient that nobody knew what the words meant. I was about to push my way into the crowd when I saw a single, lonely figure standing on the pedestal of a statue of Flora that stood in an alcove between the public bath and the new Temple of Minerva. The man was strangely erect and dignified, and even in the gloom of the alcove he seemed familiar. Curious, I walked over to the pedestal and looked up.

"Consul?" I said.

Cicero looked down. "Is that Decius Metellus? Come up and join me."

Mystified, I went behind the statue where there were steps to mount the pedestal. It was almost four months past the *Floralia,* but the statue of the goddess had been freshly draped with flowers in honor of the occasion. The smell was almost overpowering.

Gripping a fold of the goddess's gown to steady myself, I rounded the statue and found Cicero gazing upward. He was very still, and did not seem at all like his usual, public self.

"Here, out of the torchlight," he said, "it is a good night for observing the stars. I spend a part of every night in contemplating the stars."

"My father taught me to take the auguries," I said, "but except for the falling sort, those don't take great account of the stars. I'm afraid he considers stargazing to be Oriental mummery."

"Many Romans think that, but they are wrong. I have studied writings from Egypt and Persia, the Greeks, even the wild Druids agree that the stars exert great influence on us. Especially that one." He pointed and it was plain which one he meant. It was by far the brightest and the reddest, hanging like a brilliant drop of blood amid the jewellike points of white.

"Even I know that one," I said. "Sirius, the Dog Star, *Canicula,* the little dog, and a few other names. Patron of these very days, the dog days of late summer."

"What you say is what everyone knows. But why do we fear that one? What makes it a star of evil reputation?"

"I thought it was because the dog days are the time of pestilence and the beginning of the season of storms." This seemed an odd subject to be discussing at such a festive time.

"That is true, but there is more. At the festival of this gentle goddess"—he patted the knee of the statue—"at the *Floralia,* we sacrifice red dogs to appease that star.

We do the same at the *Robigalia* when we honor her male counterpart. Why do we do that?"

I shrugged, longing for some more of that Caecuban wine. "These are very ancient deities," I said. "We perform a good many rituals we no longer understand."

"That is true. It is also true that never in living memory has Sirius been as red as it has been this summer."

In the distance, faint over the chanting of the crowd, we heard the heralds proclaim the resumption of the feast. With great relief I descended and helped Cicero down. He did not need help because he was feeble. He was only forty-three at the time, astoundingly young for a Consul. He needed aid because of the awkwardness of his formal toga, which was so white that he almost glowed in the darkness of the alcove.

As we made our way through the crowd, I thought about what he had said. Even more than most people, Romans live by signs and portents. I know of no other people who maintain two separate priesthoods to interpret omens. We take no public and few private actions without consulting the auguries and the haruspices. When all else fails, we will consult the Sibylline Books, for which we maintain a college of fifteen men who are empowered to look into them in times of national danger. Besides these more serious matters, the people of Rome, from Consuls to slaves, are mad for omens, which they will find in every imaginable place and circumstance.

Birds, lightning, storms, odd things falling from the sky, monstrous births, all are noticed, remarked upon and interpreted to signify something or other, from the loss of one's lover to a military disaster overseas. When these natural phenomena are not enough, fabricated omens must suffice. Statues speak or turn their heads, nanny goats give birth to lion cubs, gods appear to shepherds on hillsides, voices come from the sea, dead snakes prophesy from within golden eggs—the list is endless.

And yet, in all my life I had never encountered definite evidence that any of this was true. Any time I have spoken of this, I have been told that it is churlish to expect anything so mundane as evidence or proof in matters of this sort. A few philosophers have told me that certain of the Greeks had a belief that one arrived at the truth by examining evidence and drawing conclusions therefrom, but these had never gained much of a following. Even so, I have always been impelled to look into things, to examine evidence and find the truth. To snoop, as my father used to say when he was displeased with me. It got me into a great deal of trouble, and it was about to again, soon after this memorable night.

Back at my place at the long table, I saw that the servers had brought out a concoction that was meant to depict the sea monster Scylla reaching for the ship of Ulysses. After some consultation with Catilina and the diner to my other side, a *quaestor* named Vatinius, who was in charge of preventing precious metals from leaving Italy, we decided that it was made of lampreys boiled in squid ink. I decided to restrain myself and wait until the next course. I have never been hungry enough to enjoy lampreys, in or out of ink.

It was not a long wait. To my great delight, the next course consisted of African gazelle, grilled over charcoal made from the thorn wood of its native land (the server assured us of this). The nautical reference in this case was an obscure one, concerning a Babylonian god or perhaps goddess. I have never been able to make much sense of the eastern mythologies, nor ever seen much sense in attempting to. Whatever the divine connection may have been, the meat was delectable. Catilina spoke with great authority on the subject of this animal, its habits and the best ways to cook and eat it, claiming to have learned these things as *Propraetor* in Africa three years before. We were pleasantly, tipsily engaged in discussing this creature and how best to devour it when I saw Catilina turn pale beneath his red complexion, his eyes turning to agate. I followed the direction of his alarming gaze and saw, weaving among the tables, servers and entertainers, none other than Publius Clodius.

He hadn't always been Clodius, naturally. He had started out as Publius Claudius Pulcher, scion of one of the noblest of the patrician families. But he had chosen to throw in his political lot with the *populares,* and so had decided to use the plebian form of his family name.

"He must be incredibly drunk to show his face here," I noted. As Lucullus's legate in Asia, Clodius had stirred up a mutiny among the general's own legionaries. Then he deserted and joined the army of Marcius Rex, who waited outside the walls along with Creticus.

"Who knows?" said Vatinius. "He might have been invited. He's the *triumphator*'s brother-in-law, after all. And another sister is married to the *Praetor* Metellus Celer. I hear Celer's wife is calling herself Clodia now, like her brother."

"Another knucklebone," I said.

"What's that?" Vatinius asked.

I was distracted by Catilina, whose face had gone positively insane with rage. His hand went into his toga and beneath his tunic, closing around something that seemed suspiciously like a dagger hilt. I twisted around and gripped his wrist firmly.

"You can't do that here!" I hissed. "Every priest and magistrate in Rome is here tonight! It's sacrilege to carry arms within the *pomerium* and murder is frowned upon! Keep that thing hidden and calm yourself, Lucius." Gradually, his face calmed and his eyes cleared. He snatched up his cup and emptied it in one long swallow, then held it out for more.

"I've longed to kill that sewer rat for ten years. Since he came back to Rome, he's gone nowhere in public without his gang of bravos." His voice shook, but he had it under control. "It seems a shame to lose the opportunity, but I thank you, Decius. It would have been impolitic."

"Think nothing of it," I said. "We've all wanted to kill Clodius from time to time. He's even set his men to kill me, in the past. Just politics." With Catilina, it was understandably more personal. Ten years before, Clodius had accused him of an illicit affair with the Vestal Fabia. The two had been cleared of all charges and there had been deadly hatred between Clodius and Catilina ever since.

Vatinius, who had carefully taken no notice of the little drama, now distracted us by violently shoving away a dish that a server had placed before him, his face twisted with disgust. I looked to see what it was: wild hare cooked with broad beans.

"Anyone who can bear to look at boiled lampreys ought to be able to face hare and beans," I said.

"Beans are unclean food," he informed me. "Eating them is contrary to the teachings of Pythagoras."

"I didn't know you were a Pythagorean," I said. There were few things that interested me less than the teachings of Pythagoras, or any other philosopher, for that matter, but it was a safe subject.

By the time gray streaks appeared in the eastern sky, I knew that I would never want to eat again and I had heard all I wanted to hear about the teachings of Pythagoras. Before departing, each of us was given a guest-gift. Mine was a massive gold ring set with a garnet, smoothed and ready for the jeweler to engrave my seal. Like everyone else, I had brought along my largest napkin to carry away leftovers for my slaves. Some of these napkins were the size of a boy's toga and we looked like a pack of drunken legionaries leaving a sacked town with our booty on our backs.

I was joyful as I walked home. It is difficult to be sad at such a time. There were days of celebrations and public games ahead, and no work for me. Yet there was sadness too. Once again we had rejoiced in Rome's increasing power and glory, but I had a feeling of something coming to an end.

With a small group of revelers, I made my way to my home in the Subura. We trod on heaps of flower petals and bawled old victory-songs, as if we had done all the fighting ourselves. They left me at my gate, but I stood outside for a while, as the street grew quiet.

I wondered what was the meaning of this melancholy, the sense that I had seen the end of something. I could make no sense of it. I looked up at the sky, but gray dawn had washed out the stars and I could not see the bloody eye of Sirius gazing down.

II

—

ather was right about the treasury. I found that the gold did indeed flow out like the Tiber in flood. Most of it went to pay the legions, since the great public works are usually given to the city as gifts by wealthy men. It seemed shocking at first, that the relatively small number of legionaries, whose pay is not high, could cost so much. But people forget that, besides the citizen legions, there are an even greater number of auxiliaries, all of whom must be paid. They must have slaves, horses and other animals, rations, tents and so forth. Forts had to be built, ships had to be purchased and manned. Since Roman citizens paid virtually no taxes, and looting opportunities such as the sack of Tigranocerta were rare and growing rarer, somebody had to be found to pay for all this.

The answer was to tax the provinces. Since the government of Rome was too august and dignified to dirty its hands on anything as base as tax collecting, this task was farmed out to the *publicani*, the men who bid at auction for the public contracts, among which was the tax-collecting franchise. It was often hard on the provincials, but people who don't want to be taxed should make sure to win their wars. It had the advantage that the provincials usually hated the local publican rather than the Roman government.

Most Romans manage to live out their lives blithely ignorant of these things, but I had to learn them as part of my job. Another part was that, as a *quaestor*, I was expected to contribute to the paving of the high roads out of my own purse. It was a sort of poll-fee for entering the life of politics. What it meant was that I had to borrow heavily from my father, who at least wouldn't charge me usurious interest.

Even with all this, I truly had little to do at the Temple of Saturn. My days were passed amid boredom, watching the slaves and freedmen laboriously adding and subtracting. I signed for contributions and disbursements. The days passed without variety: mornings at the temple, afternoons at the baths, evenings I usually had dinner at someone's home. As an official, even a lowly one, I was much in demand as a guest.

On a morning in fall, I went to the temple in a better frame of mind than usual. The year was waning, soon I would be out of office. Some other poor office holder could take over the drudgery of the dim rooms beneath the temple. By virtue of having held this office I would be a Senator, with a purple stripe on my tunic and the privilege of sitting in the *Curia* listening to speeches and pretending to have influence. Perhaps I would seek an appointment as legate in one of the provinces. I always detested having to be absent from Rome, but I was ready for a change of scenery after my dismal quaestorship and it was idle to seek higher office without a consistent military record.

With these pleasant thoughts in mind, I walked from my house toward the Forum. I was not halfway to my destination when I saw a small crowd blocking my path. There is a way that people stand, grouped in a sort of elongated oval and looking downward, often on tiptoe and over one another's shoulders, that tells you they are gawking at a body. This seemed odd to me, because there had not been any large gang fights since the elections. A man in the tunic of a *vigile* saw me and came running.

"*Quaestor*, there has been a murder. Will you take charge here until we can inform a *praetor?*"

"Certainly," I said, delighted at this break in routine. "Any idea who the victim is?"

"Well, no, sir," the man said. "We were afraid to touch him. Not that I'm afraid of ghosts or dead men's curses, but some of the men are." It was typical. We kill people enthusiastically all over the world, and we are entertained by violent death in the amphitheater, but Romans are afraid to touch dead bodies.

"Then go to the Temple of Libitina and have a priest and some attendants sent to perform the rites. We can't just leave a body lying in the street until a relative or owner comes to claim it."

"Won't be any owner, *Quaestor,*" the *vigile* said. "Look at him."

The crowd parted at my approach and I saw the body. The disarrayed toga covered the head, but enough of the tunic was uncovered to reveal the purple stripe that ran from collar to hem. It was not the broad stripe of a Senator, but the narrow one of an *eques.* It lay facedown, one hand protruding from beneath the folds of cloth to display a number of weighty gold rings glinting in the growing light of morning. In the middle of the back, a dagger pierced toga and body. A broad circle of blood surrounded the blade, marring the whiteness of the toga.

"You *vigiles,*" I called to the men who stood around, their fire-buckets dangling from their hands, "keep this crowd back and keep the street clear enough for people to pass." They did as I said.

I squatted by the body, careful to keep my toga clear of the filthy street and especially careful not to touch the corpse. It was not that I was afraid of ghosts or curses, but if I touched it I would be ritually unclean and then I could not enter the temple without a lot of tedious cleansing ceremonies.

The handle of the dagger was curiously carved, but in the still-dim light I could tell no more about it. I promised myself a closer look later. I could tell nothing about the dead man except his rank, and I would know nothing further until the *libitinarii* arrived to turn him over. I was almost disappointed that the purple stripe of the tunic was not wider. There were a few Senators I would not have minded seeing in this condition. Even worse luck, it could not be a patrician, because then I could have amused myself by hoping it would be Clodius's face I would see.

Within a few minutes, a lictor cleared a way through the crowd, the people parting magically before his *fasces.*

Behind him was a Senator I recognised. It was Caius Octavius, who had been appointed a *Iudex Quaestionis* for that year. I stood when he arrived.

"The *Praetor* Rufus has sent me to report to him on this matter," he said. "I don't suppose there were any witnesses?"

"Are there ever?" I answered.

"Who is he?"

"That is what I would like to know," I said, then: "We may know soon. Here come the corpse-takers."

Down the street came the one sight guaranteed to make Romans stand back: the *libitinarii*, preceded by their priest with his long-handled mallet. With their long, red tunics, their high buskins, their pointed Etruscan beards, wide-brimmed felt hats and high, pointed false ears they are the ghastliest sight anyone could ask for so early in the morning. People jumped back with their thumbs protruding from their clenched fists or fished out tiny phallus amulets and pointed them at the *libitinarii*.

Wordlessly, the priest stepped up to the body and touched it with his mallet, claiming it for the underworld goddess. An attendant carrying a box opened it and the priest began a long chant, from time to time taking liquids or powders from the box, sprinkling them on the corpse. When the *lustrum* was finished, the attendant closed the box.

"Turn him over," Octavius instructed. The attendants crouched by the corpse. One of them plucked out the dagger and nonchalantly tossed it to the pavement. Grasping the corpse beneath the shoulders and knees, they rolled it over.

I did not recognize the man. He appeared to be about fifty years old, with sandy, graying hair. His mouth and eyes were open, but his face bore no readable expression. I saw that the other hand was equally beringed.

"Does anyone here know him?" Octavius asked loudly. Amid muttering and shrugs a man came forward.

"That's Manius Oppius, sir. He lives ... lived not far from here. I've delivered sandals to his house a number of times. My shop's down there on the corner."

"Good. You can lead these men to his house. His family will want to claim his body." He turned to me. "Oppius. Aren't they bankers?"

"I believe so," I said. There was a commotion a little way up the street. An important man was coming, followed by a great mob of friends, clients and retainers.

"What now?" Octavius said with annoyance. Then his face registered alarm. "Oh, no! Stop him!" Then I saw who was in the lead and ran to block his way. It was Caius Julius Caesar. He smiled, puzzled, when he saw me.

"Good morning, Decius Caecilius. What is happening here?"

"There has been a murder, Caius Julius. Somebody stabbed an *eques* named Oppius. There is blood."

Caesar looked concerned. "Oppius? Not Caius Oppius, surely."

"A sandalmaker here says his name is Manius. The *Iudex* Octavius has taken over."

"I don't know any Manius Oppius, but Caius is a friend of mine. I will make inquiries. Thank you for warning me, Decius. This could have been a terrible misfortune for the city." He drew a fold of his toga over his head as if he were offering sacrifice and he held a great fold of it draped over his arm, hiding his face from the body on the ground as he went on past, followed by his entourage. It was necessary but, being Caesar, he turned it into a broad, actor's gesture.

A few weeks before, the old *pontifex maximus* had finally died. To the immense amusement of the whole city, Caesar had been elected to his place. The man known for the frequency as well as the diversity of his debaucheries had become the high priest of the Roman state. One of the restrictions of the office was that the *pontifex maximus* could not look upon human blood.

"Does anyone have a coin for the ferryman?" the priest asked. Fumbling in my purse, I came up with a copper *as* and tossed it to one of the attendants, who placed it beneath the dead man's tongue. It was the least I could do for the unfortunate man, who had relieved the tedium of my day.

As the *libitinarii* lifted the corpse onto a folding stretcher, I stooped and picked up the dagger. The man's toga was ruined anyway, so I used it to wipe off the blade. Then I thought of something. "Is there any way to tell how long he's been dead?" I asked the funeralmen.

"He's not quite cold," said one. "And he hasn't gone stiff yet. I'd say he hasn't been dead more than two or three hours."

As the body was borne away Octavius and I turned our steps toward the Forum. I held the dagger up so that he could see it. "This is evidence," I said. "I call on you to witness that I am not bearing arms within the *pomerium*."

He laughed. "If we enforced that one, the courts would have nothing else to do. What sort of dagger is it?"

I shrugged. It was not the broad-bladed *pugio* of the legions, but neither was it the curved *sica* most favored by the city cutthroats. It was straight and double-edged, with a thick midrib reinforcing the blade. The hilt was of plain bronze, the grip a piece of bone with a serpent carved on it, rather crudely. Winding its long body from the hilt to the pommel, the serpent formed a raised, spiral rib that afforded an excellent grip. The pommel was a plain, mushroom-shaped cap of bronze.

"Just an ordinary sticker as far as I can see," I told him. "The kind you can buy in any cutler's shop."

"Nothing of any real use as evidence, then," said Octavius. "Not as if the blade were engraved 'Death to the enemies of King Phraates of Parthia' or something of the sort."

"That would be convenient, but my experience of life has taught me that things are seldom ordered for our convenience." I tossed the dagger in the air and caught it again.

"Why, Decius, you've become a philosopher! Will you be growing a beard and opening a school?"

"Spare me, Octavius. Do keep me informed about this, will you? I almost feel that the poor fellow was my client, since I presided over the first part of his funeral rites." He promised to do so and we parted in the Forum.

It was a clear, cool day, one of those brilliantly lucid mornings such as one only encounters in Italy during the fall. The oppressive heat of summer was past and the chill and rains of winter had not yet begun. It made me have second thoughts about seeking an appointment that would take me out of Rome. I knew that winter would cure that. I would start thinking about the Greek islands, Africa, perhaps even an embassy to Alexandria, which I had always heard was a deliciously wicked city.

The day passed like all the others, save for the brief excitement of the morning. I found the staff waiting impatiently for me to unlock the treasury and I soothed them with a lurid account of the murder. I signed for yet another consignment of silver to the legions. I walked away when the tedious task of weighing a shipment of gold from Spain began.

I left the musty interior of the temple with its reek of old incense and older sacrifices and went out into the clean air of the city. Relatively clean, at any rate. The wind wasn't off the fish market or the slaughter yards or, worst of all, the open burial pits. It blew clean from the north, off the Alps. It was a pleasant waste of time, but it had to end and I turned toward my duties. Just within the entrance, I stopped. Something seemed to be wrong or out of place. I looked about me carefully. The statue of Saturn was as always. The pigeons nesting in the rafters cooed as usual. The temple was one of the most ancient, much of it still made of wood. There seemed to be nothing different about the various alcoves and doorways. My gaze stopped at the low doorway to the right of the entrance. It was the one old Minicius the state freedman had said led only to some disused storerooms. I walked over to it to see what was wrong.

There were fresh footprints in the dust, a great many of them. Had another train of slaves taken the wrong turn and gone in there? The question might not have concerned me had I not been so bored. Or perhaps it was because my mind was on mysterious matters such as, why had the murderer of Manius Oppius not stolen those rings, which were valuable enough to keep a poor family comfortable for two or three years? Or it might have been my *genius* whispering in my ear. *Genii* are supposed to be guardian spirits, but mine always gets me in trouble.

For the second time that day, I squatted to examine the evidence. There were prints of sandals and of bare feet. The bare feet probably belonged to slaves. I could see that at least two pairs of sandals had made prints, but little more than that. I straightened and looked around to see if anyone was observing me. I felt foolish, like a boy out climbing trees when he should be at his studies. Quietly, I went to a wall niche and took a lamp from it. Then I went back to the doorway.

The footprints were on a small landing, from which steep stairs slanted downward to the right. I descended the steps slowly, allowing my eyes to become accustomed to the dimness. By the time I reached the bottom, the illumination provided by the lamp's smoky wick was perfectly adequate. The stairs ended at another tiny landing, with barely enough room for a man to stand and turn around. Three doorways opened off the landing, one to each side and one straight ahead. The last of the steps and these three rooms were actually below the foundations of the temple, carved directly into the bedrock. It felt far older than the treasury rooms. It was a strange sensation, standing on a spot where Romulus might have stood.

I decided to try the room before me first. Ducking below the lintel, I went through and found myself in a small, cramped chamber. Its walls were decorated with faded paintings of gods and demons in the Etruscan style. On one wall, a blindfolded man was being savaged by a dog or wolf held on a leash by a figure with the long nose and ears of a death-demon. On another, two naked men were locked in mortal combat while men and women in priestly raiment looked on. One combatant grasped his opponent around the neck and thrust his sword through his body while the other's sword pierced the victor's thigh. Blood gushed profusely from both wounds. On the third wall, a warrior in antique armor grasped the hair of a bound prisoner seated on the ground before him and drew his sword across the victim's throat.

I like to think that I am not superstitious, but these ancient paintings filled me with horror. Were these long-forgotten rites of worship once demanded by Saturn? Were they scenes from the dedication of the temple? It was not the mere bloodshed, which was a common enough sight. It was the ritual, religious nature of it. We were fond of our gods as patrons of agriculture or craft or war, but we had little liking for the blood-drinking gods of the underworld. Our ancestors had not been so squeamish.

I would have to bring Cato down here, I thought. He would probably petition the Senate for a return to human sacrifice, since it had been the custom of our ancestors.

There was a heap of something on the floor, covered by a large piece of cloth. Behind me, next to the doorway, I found a lamp-niche and placed my lamp in it. Then I stooped and drew the cloth back. The flame glittered off a great deal of metal. It was a heap of weapons. The majority were swords and short spears. I saw the stout *gladius* of the legions in many styles, some recent, others dating back as far as Scipio and the Punic wars. There was the long *spatha* of the cavalry and the many shapes of sword used in the amphitheater. Some of the spears were hunting weapons such as broad-bladed boar spears. Others were military, the light javelin and the heavy *pilum* of the legions. Once again, these last were mostly of older design.

It was a strange armory, obviously gathered from many sources, but brought here for what purpose? I recovered the heap of arms and looked into the other rooms. One was empty. In the other was a small stack of shields, not the great, body-covering *scutum* of the regular legions, but the small, round or oval ones carried by light-armed auxiliaries.

I went back up the steps. At the landing, I looked to see if there was anyone about who might see me leaving the basement stair. The great shrine was vacant for the moment and I slipped out, replacing the lamp in its niche. When I returned to the treasury, Minicius looked up from beneath his white brows.

"Where have you been?" he demanded. He was only a freedman, but as one of the most important freedmen in Rome, he did not have to be humble. He sat at his table, his pen racing across a scroll of papyrus.

"I had to run over the public bath and use the jakes," I said. "It must have been something I ate this morning."

"More likely something you drank last night. Here, I've a stack of things for you to sign."

I looked them over, but I really had no idea what I was signing. Only a man who works with numbers all his life can make any sense of columns of figures. I had to trust Minicius. Since every treasury *quaestor* for the last forty years or so had done the same without coming to harm, I felt fairly safe.

I said nothing to him or anybody else about what I had found. It was the sort of thing requiring a great deal of deep, serious thought. After locking the treasury in the afternoon, I did exactly that. I went to one of the smaller baths, where I was not likely to encounter anyone I would be obliged to talk to. There I sat in the *caldarium,* stewed in the hot water, and thought.

Somebody had cached arms in the Temple of Saturn. It was clearly not part of an attempt to steal the treasury. Thieves avoid fighting at all costs. On the other hand, someone planning a coup would naturally wish to seize the treasury as one of his first acts.

But who might it be? The times had been tranquil for almost twenty years, since the dictatorship of Sulla. All the wars had been on foreign soil except for the slave rebellion led by Spartacus. Was one of our generals planning a march on Rome and preparing for it by arming cohorts within the city? It would not be the first time.

Something did not fit that theory, though. I worried at it until I saw what was not consistent: it was the haphazardness of the weaponry. Surely a general would have supplied his confederates with arms of a uniform nature, if for no other reason than a military sense of tidiness. Whoever had done this had picked up weapons wherever he could find them, probably buying them a few at a time at widely separated places to avoid suspicion.

Of course, not all of our generals were as well fixed as Pompey. Italy was full of the veterans of a dozen wars, paid off, disbanded and settled in smallholdings up and down the length of the peninsula. Every one of them had his helmet and shield, his sword and armor hanging by the hearth, waiting for his old general to call him back to the eagles. These veterans formed one of the most unstabilizing aspects of Roman life, always a potential hotbed of rebellion. Almost any one of the highest men in political life, feeling himself cheated or insulted or thwarted in some way, might remember that he was a soldier before he was a public servant, and that he had many other soldiers ready to follow him. Such a one might very well buy up old arms to equip an urban cohort.

I tried to think who I might approach about this. The problem was that almost any of the men in high office could be the instigator of this plot, or one of his adherents. Many of the men in high office were my relatives, but I could not count on that to save my neck if one of them should turn out to be a part of a conspiracy against the state.

I could see that this matter was going to call for subtlety as well as for boldness and quite possibly for violence. I decided to pay a call upon the man who was a master of all three. I went to see Titus Annius Milo.

Milo was the best representative of a type of man who had come to prominence in Rome during the last century: the political criminal. Such men, besides their usual criminal activities, performed strong-arm tasks for politicians. They broke up rivals' rallies, made sure that the voters in their districts voted properly, provided bodyguards and rioters, and so forth. In return, their highly placed patrons provided them with protection in the courts. Clodius was another such man. But I detested Clodius, while I counted Milo as a good friend. Clodius and Milo, needless to relate, were deadly enemies.

From the bath, I walked to Milo's house, which was

not far from my own, near the base of the Viminal, in a district of raucous shops that were beginning to quiet down as late afternoon sapped the vigor that had been so boundless earlier in the day. Milo had once been assistant to Macro, who had been a very distinguished gang leader. Now he ran Macro's gang and lived in the house that had belonged to Macro. Macro had died rather suddenly and Milo had produced a will that looked authentic.

A tall, gangling lout leaned against the doorpost, favoring me with a gap-toothed grin. He was a Gaul, but he must have arrived in the city very young, because he spoke without any accent. The inevitable bulge of a *sica* handle showed through his tunic beneath the armpit.

"Greeting, *Quaestor,* we haven't seen you in too long."

"No, I haven't been hanging about the criminal courts, Berbix, or we would have seen a lot of each other."

"Now, sir," he said, still grinning, "you know I'm as innocent as a little lamb. And speaking of innocence, you wouldn't be meaning my patron any harm with that sticker you've got under your tunic, would you? I know you and him is friends, but friendship only goes so far, if you take my meaning. I'm shocked, sir, you being a public official and all."

I had all but forgotten about the dagger. I had wrapped it in a scrap of cloth and tucked it beneath my tunic. He had sharp eyes to spot it through tunic and toga both.

"When did a little dagger do anyone any good against Milo?" I said.

"I won't argue with that. Come on in, I'll announce you."

The house was a fine one, which Milo had remodeled so that he had both a large courtyard and an assembly room, where he could hold mass meetings with his associates in good weather or bad. The thick, wooden door was reinforced with iron strapping and had heavy locking bars. The place was built like a fort, to withstand attack by rioting mobs led by rivals. Three streets bounded his house, and he had clearly sited the door on the narrowest street, so that enemies would have no running space to use a ram against it.

The Gaul left me in a small anteroom and sent a serving girl to search for the master, then he resumed his post by the door. It was sign of the relative tranquility of the times that Milo thought one man on the door was enough. Milo had ambitions to become a Tribune of the People, an office that had been the death of more than one Roman. Clodius likewise was angling for that office, and the inevitable collision of these two was anticipated with great glee by the idlers of the Forum. Clodius cultivated the rising fortunes of Caesar while Milo had formed an odd alliance with Cicero.

Milo arrived, his face decorated with a tremendous smile, and I took his hand. It had not grown soft despite the passage of years since he had earned his living as a rower. He was a huge man, still young, with so much energy and ambition that it made me tired just to be in his presence.

"Decius! Why have you not come to see me in so long? You look pale. That's what comes of spending your days counting money under the watchful eye of Saturn. How does it feel, being in charge of all the gold in Rome?"

"Whatever pleasure is to be had in watching it flow by is mine," I told him. "I assure you, that is very little pleasure indeed."

"Then let me cheer you up. Come with me."

He led me to a small room equipped with a single table and two small dining-couches. Next to them was a bronze basket filled with glowing-red stones that had been heated in a baker's oven. This provided heat without smoke, for which I was grateful. The afternoon had grown cool. The table was furnished with cups and a pitcher of wine and snacks of the simplest sort: olives, nuts, dates and figs. This represented not a philosopher's love of simplicity but rather a busy man's lack of time for any sort of ostentation.

We drank each other's health and passed a few pleasantries between us. Then Milo spoke in his usual, direct fashion.

"Much as we always enjoy each other's company, I take it that this is by way of being an official visit?"

"Not precisely. That is to say, it doesn't involve my present office. I've come upon evidence of a possible conspiracy against the state, and I am not sure what to do with it. I know of no one totally trustworthy in whom to confide."

"Except me." He smiled.

"You come closest," I admitted.

"Then tell me about it."

Milo was not a man with whom to prevaricate, or speak in circumlocutions or innuendo. I told him exactly what I had found and where I had found it. I told him my reasons for not going to the Consuls or *praetores*. He listened with great concentration. Milo did not have the most brilliant mind I ever encountered; that laurel would have to go to Cicero. But I never knew a man who could think harder than he did.

"I can understand your urge to caution," he said when I had finished. "So you suspect a plot against the state?"

"What else could it be?" I asked.

"I know that you have fears that Pompey will make himself king of Rome, but somehow I don't see him arming a few hundred scruffy supporters to hold the gates for him. If he truly wanted to, I think he could bring his armies to Italy and walk into the city unopposed."

"There are plenty of others, besides Pompey," I pointed out. "Men who once commanded legions and know they will never have the chance to do so again. Men who have been disappointed in their bids for high office. Men who are desperate. Who else?"

"The weapons you describe would not be much use in arming soldiers for the field, but they are just the thing for fighting in a city. No heavy shields or armor, no long pikes, no bows or arrows. They *might* be used as you fear, but there is another possibility."

"I would be glad to hear of it," I said.

"Decius, you have allowed these fears of overambitious generals to dominate your thinking. Those men have learned from what happened in the days of Marius and Sulla. I think that, in the future, they will do most of their fighting outside of Italy. But there are other men who have no ambition to command great armies and lord it over the provincials. These men want to control Rome itself, just the city. Such a cache as you describe would be of great use to one of those."

"And who," I said, "might this person be?"

"Clodius Pulcher comes immediately to mind," he said.

"And you would be another. No, it is tempting, and that makes me even more skeptical. There is nothing in the world I would love more than to impeach Clodius before the Senate. It would rid the Republic of a despicable cur and, incidentally, make my name in politics. For that reason, I can hardly believe that the gods have dropped this opportunity in my lap. I will not, of course, suggest that you might have had anything to do with this."

"Give me credit for greater subtlety. Then let us go back to the idea of a malcontent itching for a coup. It wouldn't be just one malcontent. They have a way of finding one another and talking about how unjustly they have been treated."

"Why the Temple of Saturn?" I asked him.

"It is a good location, near the Forum. It has, as you found out, disused storerooms nobody ever looks into. The treasury is always securely locked but the temple itself is open. It will only be one of several caches, you know. Keep an eye on the one in the temple and see if there are more deposited there in the next few days. But don't let anyone see you do it. I would hate to hear that you were found dead in the street one morning, like poor Manius Oppius." He would have known of the murder within minutes of the body's being found. I only hoped that he had not known of it before.

"I passed by the murder scene this morning," I told him. "I took charge until the *Iudex* Octavius arrived. Do you know anything about the man?"

"He was a banker, like a lot of that family. I didn't know him, but I know plenty of people who owed him money."

"There will be no shortage of suspects, then," I said. I took the dagger from beneath my tunic and un-wrapped it. "This is what he was killed with. Have you ever seen one like it?"

He turned the knife over in his hands, ran his thumb along the carved serpent. Then he shook his head. "It's no national type I know of. Not even very good work. If I were going to murder a man, I'd probably go to a market, pick up a thirdhand weapon like this from a junk dealer, use it once and leave it where it was or toss it into the nearest storm drain." He handed it back to me. "Sorry. I suspect that whoever used this picked it because it could not identify him."

I rose. "I thank you, Milo. I still haven't decided what to do, but you have given me some things to think about."

"Stay for dinner," he urged.

"Alas, I am having dinner with the Egyptian ambas-sador. Ptolemy the Flute-Player is in trouble again and is cultivating every official in Rome for support. He comes here so often we ought to make him a citizen."

"Well, I won't try to keep you from a good party." He rose as well and put his hand on my shoulder as he walked me to the door. "You recall what I said about how malcontents find each other?"

"I do."

"If you really want to find out if some of them are plotting to overthrow the state, let them find you. They are always looking for others like them. Don't be too obvious, but let fall a few comments about how no good offers for post-*quaestor* appointments have come your way, how your highly placed and jealous enemies are thwarting your ambitions for higher office. You know how they talk. But let them think that it is they who are suborning you." He thought for a while. "You might drop some of these words where Quintus Curius may hear them."

At the door I took my leave and thanked him again. As usually happened when I had discussed something with Milo, I felt that I had been vouchsafed a special insight, making simple what had seem a thorny, difficult problem. He had a way of cutting through the dross and the distractions to reach the core of the matter. He was not bothered by the useless fears, the ethical considerations, the nonpertinent inconsequentialities that cluttered my own mind. His fixation on the acquisition and exercise of power was as intense and single-minded as those of Clodius, Pompey, Cicero, Caesar and the rest, but he was far more likable than any of them, even Caesar, who could be incredibly likable when he wanted your support.

For instance, why had I not thought of Quintus Curius? He was a penurious malcontent of the first order, a man known to have committed half the crimes on the law tables and suspected of the rest. If anything truly villainous was being plotted in Rome, he would be involved. A few years previously, the Censors had expelled him from the Senate for outrageous behavior. He came of an old and distinguished family, and so naturally thought that he was entitled to wealth, high position and public esteem. He was one of those men who simply could not understand how a new man like Cicero could have become Consul.

I went to my home in the Subura to put on my best toga, thinking of how I might establish a link with Curius. It should not be difficult. The social life of Rome, like its political life, was dominated by a rather small group of men and women. Since I was dining out almost every evening, it should not take me more than a few days to make the necessary connections. The opportunity was to come far sooner than I had hoped.

The house of the Egyptian ambassador was located outside the city walls, on the Janiculum. This gave it almost the aspect of a country villa and allowed the ambassador to lavish his guests with entertainments restricted or forbidden within the walls. The politics of Egypt formed a source of endless entertainment for Romans. The huge, rich nation of the great river was ruled, to use the term loosely, by a Macedonian family that had adopted the quaint Egyptian custom of legitimizing one's reign by marrying one or perhaps more of one's close female kin. This family had an almost Roman paucity of names, all the men being named Ptolemy or Alexander, and all the women Cleopatra or Berenice. (There was an occasional Selene, but that was usually a third daughter. By the time you were down to marrying a Selene, your claim to the throne was shaky, indeed.) At least one of them, named Ptolemy, deposed his older brother, also named Ptolemy, married his brother's wife, Cleopatra, who was also sister to both of them, and then, just to make clean sweep of it, married her daughter (and his niece), also named Cleopatra.

The last of the legitimate Ptolomaic line had been Ptolemy X, a Roman client, who claimed the throne by marching his troops into Alexandria and marrying his elderly cousin and stepmother, Berenice, whom he assassinated within twenty days. The Alexandrians, who had been fond of that particular Berenice, promptly killed him. Needing a Ptolemy, lest the natural order of things be shaken, they found a bastard, Philopater Philadelphus Neos Dionysus, better known as *Auletes,* the flute-player, for his realm of greatest competence. At the same time, for incredibly complicated dynastic reasons comprehensible only to Egyptians, they made his brother king of Cyprus. Since that time, several cousins had laid claim to the throne of Egypt. Since it was generally understood that the legitimate king in Egypt was the one who had Roman support, all of them, cousins, ambassadors and frequently the Flute-Player himself, were in Rome, passing extravagant bribes and entertaining lavishly. This was a source of great fun and profit for us Romans, and I was a frequent guest there, as was every man likely to reach high office.

The villa itself was a wonderful mishmash of architectural motifs, with Greek sculptures, landscaping in the Roman fashion, Egyptian lotus and papyrus pillars, shrines to the Roman gods, to the Divine Alexander, to Isis and a horde of animal-headed Egyptian divinities. There was a beautiful fishpond in the gardens with a huge obelisk in its center, and another pond full of crocodiles, presided over by a loathsome crocodile-headed god named Sobek. There was a rumor in the city that the Egyptians fed these huge reptiles on unclaimed corpses they obtained by bribing the attendants at the public burial pits, but I never saw any proof of this.

The ambassador at that time was a fat old degenerate named Lisas, an Alexandrian. Alexandria was virtually a nation in itself, the most cosmopolitan of cities, and Lisas was typical of its inhabitants: a nameless mixture of Greek, Egyptian, Nubian, Asiatic and Jupiter alone knows what else. It is a blend of races that produces exotically beautiful women and some of the ugliest men to blight the face of the earth. Of Alexandria it is said that few cities are so beautiful, but it must be viewed from a distance.

Lisas greeted me in his usual fashion, all smiles and oil. "My friend, Decius Caecilius Metellus the Younger! How your presence brightens this house of the king! How generous of you to look with favor upon my humble invitation! How splendid of you ..." He went on breathlessly in this vein for some time.

"And most pleased I am to be here," I assured him. The smells drifting from within almost made up for the scent in which he was drenched. Effusively, he led me inside and announced me to the guests, of which there were some thirty or so. Since large-scale currying of favor was the whole purpose of the embassy, Lisas did not restrict himself to the Roman custom of inviting no more than nine guests for dinner—"not fewer than the Fates, nor more than the Muses," as some wit or other once said.

The gathering ran the gamut of social and political life, with as many elected officials as he could persuade to come, some fashionable poets and scholars for dignity, and a sprinkling of clowns for levity. There were a number of women noted for beauty and social graces and for less reputable accomplishments. It looked like a good party.

The musicians played exotic instruments such as harps and sistra, garbed in pleated Egyptian linen, while dancers, clad in less of the same material, clapped and gyrated, swinging their weighted braids orgiastically. The servitors were all black Nubians dressed in animal skins and paint. Many of them were carved with ritual scars and had their teeth filed to points. These offered the thick, sweet wines of Egypt as well as the more palatable vintages of the civilized world.

These evenings were always leisurely, beginning early and running far later into the night than was the Roman custom. The thoughtful Lisas maintained a whole corps of linkboys and guards to escort his guests safely to their homes.

The atrium where the guests assembled was a large, circular room, drawn from no architecture with which I was familiar. Its floor mosaics depicted a menagerie of Egyptian fauna, with crocodiles and hippos disporting themselves among water and reeds, ostriches, cobras and lions frolicking in the desert, vultures and hawks soaring through the skies. The wall paintings depicted Nile pygmies fighting a battle with long-beaked cranes. Travelers insisted that these tiny folk actually existed, somewhere near the source waters of the great river, but I never saw any.

I did see one thing that interested me. The beautiful Sempronia was present. She was one of those infamous women of whom I made mention earlier. That is to say, she was educated, outspoken, independent, intelligent and rich enough to carry it all off. She was of matronly years but still one of Rome's great beauties, combining a fine-boned, aristocratic face with that arrogance of bearing that Romans find most admirable. Her husband, Decimus Junius Brutus, was a busy drudge who took no interest in his wife's doings, and the two had not lived together in years. She was also on the best of the terms with Rome's lowest and most prodigal reprobates, finding them far more stimulating company than her husband's respectable friends.

"Decius!" she said, when I approached her. "How good to see you again!" She offered me her cheek, which I kissed, amazed to find that it bore no makeup. Her complexion was adornment enough. She held me by the shoulders at arm's length. "You are even handsomer than you were last week, although I shouldn't say it, having a son near your age."

"Please," I said, taking her hand, "say it as often as you like. And you exaggerate the disparity in our years, since young Decimus is surely no more than seven years old."

She laughed her wonderful, honking laugh. "How good of you to say that!" With a fingertip she traced the ragged scar that decorates my face. "You never told me how you got that. Most men brag about their scars."

"Spanish spear," I said. "That was when I served with Metellus Pius, during Sertorius's insurrection. I don't brag about it because I acquired it very foolishly. It embarrasses me to this day."

"It's good to find a Roman who doesn't think getting cut up is a fine idea." She surveyed the room. "Isn't this a delightful gathering?"

"After spending my days at the treasury, a gathering of cobblers would look inviting." I tried to sound petulant, an attitude that does not come naturally to me.

"Oh, that sort of work doesn't suit you, Decius?" She sounded honestly solicitous.

I shrugged. "Everybody knows it's the job given to the *quaestores* who lack influence in high places."

Her eyebrows went up. "With *your* family?"

"That's just the problem. There are so many of us that one more Metellus at the bottom of the political ladder scarcely rates a pat on the back. If you want to know the truth, the old men of the family think the high offices are theirs by right and they don't want to see any ambitious young kinsman coming along to challenge them."

She flashed me a brief, calculating look, then took a cup from a passing slave to cover it. "And I suppose you've gotten yourself into debt fulfilling your duties?" This seemed an odd comment, but it sounded promising. I had only borrowed from my father, but many penurious politicians ruined themselves trying to support the requirements and dignity of office.

"Head over heels," I told her. "Paving the high roads isn't cheap, I've found. I'm not certain I'll even be able to run for *aedile* with all the cost that entails."

"But surely," she said, "you've been offered a good posting when you leave office, someplace where there are opportunities for a bright, wellborn man? Many a *proquaestor* or *legatus* comes home rich and ready to stand for the higher offices even if he wasn't born wealthy." She watched me closely.

"That's what I was hoping, but nothing's been offered me so far, and it will be many years before a profitable war comes along. Pompey's cronies have all the good postings sewn up." I thought I might be laying it on too thick and changed the subject. "But who knows? Something may well turn up. Now, Sempronia, who is here aside from the usual hangers-on?"

"Let me see ..." She scanned the room. "There is young Catullus. He's recently arrived in the city from Verona."

"The poet?" I said, having heard the name. He was supposed to be the leading light of the "new poets." I preferred the old ones.

"Yes, you must meet him." She took my arm and dragged me over to the young man's side. I was amazed to see that he could not have been older than nineteen or twenty. Sempronia made the introductions. He was slightly diffident, still obviously a little overwhelmed at being in the high life of the great city and trying to cover it with a confident pose bordering on arrogance.

"I hear great things about your work," I said.

"Meaning you haven't read them. Just as well, I feel that my best work is ahead of me. I am embarrassed to look at my earlier writing now."

"What are you working on now?" asked Sempronia, knowing that poets rarely like to talk about anything except their art.

"I am laboring over a series of love poems in the Alexandrian fashion. That is one reason why I was happy to be invited here tonight. I have always admired the Alexandrian school of Greek verse." The other reason was a chance for a free meal, I thought. I was not being disparaging in this, having been in the same position many, many times myself. Before we turned him over to his literary admirers, he asked me a question.

"Your pardon, but are you a relative of Metellus Celer, the *praetor*?"

"He is a cousin of my father, but that doesn't mean I know him well. Throw a rock into the *Curia,* and chances are good that you'll hit a Metellus." He laughed at the witticism, and I could see him filing it away for use in a political lampoon. That was all right with me. I had stolen it from an acquaintance.

"Why was he curious about Celer?" I asked Sempronia when we were alone in a garden. She leaned close and spoke conspiratorially.

"Didn't you know? He's in love with Clodia!"

"Really? She and Celer have only been married for eight months. Isn't it early for an intrigue?"

"Well, you know Clodia." Indeed I did, all too well. She was a woman about whom I had decidedly mixed feelings. "Actually," Sempronia went on, "I think he just worships her from afar, writes love lyrics to her, that sort of thing. She's flattered, as who wouldn't be?"

"But you think it's nothing more than that?" I said, cursing myself for even caring. She shot me another evaluating glance.

"Dear Clodia hasn't let marriage interfere with her social activities," she said, "she's as wild as ever. But since she has married, she has been extremely discreet where men are concerned. I think she is being faithful, within her limits."

Well, how could I blame a sensitive young poet for being in love with Clodia? I certainly had been, at one time. We were strolling by a rather graceful shrine to Isis when we encountered a man surrounded by the Egyptian staff, including Lisas. He wore the tunic of an *eques,* but they treated him with the fawning deference usually reserved for kings. He saw Sempronia, smiled, and walked from his circle of Egyptians, who parted for him as if he were preceded by a hundred lictors. He was a tall, fine-looking man of middle years whose clothes were of a quality I could only envy, although he wore no jewelry except for the plain gold ring of his rank. This, I learned, was Caius Rabirius Postumus, a famous banker and son of that elderly, distinguished Senator whom Caesar had tried to prosecute for a crime almost forty years past. I now understood the deference of the

Egyptians. Although I had never met him, it was known that Postumus had lent huge sums to Auletes.

"Decius Caecilius," he said after we had exchanged the usual pleasantries, "did I not hear that you discovered the body of my friend Oppius this morning?"

"I merely happened by. He was your friend?"

"We had a number of business dealings. He was a part of the banking community. I was terribly shocked when I heard of the murder."

"Did he have enemies?" I asked him.

"Just the ones that bankers always have. He was a quiet family man, no political ambitions or intrigues I ever heard about."

"Then it was probably a debtor," I said.

"That would make little sense," Postumus said. "He had heirs, business associates, others who will surely assume any outstanding accounts. Believe me, if the death of a creditor canceled debts, none of us bankers would be alive tomorrow. Not all debtors are as reasonable as King Ptolemy."

"How is that?" Sempronia asked.

"He has named me minister of finance to the kingdom."

"He can use one," I noted. "I have never been able to understand how the king of the richest nation in the world can be so poor."

"It's amazing, isn't it?" he agreed. "Perhaps it's because Egypt hasn't been a true nation since the days of the pharaohs, hundreds of years ago. Nothing but conquerors since then. The Macedonians are just the most recent."

"There hasn't been a worthwhile Macedonian since Alexander," I opined, the wine sharpening my wit. "And he didn't amount to much. What does it take to beat Greeks and Persians, after all? Still, they were perfectly good barbarians while they were up in their mountains. A couple of generations after Alexander, what are they? Lunatics and drunkards, growing more degenerate with each inbred generation."

"Shame on you two!" Sempronia said. "Speaking that way about the man whose wine you are drinking."

"When Alexander was romping all the way to India,"
I said, "Rome was a little Italian town fighting other
Italian towns. Now we're master of the world, and we
didn't need any boyish god-king to accomplish it, either."

She took my arm and steered me toward the dining
room. "It's time to get some food into you, Decius. I
believe I hear dinner being announced."

That sounded good to me. All this learned discourse
had sharpened my appetite. The rest of the evening
passed pleasantly, but something nibbled at the edges
of my admittedly sodden consciousness like a mouse
nibbling a crust of bread. It was something Postumus
had said, but I could not bring it into full clarity. The
party was too full of attractions to let it bother me for
long.

III

___

I woke the next morning with a ringing head and a
mouth that told me the final course in last night's
banquet must have been Egyptian mummy. My aged
slaves, Cato (no relation to the Senator) and Cassandra,
were not sympathetic. They never were when it came to
my excesses, and I could not explain to them that I had
only been pursuing my public duties.

We have a tradition of allowing ourselves to be tyr-
annized and bullied by old domestics. It is certain that
I got no respect from these two. Having raised me from
infancy, they had no illusions about me. They stoutly
refused to accept manumission. They could no more
have fended for themselves than a pair of old plow-
oxen, but as long as they could make my life miserable,
they had a purpose.

"That's what you get, master!" Cato shouted cheerily,
throwing open the shutter and letting in a horrid, sear-
ing beam of morning sunlight, the vengeance of Apollo.
"That's what you get for being out to all hours, carous-
ing with those foreigners, then coming home to wake
your poor old retainers that have given up their whole
lives to your service and acting as if they didn't deserve
a little rest."

"Peace, Cato," I croaked. "I am going to die soon, and
then what will you do? Go back to my father? If he could
stand to have you around, he wouldn't have given you
to me in the first place." Suppressing a groan, I lurched
to my feet, steadying myself on the little writing-table
by my bed. Something unfamiliar shifted on it and I saw
that it was a roll of something white. Then I remem-

bered accepting my guest-gift before leaving the previous night's banquet. Lisas, knowing that I was a public official with much correspondence to carry out, had given me a truly useful gift. It was a great scroll of the very finest Egyptian papyrus. For a fat Alexandrian pervert, Lisas was a most thoughtful man.

"Are my clients outside?" I asked.

"Already gone, master," Cato said, "and it's been ages since you paid your morning call on your father."

"He does not require that duty while I am in office," I reminded him.

"Yes, but today is a market day," Cato reminded me. "Official business is forbidden, and it should be only good manners to pay your *salutatio* when you don't have to go to the temple. Too late now, though."

"A market day?" I said, cheering up a little. That meant a chance to prowl the city and see what I might turn up. Rome was the mistress of the world, but it was still, in most aspects, a small Italian hill-town. It thrived on gossip and market days were relished almost as much as public holidays. I splashed water in my face, threw on my third-best toga and left my house, not bothering with breakfast, which I could not have faced.

At that time, markets were still held in the *forum boarium*, the ancient cattle-market. It was in full roar when I arrived, with farmers' stalls everywhere. The larger livestock were no longer sold there, but poultry, rabbits and pigs were slaughtered on the spot for customers, and they were raising their usual clamor. The farming season had been exceptional, so that even this late in the year the stalls were heaped with fresh produce.

Besides the farmers, all manner of small merchants and mountebanks had set up shop. I availed myself of one of these, a public barber. While he scraped my bristled face smooth, I watched the bustling scene. The fortune-tellers' booths were well attended. Fortune-tellers were expelled from the city regularly, but they always came back. Near the barber's stool, an old woman sat on the ground, selling herbs and philters from a display laid out on a blanket.

"Look at those two," the barber said. I followed the

direction of his nod and saw a pair of young men going into a fortune-teller's booth. Both wore full beards, a fashion ordinarily affected only by barbarians and philosophers, but enjoying something of a vogue among the city youth.

"Disgusting to see Roman youths bearded up like so many Gauls. Bad for business, too," he added.

"Gauls wear mustaches, not beards," I said. "Anyway, at that age, they're just enthralled with being *able* to raise a beard."

"They're all troublemakers," the barber asserted stoutly. "Those bearded ones are the brawlers and drunks. They come of decent families, mind you. You can tell that by the quality of their clothes. But then, that's why they wear the beards, so they won't look respectable."

I paid the barber and made my way among the stalls, being careful where I stepped. Since the barber called it to my attention, it seemed that I could not look anywhere without seeing bearded young men. There were not really that many of them, but once a thing impinges itself on my consciousness, I tend to seek it out without conscious volition. It was unlikely to be a sign of mourning, for none of the youths wore the shabby clothes one wears while mourning, going unshaven and unshorn in the process.

Among the stalls of the craftsmen I found what I was looking for: a cutlery merchant. I did not want one who sold only his own wares, but one who traveled, buying and selling the wares of others. The one I found sold edged implements from a number of display cases, the sort that stand up, with doors that swing wide and are themselves lined with racks. These cases glittered with kitchen knives, butcher's cleavers, scissors and shears, awls, sickles and pruning knives and other farm implements, and a few daggers and short swords.

"Are you looking for anything in particular, sir?" the merchant asked. "I have some elegant military weaponry still packed away. A gentleman of your evident rank must spend time with the legions. I have swords decorated with gold and silver and parade pieces inlaid with carved amber, some with hilts of ivory. This is a largely rustic crowd, so I did not take them out. However, if you are interested, my slave can—"

"Actually," I interrupted, "I was wondering if you could tell me anything about this." I took out the snake-hilted dagger and handed it to him. His look of disappointment was so piercing that I thought it best to brighten his day.

"I am the *Quaestor* Decius Caecilius Metellus and I am investigating a murder. This is the murder weapon." Actually I had no authority whatever, but there was no need to tell him that.

"A murder!" He examined the dagger eagerly. People are always willing to lend you their expertise if they can feel important by doing so. He turned it over in his hands, admiring the discolorations left where the blood had been wiped off.

"Can you tell anything about it?" I asked impatiently.

"Well, it's African. You see this kind of heavy central spine on blades made there. And I've seen this kind of serpent carving before. They had some sort of serpent-god in Carthage, and they still make hilts like this around Utica and Thapsus."

"Do you see them very often?"

"Just the occasional souvenir brought back by a soldier. There were a lot of them brought back after the war with Jugurtha, but that's getting on toward fifty years ago, so you don't see many of those left. There's no demand for them here, since better knives are made here in Italy, and in Gaul."

"I thank you. This may turn out to be very valuable information."

He preened. "Always ready to be of service to the Senate and People, sir. Sure I can't interest you in a fine parade *gladius*? One worked with jet and coral, perhaps?"

"Thank you, but my arms have a few campaigns left in them."

"Well, sir, keep me in mind should you need any. And I hope you catch the murderer. Is it about that *eques* I heard about this morning?"

"Yes. A banker named Oppius."

He looked puzzled. "I thought it was a building contractor named Calenus."

I thanked him again and hurried away. All government offices were closed on a market day and free men did not have to work, but slave work went on as always. I decided that the quickest way to locate a contractor was through the great brick manufactory owned by the Afer family. It was located near the river, not a long walk from the *forum boarium*.

I felt the heat from the huge kilns while I was still a hundred paces away from the brickyards. A slave took me to an overseer who sat behind a table in an open shed, writing on wax tablets. He stood when I came in and identified myself.

"How many I help you, sir?"

"Do you have dealings with a contractor named Calenus?"

"Certainly, sir. He is involved with a number of large public projects. We supply all his bricks within the urban area."

"I must locate his house. Can you tell me where it is?"

"I will lend you one of our messengers to guide you there, sir. Hector!" he bellowed.

"That would be most helpful," I assured him. The heroically named slave appeared, a boy of about twelve.

"Hector, guide this gentleman to the home of Sextus Calenus, and then come back without delay."

I followed the boy, who was obviously delighted to be away from the brickyards, if only for a short time. "It's simple to find Calenus's house, master," he assured me. "You start by the Ostian gate and head up the alley just off the fountain with the statue of Neptune. You follow that alley to the shrine of Mercury and then you go up the steps between the fuller's and the tavern with the picture of Hercules painted on the front. At the top of the steps, you go left along the little courtyard and you pass three doors and then go up some more stairs to where there's a mill turned by a blind donkey. Calenus's house is right next to the mill."

"Why don't you just guide me?" I said. Unlike the new, provincial cities we had built, Rome was an un-

planned sprawl where it was difficult to find any given
house without a guide. Once in a while, some reform-
minded Senator would propose instituting a system for
naming or numbering the streets, but Romans are far
too conservative for anything so sensible. If you wanted
someone to come to your house, you sent a slave to
fetch him. If you could not afford a slave, it was unlikely
that anyone would want to visit you anyway.

The house of Calenus was crowded when I got there.
I gave the boy a copper *as* and he ran off happily, doubt-
less planning where he was going to spend it. I doubted
that the overseer at the brickyard would see him any-
time soon. I pushed through a crowd of household slaves
until I found a group surrounding a body laid out in
the atrium. The *designator* was there with his assistants,
standing well back, by the walls of the room. They would
prepare the body for burial when the initial viewing of
the body was over. I saw that they had already dressed
him in a new toga. He was a balding man of about fifty
years and his face had been artfully set with an expression of serenity.

A group of young men—sons, I guessed—stood com-
forting a sobbing, middle-aged woman. Other women
and slaves wept loudly and bitterly, but with none of the
verve the professional mourners would show at the funeral. Among those who had come to view the body
were several men in senatorial tunics. I looked for a familiar face and found one: a friend of my father's named
Quintus Crispus. I caught his eye and he came to join me.

"Isn't this terrible, Decius?" he said. "Who would want
to murder a man like Sextus Calenus? He hadn't an enemy in the world, that I ever heard of."

"He was a friend of yours?" I asked. We spoke in low
voices, the way one usually does in the presence of the
dead, although nobody could have heard us over the
wailing.

"A client. His family have been clients of mine for
generations, since before they gained equestrian status."

"How did it happen?" I asked him.

"It was late last night. I saw him yesterday afternoon,
on a matter of business. As his patron, I have always

worked to secure him public contracts. From there he went to have dinner with friends and didn't leave for home until well after dark. He was waylaid and killed right outside the door of his house. Robbed, so I hear."

"Were there any witnesses?"

"He had a slave linkboy with him, borrowed from the house where he had dinner. The fellow's around here someplace. He was clouted over the head and gashed a bit, but he wasn't badly hurt. Are you investigating?"

"Yes, I am." Well, I *was* investigating. I just had no authority to. "I'll question the slave presently."

I went to the *designator,* a skeletal man whose face had the lugubrious solemnity of one whose task it is to prepare corpses for burial. I identified myself and asked about the nature of the wound that had killed Calenus.

"The murder weapon was not left with the body, *Quaestor,*" he said. "The gentleman was stabbed five times. I think that the murderer tried three times, but the blade struck ribs and failed to penetrate. Then he stabbed twice beneath the rib cage and one of these thrusts pierced the heart."

"Have you any idea what type of weapon was used?" I inquired.

"The stab wounds were wide, about four fingers. It was either a very broad-bladed dagger or a short sword, perhaps a *gladius.*"

I went in search of the slave and found him in the kitchen, seated on a stool, his head bandaged and holding a compress to his neck. The compress was soaked through with blood. He was perhaps sixteen, with sandy hair and an intelligent if somewhat pained face. His tunic, now much stained, was of excellent quality and bespoke a rich owner. I asked him to describe the events of the previous night.

"My name is Ariston, and I belong to the house of Marcus Duronius. Last night I was given a torch and assigned the task of walking Master Sextus home. My master is out there with the family, he will confirm that. We'd just got to the door out there, and I hadn't even time to knock when two men jumped out of the shadows. I saw one grab Master Sextus from behind and that was when the other one hit me alongside the head with his sword hilt. I don't think I was quite knocked out, but I don't remember getting this." He took away the compress and showed an ugly gash in his neck. It was still seeping blood, but it did not look dangerous. "I think this was all that saved me." He touched a narrow copper ring that encircled his neck. "I ran away once and my master put this on me."

I leaned close and studied it. As usual with such rings, it gave the slave's name, the master's, and a promise of reward if the runaway were apprehended and returned. It bore a deep gouge where a point had dug in and then skittered off, gashing the boy's neck. I pushed his hair back and saw that his forehead had not been branded with an F for *fugitivus*, so the ring was just for temporary discipline.

"Tell your master you need a new ring, his name has almost been obliterated on this one. Then keep it as a lucky piece for the rest of your life. Now, what else can you tell me?"

"Not much. I only saw them for an instant. I couldn't recognize them if I saw them again. It only took a few seconds, because I remember the *janitor* coming out to see what the commotion was. I won't have to testify in court, will I, sir?" He was frightened because slaves can only testify under torture.

"Don't worry," I said, patting his shoulder. "Since you are not suspected of any wrongdoing, it would only be a matter of form. They just pour a little water up your nose."

"But I don't *like* water up my nose!" He winced at the pain in his neck. It almost did me good to see someone who felt even worse than I did.

"There's nothing else you can tell me? Did the torch go out?"

He though a moment. "As I said, I didn't see much, but I remember the torch was still burning on the street when the *janitor* came out and helped me get up." He rubbed his sore head with his free hand. "Of course, he dropped me when he saw his master lying there like a sacrificial ram." He thought a while longer. "I think they were foreigners, sir, Greeks or maybe Asiatics."

"Why do you say that?" I asked.

"Well, who else wears beards?"

I walked back to my house pondering. I felt that the two murders must be related, but there was nothing to connect them save the rank of the victims. The *equites* were a large class, and Rome was a populous city, where murder was not uncommon. I doubted that anyone else shared my belief that there was a connection. One victim had been a banker, the other a building contractor. One had been stabbed in the back by someone using an African dagger, the other run through the body from in front by someone using a sword and working with a confederate.

It was clear that the killers of Calenus had not been professionals. The *sicarii* who infested the city used curved knives and their preferred technique was throat cutting. An experienced swordsman, an ex-soldier or gladiator, would have killed him with one clean thrust, even in the dark. This one, with a friend to hold the victim and torchlight to see by, had required five clumsy thrusts to dispatch the victim and had even bungled killing a slave who lay semiconscious on the street. They had robbed the body, but that may have been to disguise what was actually an assassination, something the killer of Oppius had not thought to do, another amateur mistake. The meaning of the beards? There my ponderings failed to enlighten me.

The day was still young, although I felt old. After forcing down some lunch I felt marginally better and went to the baths, where I sweated out the last of the excesses of the night before.

From the baths I went to the Temple of Saturn. It was nearly deserted, since there was no work done that day in the treasury and there were no rites to be performed. An elderly priest nodded to me as I entered and I pretended to be examining the racked military standards until I was alone. Then, taking the same lamp I had used the day before, I went into the storerooms.

The room with the shields now contained another

forty or so shields and a sheaf of javelins. The previously empty room now contained a small heap of swords. This batch was as mismatched as those in the other room, but two attracted my attention and I slid them from the heap for a closer look. Both were short swords of a rather antiquated design. The handle of one was of horn, the other of wood. Both were crudely carved with serpents wound spirally. I slid them back into the heap and ascended the stairs.

Was this a coincidence? The cutlery merchant had said that such weapons had been common in Italy after the Jugurthine war, and these two swords looked as if they might have been that old. But that I should encounter such oddities on two successive days in connection with two different offenses smacked of more coincidence than I was prepared to accept.

I knew that I had to do something, but I needed more information. Perhaps more important, I needed some sort of semi-legal status for what I was doing. Of the Praetors of that year who were empowered to grant me such status, only one was a kinsman I knew fairly well. This was Metellus Celer, who since the death of Metellus Pius was the virtual head of our family. His prestige in Rome was great, so that, when Cicero for reasons of his own had turned down the governorship of Cisalpine Gaul upon the end of his term of office, Celer had been given the province. It was rare for a *praetor* to receive a proconsular appointment, but Celer was of sufficient prestige.

Taking my courage in both hands, I presented myself at his gate. It was not Celer who made me nervous, but rather his wife, Clodia, a woman with whom I had a rather tangled relationship. I doubt that Clodia ever had an uncomplicated relationship with anyone. She was suspected of a number of murders in her scandalous lifetime, and I know that she was guilty of some of them.

"The *Quaestor* Decius Caecilius Metellus to see the *praetor*," I said to the *janitor* who guarded the gate. He summoned a majordomo who then ushered me into the atrium.

My fears were realized when Clodia came in. "Decius,

we haven't seen you in far too long!" She was as beautiful as I remembered her, and her smiling face showed no hint of the demon I knew to lurk there.

"My work prevents me from circulating," I told her.

"It didn't keep you from the party at the Egyptian ambassador's residence last night," she said. I felt an immediate stab of alarm that she might be having me followed. "Young Catullus told me that he met you there." I sighed with relief.

"That young man seems quite smitten with you," I said. "Dare I speculate that his new cycle of love poems is addressed to you?"

"Oh, well, you know these new poets. They prefer to address their verses to living women rather than the mythological sort. He has been living as a guest in my sister's house and he pays me extravagant court when I visit, as I did this morning."

"Which sister is that?" I asked, wishing Celer would show up.

"Lucullus's wife. Dear Lucius has decided to leave public life altogether to be a patron of the arts." She could not hide a certain tone of contempt. Clodia was interested only in men who strove for ultimate power. "Have you seen their new mansion? It's the size of a small town and Lucius is building a country house even bigger."

"All the more room for poets," I said. By the glaze in her eyes I could see that she was already growing bored with me, an attitude I much preferred to an excess of interest.

"Well, we have dinner guests arriving soon, Decius, and I must see to the dining room. Will you stay for dinner?"

"Alas," I said hastily, "I have another obligation this evening. Another time, perhaps." She smiled and left and I commenced breathing easier. A few minutes later, Celer arrived. He was a short, bald-headed man with a froglike face. He was blocky and compact, with hairy legs showing beneath his casual tunic.

"Good afternoon, Decius," he said. "I trust your father is well?"

"In the best of health," I assured him.

"That is good to hear. I shall be backing him for the Censorship in next year's elections. If necessary, I'll send a *legatus* from my post in Gaul to represent me here in the city. I am sure that he will be one of the two elected."

"He is very grateful for your support."

That took care of the social amenities. "Now, Decius, how may I help you? I have a few minutes before my guests begin to arrive."

"I apologize for coming to you on a noncourt day, but this is a matter requiring discretion."

"There's no such thing as a nonbusiness day for a public official," he said, "any more than there's a non-duty day for a soldier. What is this mysterious matter?"

"You know of the two murders of the *equites* Oppius and Calenus?"

"Naturally. Rome is not a safe place, but then it never was. I've known mornings when there were forty men of senatorial or equestrian rank dead in the streets, and nobody bothered to count the lesser corpses."

"That was in rougher times," I said. "That was when the gang and faction fighting was at its height, when Sulla published his proscription lists and when Marius led mobs of cutthroats in the streets. Times have been settled lately."

"Even so, there are always robbers and jealous hus-bands. The *equites* are involved in business and money-lending. Business rivals can be as ruthless as the political kind."

"Even so, I think that these two murders are connected, and I fear that there will be more." I did not yet want to tell him about the arms cache in the temple. "I want you to appoint me investigator for these murders. In secrecy, of course, but I wish to have some sort of legal footing when I have enough evidence to bring forth charges."

"Hmm. I think you are making something out of nothing, Decius. You have always had this propensity for snooping."

"It has paid off in the past," I reminded him. "I have ferreted out crimes and conspiracies no one else sus-pected."

"And gotten yourself into a great deal of trouble

thereby," he said. "Your father and I and your uncles have all had to exert ourselves to preserve your young hide when you have troubled powerful men."

"For which I am exceedingly grateful. Even so, I would ask for your support in this. I have reason to believe that the murders are only a part of a far greater conspiracy, one that threatens the public order and possibly the security of the state."

"This is a lot to infer from two wretched murders," he grumbled. Then, "Oh, very well. I appoint you special investigator into these murders. You are to report to me before you go haling anyone into court and you are to bring to me any evidence you turn up. And I do not want you going over my head and consulting with the Consuls without my permission, is that clear?"

"It is. What I discover will redound solely to your credit," I promised.

"Very good. But if you do something disgraceful, I will try to pretend I'm not even related to you. The times are perilous now and it is difficult for us to steer a middle course. It is easier than usual to make enemies. Now, Decius, I must prepare for my guests."

I thanked him profusely and left his house. I was all too aware of what his warning meant. Romans were growing dangerously divided along faction lines. We Metelli were moderates by the standards of the times, but we had historically backed the aristocratic *optimates* and had supported Sulla, the champion of that party. In fact, for the past twenty years, nearly all the men in power had been Sulla's supporters while his Marian enemies were mostly in exile.

Now, though, Sulla's men were growing old, the sons of the old Marians were trickling back into Rome and into Roman politics, and the power of the *populares* were reviving. Sulla's constitution had stripped the Tribunes of the People of most of their old powers, but legislation of the past few years had restored the greater part of it. Many new politicians had arisen to challenge the ascendancy of the *optimates*. Caesar was the nephew by marriage of Gaius Marius, and he used that connection to curry favor with the populace, who still revered the name of the old tyrant.

The time was fast approaching when there would be no space in the middle for anyone who had no wish to align himself with either faction. The Senate was primarily *optimate*. The moneyed class of the *equites* had long been at odds with the Senate, but was, as a group, beginning to coalesce into the *optimate* camp. The Centuriate Assembly was closely tied to the senatorial class by clientage and patronage while the Popular Assemblies were, naturally overwhelmingly *populare*.

Pompey was the darling of the *populares*. The Senate had once supported him, but now it feared him. He used the power of the Tribunes to block other generals' triumphs. He was popular with the veterans in their settlements throughout Italy.

Two years before, Caesar, as *aedile*, had put on public games more lavish than anyone had ever seen before. He had bought and trained so many gladiators that the Senate had hastily put through legislation limiting the number a citizen could own, for fear that he was building his own army. He had subsidised the people's housing for his year in office, and given free doles of grain above what was already allotted. In doing this, he had gone into debt to such an extravagant degree that many believed him to be mad. In this Caesar proved himself to be the shrewdest politician of all time. He had bought popularity with the masses at the expense of moneylenders. Besides the professional financiers, he had borrowed from friends, from Senators, from provincial governors, from anyone with money to lend. Now those men were beginning to realize that the only way they were ever going to collect on those loans was to push Caesar's career, to make sure that he received lucrative commands where there was loot to be had, high offices where rich bribes would come his way, and the governorship of wealthy provinces. He had built a spectacular political future for himself with other people's money.

The great and rich Crassus had tried to steer clear of faction politics, but he was drifting into the *populare* camp. Like Pompey, he had been a supporter of Sulla, but he saw the future belonging to the rising politicians. Like the other financiers, he had been hurt by Lucullus's magnanimous cancellation of the Asian debt, but he was too rich to be truly hurt by anything.

It must be said in all honesty that none of these men had the good of the Roman people at heart. The *optimates* spoke of saving the Roman state from would-be tyrants, but they merely wanted to perpetuate aristocratic privilege. The leaders of the *populares* claimed to be on the side of the common man, but they sought only to aggrandize themselves. It was a struggle for raw power by two groups of self-seeking men. The only truly enlightened men of the times, Lucullus and Sertorius, had done their good work outside of Italy, in places where the corruptions of Roman Government had not yet taken hold.

And me? Sometimes I wonder myself. I fondly believed that I was trying to save the Republic in something like its old form, even though my own cynicism told me that it had never been as good and just as we liked to think it was. I did not want to see our whole empire fall into the hands of men like Caesar, or Pompey, or Crassus or, most unthinkable of all, Clodius.

But I was soon to find that there were even more ominous developments in store.

When I arrived at my house I found a slave messenger waiting for me. He gave me a tiny scroll tied with a ribbon, my name written on its outside in a feminine hand.

The Lady Fulvia, it said, *requests the company of the* Quaestor *Decius Caecilius Metellus the Younger for dinner tomorrow evening. If you can come, as I pray you will, please send your reply by this slave.*

I promptly sat and wrote out my acceptance and gave it to the slave. Things were looking up. Fulvia was a beautiful young widow of excellent family, as lively and accomplished as Sempronia. She was also, as everyone in Rome knew, the mistress of Quintus Curius.

IV

A Greek slave woman conducted me into the atrium, where other slaves were hanging flower chains and fussing with plants in huge Persian vases. As was common with women who were mistresses of their own households, Fulvia owned a staff made up largely of women. Hers were quiet, efficient and well educated, almost all of them Greek. The lady of the house was more than fluent in that language.

It was an oddity of the times that the women of the better classes were often better educated than the men, who were usually so busy with business, politics and war that they had little time for the gentler arts of civilization. Beyond the necessities of war, politics and estate management, a man was expected to be proficient in public speaking and rhetoric, subjects of limited interest outside the political arena.

Women like Fulvia and Sempronia knew more about poetry, history, drama, painting and sculpture and so forth than almost any man in Rome. For men, proficiency in these subjects was suspect, a sign of Greek decadence and probable effeminacy. Many men did not like their women carrying on in such a fashion. After all, if one wanted to have educated persons in one's home, one simply bought them.

Truth to tell, there was little for a highborn woman to do in the home anymore. There was no point in sitting and spinning and weaving like Penelope. The slave staff took care of the house and nurses raised the children. No woman could practice law or enter politics or.

join a legion. The alternatives were to become scholars or behave scandalously; there were some who did both.

Fulvia came to greet me dressed in a gown that did little to stop the passage of lamplight. Her hair, like that of many Roman ladies, was a mass of elaborate blonde curls. Unlike most, hers had not been shorn from the scalp of a Gallic girl. We exchanged the usual greetings and compliments.

"I am so happy you could come, Decius. It was thoughtless of me to expect you to accept an invitation on such short notice."

"Nothing could have prevented me," I assured her. "I would have canceled an appointment with a Consul to attend one of your famous gatherings." This was only moderately insincere. Fulvia was famed for having varied and interesting guests at her entertainments. Poets and playwrights, philosophers, noted wits and women of questionable antecedents. Neither wealth nor high birth were necessary, but one had to be amusing. Fulvia was one of the first highborn Romans to allow actors into her house as guests rather than as performers. There were those, of course, who considered this the very nadir of degeneracy, but invitations to her evenings were much sought-after.

Her taste in men was more questionable. Her long liaison with Quintus Curius was a matter of much city gossip. He had been a Senator, but was expelled by the Censors for scandalous behavior. When one considers what a Senator could get away with and remain in the Senate in those days, some idea of the enormity of his transgressions may be formed. By all accounts, his courtship of Fulvia had been stormy, including threats against her life. Politically, he was of no consequence, a mere hanger-on of greater men, whose favor he cultivated in hopes that they would help defray his crushing debts.

I could never understand how a woman like Fulvia could dote on a loathsome, worthless parasite like Curius, but then there is much about women I have never understood. Philosophers tell me that women and men do not properly belong to the same species, and therefore can never understand each other. This may well be true. I have noticed that the finest women are often drawn to the very worst men, while my own fortune in that area has not been of the best.

The man in question had already arrived, and Curius greeted me as if we were long-separated friends. I expected a touch for a loan before the night was over.

"Decius! How good to see you! I hear great things of your work." How he could have heard any such thing was beyond me. "And in less than three months you will take your place in the Senate. Richly deserved, my friend." I am not averse to flattery, but I prefer it from a more savory source.

"You must miss that august body of men," I said.

He shrugged. "What is done by one Censor may be undone by another." That sounded ominous. He took me to a pair of men who had also arrived early. "Decius, I believe you know Marcus Laeca and Caius Cethegus?" I did, slightly. They were Senators by virtue of having held, like me, the quaestorship, and were unlikely to rise any higher in office. We exchanged small talk for a few minutes. It seemed that this gathering was going to be entirely political. Dull as the company was, it looked promising as far as my investigation was concerned. Low-level functionaries with no prospects for higher office form the classic breeding ground for rebellion. Neither Curius nor Laeca, though, seemed to me to be either desperate or courageous enough for any truly violent enterprise, however great the rewards. Caius Cornelius Cethegus Sura, on the other hand, was a notorious firebrand and a well-known scatterbrain, just the sort to be involved in something sublimely violent and stupid.

Sempronia arrived, accompanied by a matched pair of Nubian slaves dressed in feathers and zebra skins. She was explaining to Fulvia that the two were gifts from Lisas, the Egyptian ambassador. They were twins and therefore a great rarity, because the Nubians usually smothered twins at birth for some barbaric reason of their own. I wondered what favor Sempronia had done for Lisas to earn such a gift.

Soon after, the last guests arrived. They were a man

and a woman. I instantly recognized the red hair and ruddy face of Lucius Sergius Catilina. The way the others fell silent and turned toward him, I knew that he was the reason for this night's gathering. I shuddered to think that Catilina might be behind the matter I was investigating. He was a dangerous man. He went around the room greeting and clasping hands. When he reached me he brought the young woman forward.

"Decius, have you met my stepdaughter, Aurelia?"

"No," I said, "but I am happy to say that she greatly favors her mother." Orestilla, Catilina's second or perhaps third wife, was a famous beauty. Her daughter was about nineteen or twenty, but she had as much poise as Sempronia or Fulvia. She was not as brazenly clad as the older women, but she was so lavishly endowed by nature that she needed nothing artful to call attention to her figure. Her chestnut hair was short, set in tight ringlets. She had huge gray eyes, startlingly direct.

"Your mother and mine were close friends," she said. "She still speaks often of Servilla." The young face was beautiful but solemn, as if she did not smile frequently. I did not remember my mother mentioning Orestilla, but she had died when I was very young.

"Young Decius is marked out for a remarkable career," Catilina said heartily. He looked at me searchingly. "I suppose you have a good position lined up when you leave office?"

"I'd expected a decent offer from one of the Consuls or *Praetores*," I said, playing the role, "but nothing so far."

"Incredible!" Catilina said. "Why, a staff appointment should come almost automatically to a young man of your birth and experience."

"So you would think," I said. Aurelia was giving me disturbingly close attention. She did not wear the rings, bracelets, necklaces, tiaras and other jewelry that adorned the other women. To make up for it, she wore the longest rope of pearls I had ever seen. It looped behind her neck, crossed between her breasts and circled her waist three times. I did not know whether it was intended to emphasize the shapeliness of her neck, the size of her breasts or the slenderness of her waist, but it did all three and damaged my concentration. It must have been worth a small city.

"Disgraceful that our officials do so little to advance the careers of deserving young statesmen." I must admit that this was much better than being flattered by Quintus Curius. Catilina could at least sound as if he meant it.

"There is little I can do about it," I said. "Junior officials have little enough power, and soon I'll be an ex-junior official."

"Perhaps there is something you can do," Catilina said. "We must speak more of this."

At that moment the female majordomo announced dinner and we filed into the dining room. To my great delight, I found myself reclining next to Aurelia. This should have been an irrelevance, since I was supposed to be uncovering a seditious plot, but I saw no reason why I should be deprived of pleasant feminine company while I pursued my duties. I was still very young.

I will not bore you with a recitation of the wines and dishes served, although my memory for this sort of detail improves as the years advance. More important was the company. Each of the men present, saving myself, had been prosecuted at some time or other for corruption, although it was a rare politician in those days who escaped that charge. The traditional way for a newly arrived Senator to make his name was to prosecute somebody for corruption, the usual charges being graft, bribe taking and extortion. These men, however, had been proven guilty on every count with overwhelming evidence. And all of them were deeply in debt.

Catilina was the same sort, only to a far higher degree, and the crimes imputed to him were not all political. His bloodthirstiness in carrying out Sulla's proscriptions was legendary, but that had typed him as merely one of the more opportunistic young men of a rough time. I have already made mention of his alleged illicit liaison with the Vestal Fabia, a charge brought against him by Clodius. Even in the usually gentle realm of courtship, Catilina's behavior had been more than ordinarily violent. When he had wished to marry Orestilla, his grown son by a former marriage had objected. Rumor had it that Catilina had then murdered his son. True or not, he was the sort of man around whom this sort of story grew. More recently, each time he had announced himself a candidate for Consul, charges of extortion had been brought against him, barring him from candidacy. At the time of the last election, charges of more direct criminal activity had been brought against him. Cicero had charged him with plotting against his life and had surrounded himself with bodyguards, contributing to Catilina's already bad reputation. I cannot say how many of these charges may have been true. Catilina always complained bitterly that he had many enemies in high places. But then, few men have deserved enemies more.

I was more interested in who his friends were. Boisterous as he was, I could not believe that Catilina, unaided, represented a credible threat to the state. He was too profligate, too headstrong, too heedless of future consequences. And he was notoriously poor. He was not as intelligent as Caesar, who could turn indebtedness to his own advantage. Even less threatening were his lackeys. But just being in their company made me suspect, and I was glad that I had gone to Celer for semi-official status. If Catilina was truly behind a conspiracy against the state, then someone was behind Catilina.

"Do you know my stepfather well?" Aurelia asked. All the diners were conversing among themselves in low voices.

"Lucius Sergius and I have met from time to time, mostly under informal circumstances, such as this. We haven't had much call to meet officially. He was a *praetor* long before I was even eligible to stand for *quaestor*."

"I was wondering." Her voice was languorous, her eyes hooded and inward-looking. "He is always surrounded by younger men these days." That was a statement open to various interpretations. I said nothing. "You don't look like them, though."

"Oh. They run to a type, then?" I asked. I was truly

interested to learn what type of men I had thrown in with.

"Wellborn and worthless," she said succinctly. "Greek tutors, good clothes, no money, old enough for the legions but never served." She looked at my scar. "You've been with the legions. And you've taken the trouble to actually stand for office. And you don't wear a beard."

The back of my neck prickled and I took a sip of lightly watered wine to cover my excitement. "They wear beards?"

"Yes." She looked puzzled. "Most of them. It's their way of being unconventional, I think. It may be the only gesture within their capabilities. Surely you've noticed them?"

"My work keeps me underground most days," I said. "But I've seen them here and there around the city. I thought it was some horrid outbreak of philosophy."

"Far from it. Some are from old Marian families. At least, that's their excuse for being kept out of power. I think it more likely to be good taste on the part of the assemblies."

"Am I to take it that you do not admire your stepfather's friends?" I asked.

"It's sufficient that they admire him." She shrugged, a difficult gesture when reclining, and one which she performed to perfection, causing those superb breasts to roll enticingly. "There are always only a few to lead, and a great many cattle."

"I trust I am not one of the cattle," I said.

She looked me over coolly. "That may be," she said after she had surveyed me, presumably for bovine qualities.

"Why are these impecunious young men so drawn to Lucius?" I asked ingenuously.

"Who would not be? He's like Sulla. He can raise men from obscurity to the highest rank. That is a great attraction to men who could never accomplish such a thing on their own."

"If you will forgive my observation," I said, "he has thus far been in no position to raise anyone from obscurity."

"For the moment," she said, holding out her cup for refilling. "But that was the way it was with Sulla, once. He fought the battles and he captured Jugurtha, but old Marius took the credit. But the men who supported Sulla did well out of it in the end."

That was shrewdly put. My own family had done well out of Sulla's reign as dictator. They had thought a man of intelligent, calculated violence preferable to a crazed old loon like Gaius Marius. At least, I had always accepted the accounts of men like my father that that had been their reasoning. Perhaps they just wanted to be on the winning side.

"So does Lucius plan to stand for Consul yet again?" I asked.

"I think it's something like that," she said, her expression unreadable as she raised her winecup and the rim obscured her face.

"Decius," Catilina said. He lay on the couch opposite me so we were separated by several feet and he had to speak loudly. "What is your opinion on the consulship of Cicero? We have just been discussing him."

"He is the best orator in Rome," I said. "Perhaps the best who ever lived. He writes wonderfully and his grasp of the niceties of law and legal practice is legendary."

Catilina snorted. "In other words, he governs like a lawyer. Is this what Rome needs? Where are the soldiers who made us great? When did Cicero ever win glory in the field?"

"Antonius is no lawyer," I reminded him. Catilina looked sour. He had sought a *coitio* with Antonius for the election of the previous year, but something had gone wrong and Antonius had thrown in with Cicero instead.

"Yes, well, he's no soldier either, and I predict the Macedonians will have a rough time of it when he gets there next year." Catilina lacked military distinction himself but, like most such men, he conceived of himself as a glorious general. His mediocre record he attributed to lack of opportunity.

"I confess I was surprised that Cicero turned down

the proconsular governorship of Macedonia," I said, giving him an opening.

He pounced. "It's because Cicero is a coward! He knows that it will mean fighting and he has no stomach for it. He would rather stay here in Rome and be a nuisance, troubling better men with his piddling legal tricks."

"If his last accusations against you are true," I said, "he hasn't been very safe here in Rome either."

Catilina laughed uproariously and, I think, honestly. "He sees plots against his life everywhere. That is simply the way it is with cowards. Believe me, Decius"—now he looked at me very seriously and directly—"if I were to commit myself to desperate action, I would not confine myself to murdering the likes of Marcus Tullius Cicero." He pronounced the name as if it were some rare disease.

"I doubt our Decius has the nerve for truly desperate action," said Cethegus, with precisely the same look and intonation as a ten-year-old bully. He was a dark man, with a saturnine face and a mouth that turned down at the corners. He was an easy man to hate.

"I do suffer from an excess of intelligence," I told him. "Only the truly stupid hazard their lives and fortunes without a chance of victory."

"Men like you can afford to be patient," Cethegus said, contemptuously. "Not all of us have illustrious families to support us and push our careers." Catilina was watching us both carefully. For some reason he was letting his flunky have his head.

"Isn't the curule *Aedile* Lentulus Spinther a close kinsman of yours?" I asked.

"And what does that amount to?" he said hastily, as if it were a disgrace to be related to a high official.

"I think I know what Decius means," Laeca said. I had the distinct impression that some sort of signal had passed between him and Catilina, telling him to take my part. "There are so many Caecilii Metelli that one of many young men, just beginning public life, does not sit high in family councils, am I right, Decius?"

I forced a good malcontent's scowl. "I won't deny it."

"And," Laeca continued, "I daresay that the expenses of your office have been painful. When I was *quaestor,* it seemed as if the *quaestores* of the past decade had neglected the highways. I had to go deeply into debt to see to their paving." He was a fat man, who spoke smoothly and agreeably.

"How about it, Decius?" Catilina asked. "Have the expenses of the office sent you to the moneylenders?"

I saw an opportunity. "Expenses! Do you think it is just a matter of paving the roads? No longer!" I tried to act slightly drunk, which, I swear, I was not. "Next I must stand for *aedile.* Since Caesar's games two years ago, the people expect such entertainment from the *aediles.* That means I must borrow *now* to support that office. A few years ago, people thought that twenty pairs of gladiators was a fine show. Caesar has taught them to expect five hundred pairs at a single set of games! Not to mention the lions and bears and aurochs and so forth."

"Very true," Laeca said. "Not just gladiators, but *Campanian* gladiators, from the best schools. Not just a public banquet after the games, but fresh meat and fish and foreign fruits for every last bricklayer in Rome. Who can compete with that sort of profligacy?" His fat face creased in a rueful, mock-sympathetic smile. "But surely your family will defray some of your expenses?"

"They would for some of us," I said, frowning. "My father has been helpful, but we're not among the really rich Metelli, and none of the Metelli have wealth like Crassus or Lucullus. We are spread too thin for wealth to concentrate." This last made a very neat wordplay in the Latin still in use at the time, and was applauded. The ladies applauded with special warmth, and it occurred to me that Fulvia and Sempronia had said nothing, a very suspicious circumstance. It was clear that Catilina was directing this conversation, and had forbidden them to speak until he was satisfied about something.

"And have you been so fortunate as to find financial backers?" Laeca asked solicitously.

"One is never sufficient," I said a little stiffly. "Unless you have Crassus behind you."

"Crassus has recently forged ties with your family," Catilina pointed out.

"As I have said, there are a great many Metelli, and we are not held in equal esteem by Crassus, who considers me a personal enemy." In this age of the First Citizen, people may have forgotten how great a man Crassus was in those days. Suffice it to say that for a mere *quaestor* to think that Crassus took enough notice of him to consider the wretch a personal enemy was the height of presumption. It was exactly the sort of thing men like these would find endearing.

"And you can't very well go to Pompey," Laeca said, "if the rumors of a few years ago are true. He had you exiled."

"I found it expedient to leave the city for a year or two," I said cryptically. What was true of Crassus was doubly true of Pompey. In truth, I was never more than a nuisance to Pompey. At this time, he might have had difficulty remembering me. He had more important things on his mind.

"Your family," Laeca said, "while famed for moderation, generally oppose the ambitions of Pompey. Yet your cousin, Metellus Nepos, is Pompey's faithful legate. He has been elected Tribune of the *plebs* for next year and will be pushing legislation to further Pompey's ambitions."

"A wise family always keeps a few members in every camp," I said. "That way, you don't lose everything if you've backed the wrong side. And Nepos will accomplish nothing as Tribune, because Cato will be his colleague and Cato will block every piece of pro-Pompey legislation he introduces. Cato stood for the tribunate just to oppose Nepos."

"There is always Lucullus," Cethegus said, making it sound sarcastic. Everything he said sounded sarcastic.

"Lucullus and I have never been at odds," I said, "but I would not approach him. He is married to one of the sisters of Clodius, and Clodius hates me more than Pompey and Crassus combined."

"You have a rare knack for making enemies," Catilina said, laughing. Taking their cue, the others laughed as well. Aurelia didn't. "Well, any man Clodius hates is a friend of mine. So you've had to go to the professional moneylenders, then?"

"Why all this curiosity about my financial affairs?" I asked.

"Every man with ambition who was not born rich is in debt by definition," Catilina said, "but any man indebted to one of the three we mentioned is in that man's purse and cannot be trusted."

"Trusted?" I said. "Trusted in what fashion?"

"We are all ambitious men," Catilina said quietly, "and we know who stands between us and the power we are qualified to wield, the honors we deserve. They sequester to themselves every high office and command while keeping better men crushed beneath a burden of debt. Surely you don't think that it is some form of accident that for the last twenty years the expenses of holding office have risen so tremendously?" His face was growing redder. "Is it any coincidence that we are pushed into the grasp of the moneylenders? How did it come about that highborn men, whose families have produced Rome's Consuls and generals for centuries, are beholden to baseborn cash-breeders our ancestors would not have considered worthy to be spat upon?"

"Freedmen, most of them," Cethegus said, "men who should have stayed slaves, even if they pretend to be citizens and *equites.*"

"It is convenient for our higher officeholders," I allowed.

"It's more than convenient," Catilina insisted. "It is the result of plotting by a tiny clique of powerful men who will never willingly relinquish power. Who among us can live with such infamy and still call himself a man?" He was getting warmed up now, and the others were hanging on every word. I glanced at Aurelia and she was looking at him with adoration, but I detected something else in her expression. Was it mockery?

"And now," Catilina went on, "what sort of man assumes the leadership of Rome? Marcus Tullius Cicero! A lawyer! A man who has no qualification for office save a facility for bending words to his will. And there are

more just like him. Such men could never bring themselves to make the sort of hard, quick, ruthless decisions
a real Consul must make. They believe only in words,
not deeds."

"So what sort of man does Rome need?" I asked him.

"A man like Sulla," Catilina said, surprising me. "Sulla
took power when all had fallen into chaos. He sought
neither the fawning favor of the mob nor the patronage
of the aristocrats. He purged the Senate, proscribed enemies of the state, reformed the courts, gave us a new
constitution and then, when he was done, he dismissed
his lictors and walked from the Forum a private citizen,
to retire to his country house and write his memoirs.
That is the sort of man Rome needs."

There was much in what he said, but Catilina had left
out a few details for rhetorical effect. For instance, that
Sulla had been the cause as well as the queller of political chaos. Also, he could well afford to retire after his
dictatorship, since he had killed or exiled all his enemies and left behind him his own partisans, firmly in
power. There was no doubt of the identity of this pu-
tative new Sulla. I stared frowningly into my winecup,
as if pondering, finally coming to a momentous decision.

"I think," I said solemnly, "that I could follow such a
man. Twenty years ago, the Metelli were among the
foremost supporters of Sulla. Why should I be less bold
than they?"

"Why, indeed," Catilina said. He seemed to be satisfied, for now the women began to join the conversation.
There was no more said of power or of cabals preventing worthy men from gaining office. I paid much attention to Aurelia, who seemed to be warming to me.

As the wine flowed, the dice and knucklebones came
out and we began to gamble. I joined in, although I
ordinarily confine my betting to races or fights, where I
flatter myself that I have some skill in predicting the
outcome. I have little taste for wagering on pure chance.

Although I did not lose heavily, I was a bit alarmed
to see the sums the others were betting. For self-
proclaimed poor men they seemed inordinately well

furnished with cash. Although they all shouted loud, traditional curses when they lost, none of them seemed overly upset.

"Are you a lucky man?" Aurelia asked as the dice cup made its way back around to me.

"I wouldn't be alive if I weren't," I said. "But when it comes to dice and knucklebones, I have never been lucky."

"Let me lend you some luck," she whispered as I took the cup. She leaned toward me, as if watching the play over my shoulder, and I felt one prodigious breast pressing into my back. Through the cloth of my tunic and her gown, I could feel the hardness of her nipple. Almost as intimate was the softness of her breath on my ear. A surge of lust flooded me and I knew that it would be some time before I would be able to stand up without making a raucous spectacle of myself. To cover my discomfiture, I shook the leather cup with great vigor and smacked it down loudly upon the table, then jerked it back.

"Venus!" Aurelia breathed, making it sound almost like a prayer. Indeed, it was venus, the highest score. Each of the knucklebones showed a different surface.

"It will take some luck to match that," Catilina said, taking the cup. "But I have always been a lucky gambler." He shook the cup and slammed it down. He jerked the cup back and cursed, loudly and sincerely. I did not think it was because of the money he had lost. The knucklebones each showed the same surface, and it was the surface given the value of one. It was the lowest score, *canicula,* the little dog.

V

Over the next week, there were four more murders. All the victims were *equites*. Even for Rome, this was something unusual and the city was abuzz. One was bludgeoned, one had his throat cut, one was stabbed and the fourth was found floating in the Tiber, drowned. This last may have been accidental, but after five clear murders, nobody was ready to believe that.

The usual wild ideas made the rounds. Soothsayers offered murky revelations. But the city was not really alarmed. In fact, the general attitude was one of quiet satisfaction. The *equites* were not popular. They lacked the prestige of the *nobiles* and the senatorial class and they did not have the numbers of the commons. Too many people were in debt to them. They had wealth and comfort and thus were envied. There was still much hard feeling over the *Praetor* Otho's infamous action in reserving for the *equites* the fourteen rows of theater seats behind those traditionally reserved for the Senators and the Vestals. Overall, the general feeling in the city was that a few murders were just what that upstart class needed.

One of the murdered men, named Decimus Flavius, was a director of the Red faction in the circus. I decided to investigate him first, for no better reason than that the Caecilii were traditionally members of the Red faction, although the rest of the Metelli were Whites. Both of these factions were dwindling as the Blues and Greens came to dominate the races. The Greens had become the faction of the common man, while the Blues were the faction of the aristocratic *optimates,* their clients and supporters. Most of the *equites* were also Blues. These two factions would occupy facing sections of the circus and engage in great shouting matches before the races. Riots were still rare at that time, though.

The logical place to find out about Flavius was the Circus Maximus, and so on the morning after the murder was reported I made my way down from the Forum to the ancient Valley of Murcia between the Aventine and Palatine hills. Here was where Tarquin the Old had laid out Rome's racecourse when the city was still little more than a cluster of villages atop the seven hills. The place was so ancient that nobody could remember why its Temple of Consus was underground.

The Circus Maximus was the largest structure in Rome, a huge building complex housing everything necessary for getting four chariots, each with four horses and a charioteer, onto the sand in time for the race. This is not as simple as one might think. Horses were brought from as far away as Spain, Africa and Antioch. They were trained for a minimum of three years. The charioteers began their training in childhood and losses were high, so there had to be a steady supply of them. Chariots were made as light as possible to make them faster, so they had to be replaced constantly. Charioteers and horses needed a special diet. There were slaves to care for the chariots and harness, slaves to care for the charioteers, and immense numbers of slaves to care for the horses, cleaning out their stalls, seeing to their exercise, grooming them and doctoring them. There were even slaves who did nothing but talk to the horses to keep them contented and run alongside them on the way to the races, cheering them and raising their spirits.

Wherever Rome went, the circus went, and the factions maintained headquarters wherever there was a circus. It was not unusual for a single faction to maintain a stud of eight or ten thousand stallions to keep a single, small province supplied. In short, the circus was the largest institution in our empire. And the Circus Maximus was the largest such building in the world.

Its lowest courses of seats were of stone, but the rest

of the building was wooden. When filled to capacity with more than 200,000 spectators, the timber superstructure emitted the most alarming squeaks and groans, although it had never collapsed. There was always talk of building a permanent structure of stone, but no steps had been made in that direction. I think the populace just liked the rickety old place, even if it was the most significant fire hazard in the city. The arches beneath the stands constituted a minor forum, with shops and stalls selling everything from sausages to the services of inexpensive prostitutes. It was said in Rome that, should anything be stolen from you, all that you had to do was loiter around the Circus Maximus for a while and someone would offer to sell it to you. The citizenry had never conceived quite as much affection for the Circus Flaminius, which lay outside the old city walls. It was not as large and was only a little more than 150 years old.

When I arrived at the circus, it was bustling with activity. There would be races in just a few days, and those who were to participate in the preliminary procession were rehearsing. The slaves who bore the images of the gods practiced hoisting the platforms to their shoulders and marching in step to the music of horn, lyre and flute. Small, gilded chariots drawn by tiny ponies bore images such as thunderbolts, owls, peacocks and so forth, the attributes of the gods. These charming vehicles were driven by children who, for some reason, had to have both parents living. These white-robed little boys put their ponies through their paces with great seriousness. The musicians set up a great din and wild-haired women with tambourines danced like maenads in honor of Bacchus. A group of men in plumed helmets and scarlet tunics, bearing spear and shield, went through a slow, solemn war dance while behind them a pack of men dressed as satyrs, with goat tails attached to their rumps and huge, red phalluses to their loins, performed a bawdy parody of the same dance. All that was missing was the crowd in the stands.

On the sand, horses were being exercised, allowing them to grow accustomed to the racecourse and its immense environs. I walked along the whole length of the course, beside the *spina*, which had not yet acquired the crowd of statues that graces it now. At each end were the spikes tipped with seven gilded eggs marking each of the seven laps of a race, one egg being removed to mark each lap. This was before the water-spitting dolphins were added to aid the spectators in keeping track of how fast they were losing their money.

The sand, specially imported from Africa, was continually raked smooth after each batch of chariots rattled by. I was gladdened to see that the sand was its accustomed tan. When Caesar was *aedile*, he had spread green-tinted sand in the circuses, the color of his faction. He had achieved this remarkable effect by mixing pulverized copper ore with the sand. Past the *spina*, and careful not to be trampled by the practicing charioteers, I crossed the track and passed out through the open end of the great stadium where the starting gates stood open.

Beyond these gates was the stable area, almost as large as the circus itself. Since White and Red were the oldest factions, their stables and headquarters were nearest the circus. Red headquarters was a six-story building the size of a tenement built directly above their brick stables. The stables themselves were three-storied; two above ground and one below, connected by ramps broad enough for a pair of four-horse chariots to pass. The timber and plaster building above was painted, naturally enough, red. Outside were statues of famous horses from the stables, and the facade was decorated with plaques bearing the names of hundreds of others, listing the victories of each. The smell of horses was overwhelming, but it was more agreeable than many scents the city had to offer.

The office of the directors took up most of the second floor of the timber structure. It was spacious and rather luxuriously appointed, for a place of business. Entering this building was like stepping into another world. There were shrines to gods I had never seen before, and the walls bore enigmatic inscriptions and decorations, all having to do with the rites of the racing guild. Slave, freedmen and freemen, they all belonged to the guild and took part in its rituals. Within the guild, the various specialists had their own subguilds, shrines and even temples. That of the charioteers was especially fine and they got the most splendid, as well as the most frequent, funerals.

As I entered the office, slaves were setting up a crudely carved statue of a woman seated sideways on a horse, holding a key. The man supervising the work wore the clothes of an *eques* and noticed my interest.

"Epona," he said. "A Gallic horse-goddess. Some of our breeders in transalpine Gaul sent her as a gift."

"What is the key for?" I asked.

"It's a stable key, I think." He turned to me and introduced himself. "I am Helvidius Priscus, one of the directors of the Reds. How may I be of service to the Senate and People?"

I have often noticed this quality in Romans; an ability to recognize a public official. As a mere *quaestor* I had no lictors and no insignia of office and I dressed like a private citizen, but this man knew that I was some sort of official. I did not flatter myself that he remembered my face from the election. In that great mob it would take a twenty-foot statue of Jupiter to register a memorable impression. I was elected because I had announced my name in candidacy and the clients of the Metelli outnumber any other voting bloc. The lower offices are our birthright. The higher ones we have to fight for like everyone else.

"I am here to inquire into the murder of Decimus Flavius. I am Decius Metellus."

"The *quaestor?* Welcome, sir, you honor our establishment. I apologize for the clutter and rush, but we are getting ready for the next races, as well as picking the stallions to run in the festival of the October Horse. Please, come this way." I followed him into a broad room, one wall of which was mostly open to a balcony overlooking the circus gates. In the wide esplanade between, grooms from every nation walked their horses, talking to them in languages the beasts understood.

There was a broad table in the room, heaped with scrolls and sheets of papyrus. There were stacks of bronze plates upon which were inscribed the pedigrees of horses, some of them going back centuries. Around the table were seated several *equites*, a few freedmen secretaries, and a distinguished man who wore the strange, spindle-topped cap and other insignia of a *flamen*. This, as it turned out, was Lucius Cornelius Lentulus Niger, the *Flamen Martialis*. He was here in his capacity as high priest of Mars to oversee the choosing of the horses to run in the race of the October Horse. It was rare to encounter a *flamen* away from his home except when he was performing his sacerdotal functions because the *flamines* were so surrounded by ritual taboos that life was difficult for them. The highest priesthood of them all, *Flamen Dialis*, had been vacant for twenty-four years because nobody wanted it.

"Decimus Flavius was a most energetic director of the company," said one of the *equites*. "It came as a great shock to us all when he was so foully murdered."

"Under what circumstances was he found?" I asked.

"A cleaner found him over there in the circus," said Priscus. "He left here yesterday evening, just before dark. His home is just on the other side of the circus and he usually walked home that way."

"Would you be so good as to summon the cleaner?" I requested. A slave was dispatched to find the man. "Was the murder weapon left at the scene?"

"Yes, it's right here," said one of the directors. He reached into a box and rummaged among scraps of papyrus, ribbons and broken wax seals, and withdrew a knife, handing it to me. It was an unusual weapon, with a blade about eight inches long, straight for most of its length, then curving abruptly near the tip, doubling back to form a hook. It was keen on both edges. Someone had wiped the blade clean. There was no cross guard and the grip was of plain horn.

"This is a charioteer's knife, is it not?" I asked. Since a charioteer's reins are knotted around his waist, he has only a few seconds to cut himself loose after being thrown. Thus he may avoid being dragged to death or dashed against the arena wall or against the *spina*. If he succeeds in this, he need only fear being trampled by the other horses.

"It is," Priscus affirmed.

"Might he have been killed by a charioteer, then?" I asked.

"Charioteers only carry these knives when they are racing," said a director. "A dresser tucks one in the driver's body bindings just before he gets into his chariot."

"There are hundreds of them in our supply rooms," Priscus said. "But there must be thousands out in the city. The race enthusiasts beg them from victorious drivers and carry them for luck. They bribe track attendants to get them knives that charioteers have successfully freed themselves with. You know how superstitious those people are." This seemed to be another dead end as far as the murder weapon was concerned.

"Do any of you know if Flavius was in the business of lending money at interest?"

"I know that he was not," Priscus said. "At least, not in recent years. He made his fortune breeding horses, and here at the circus. He lost heavily after Lucullus's cutting the debt of the Asian cities, and swore he'd never lend money again." Thus was my theory that money-lenders were being systematically eradicated further undercut.

The cleaner arrived and, thanking the directors, I excused myself. I kept the knife and tucked it into my tunic belt. I was acquiring quite a collection of these sinister souvenirs. Its shape was highly specialized, which made it seem an odd choice for a murder weapon. A straight dagger or a *sica* made far more sense. Perhaps this murder had been unplanned.

"It was over here, master." The slave was a middle-aged man with a Bruttian accent. The Bruttians are worthless people, as all Romans know. Bruttium surrendered to Hannibal without a fight. They make adequate slaves, though. "I was taking some trash to this heap that's going to be hauled away sometime around Saturnalia."

We were walking beneath the wooden arcades of the circus. The great structure above us creaked and groaned as the morning sun warmed it. Despite that, the gloom belowstairs was deep. Some light came in through the arches, but the nearby buildings allowed little light to reach them. We turned from the main arcade into a short tunnel that ended at a great heap of trash of the sort that only a circus accumulates: broken spokes and other wreckage of the flimsy racing chariots, wax tablets recording bets flung down and smashed by enraged losers, polishing rags discarded by handlers, straw packing left by vendors and a multitude of other trash, probably a year's worth of it.

"He was right here," the slave said, pointing to a large, dark stain at the foot of the trash heap. It seemed an odd place for a prosperous *eques* to die. The others seemed to have been murdered in places that made some sense. Might he have been killed outside, in the arcade, and dragged in here? But there was no trail of blood, as there surely would have been in such a case. He must have been killed right on that spot. Perhaps he had been waylaid outside and forced into this tunnel.

"Who works in this area at night?" I asked the slave.

"Nobody. When it's not a race day, the circus is empty by late afternoon. We slaves must be in our barracks by dusk and there is no cause for freemen to be here. Maybe a few whores are here after dark."

I knew it would be worse than useless to canvass the area, asking if anyone had happened to notice a murder being committed. Few people are out of their homes after dark in the fall, and those who are seldom like to cooperate with the authorities.

I dismissed the slave and stood there for a while, pondering. My perplexity only deepened. I turned and walked out of the short tunnel and all but collided with a pair of young men, both of whom were bearded.

My hand slid beneath my toga and I gripped the handle of the charioteer's dagger. They stared at me, as astonished as I was. Then a woman pushed in front of them. In the poor light I had not noticed her standing behind the two.

"Is it Decius Metellus?" The light was poor but I knew the voice.

"Aurelia?" I said. It was she. Even in her heavy wool *stola* and in dim light, her luxuriant form was unmistakable. She had drawn her palla over her head, and I could not make out her expression.

"Decius, how odd to meet you here! Let me introduce my companions, Marcus Thorius and Quintus Valgius. They are friends of my stepfather. Gentlemen, this is Decius Caecilius Metellus the Younger, *quaestor* of the treasury." There was a slight edge to her voice as she addressed the two, as if reminding them to be on their best behavior.

"I am always happy to encounter you," I assured her, "any time and under any circumstances. Gentlemen, good day to you." They nodded rather churlishly. Both seemed to be about twenty years old. With their identical stubbled scalps and bushy beards they looked like a pair of Greek wrestling instructors.

"What brings you to the circus on a dull morning, Decius?" she asked.

"One of those murders that the city is so enthralled with," I said. "I had to come down here to make some inquiries. The victim was a director of the Reds. I came here to see the murder site."

"Oh, was it here?" she said, peering past me into the dark tunnel.

"There's nothing to see," I said. "Just a rather large but ordinary bloodstain. What brings you here?"

"We came to see Silverwing exercise," she said. "Paris will be racing him for the Whites in the next races. Quintus knows everything about the White stables."

"Silverwing has raced as inside trace horse for six years," Valgius said. "He has won 237 races." He recited this with a fanatical gleam in his eye. I knew the type. He would know the records and pedigrees of hundreds of horses. I have always loved the races, but there are limits. People like Valgius could be as boring as Cato.

"Would you care to join us?" Aurelia asked. The two men looked sour-faced but I was a long way from caring what they thought.

"Most certainly," I said. I fell in beside her as we walked toward one of the galleries that gave access to the stands.

"What do you think, *Quaestor*?" Thorius asked. "About the murder, I mean?"

I shrugged. "Probably just another murder and robbery. I think he was knocked on the head when he walked home and was dragged back there and had his throat cut. That's where all the blood is."

"Doesn't it seem to you that a lot of *equites* are being murdered lately?" Aurelia asked.

"Who has more money?" I replied. "There's little gain to be had in robbing a poor man. Anyway, I'm not here to investigate the murder, just to clear up some questions about the man. Treasury business." I told the lie on a sudden impulse, and it seemed to me that a little of the tension left the shoulders of the two hirsute youths.

The gallery opened into the stands about twenty rows up, and directly above the *loggia*, where the giver of the games or the presiding magistrate in charge would sit on race days. A loose group of men stood there that morning, observing the horses and the charioteers as they practiced. It was a beautiful morning, and on the slopes of the Aventine above the Circus the beautiful Temple of Ceres gleamed as if carved from pure alabaster. Here and there were the shrines of other, even older deities. Now that we have all become imitation Greeks, we have forgotten that once our gods were purely Italian. They lingered here in the Valley of Murcia, once a myrtle-draped site of our harvest festivals, when the circus had been a mere dirt track. The sanctuaries of Seia, Segesta, Tutilina, and other half-forgotten goddesses of the harvest stood nearby. The goddess Murcia herself, for whom the valley was named, was already being confused with Venus, who was in turn being absorbed by the Greek Aphrodite. For a people in love with our religious ceremonies, we Romans are remarkably confused in our attitudes toward the gods.

"What a glorious morning!" Aurelia exclaimed, rousing from her usual half-somnolent abstraction. We descended the steps to the *loggia* and she strode to the marble railing and stood beside the statue of Victory that crowned one of its corners. Below, the chariots roared by, the charioteers garbed in their tunics of red, white, blue or green, their heads encased in close-fitting leather helmets, some of them wearing padded leather leg-guards, their bodies harnessed in the complicated system of leather straps and thongs intended to protect them in case of a fall and relieve the tremendous strain of the four-horse reins.

"Silverwing!" Valgius cried, pointing, his eyes gleaming like those of a man who has seen a vision.

Silverwing was, indeed, a beautiful animal. All race-horses are beautiful, but Silverwing stood out like a god even among these. He belonged to that rare, ancient breed of striped horses, now all but bred out of existence. He was deep gray, with white stripes, brightest on his shoulders and withers and from these he was named. That morning he was not pulling a chariot, but was instead being ridden by one of the Numidian handlers. With only the slight, brown man for a burden, the beast truly seemed to fly.

Near us two men argued in low but heated voices. One had his back to us, and the other I did not recognize. The other people on the *loggia* stood well away from them, as men do when they do not wish to be noticed by someone who is both angry and important. Aurelia, it seemed, was not so overawed.

"I need to talk to him," she said, walking over to the two men. Not wishing to give up her company so easily, I followed. The one with his back to us turned at her approach and I wished that I had not been so eager to stay with Aurelia. It was Marcus Licinius Crassus.

The anger swept from his face and he smiled. "Aurelia! You make the morning twice as beautiful." He bestowed a properly chaste kiss upon her cheek and looked at the rest of us. "Let me see, I know Decius Caecilius, of course, but I don't believe I've met your other companions." Aurelia introduced Thorius and Valgius. Crassus's blue eyes were as cold as always, but he displayed no particular hostility toward me. He introduced the man with whom he had been arguing, and who also had regained his composure.

"This is Quintus Fabius Sanga, who is here to see his

horses run." I glanced at the man's sandal and saw the small, ivory crescent fixed at the ankle, the mark of a patrician. I took his proffered hand.

"My father has spoken of you," I told him. "He says that your estates in Gaul produce the finest horses in the world."

Sanga smiled. "I did business with Cut-Nose when he was proconsul. He has a sharp eye for horseflesh. He insisted on personally inspecting every horse bought for the *auxilia*." Farming and livestock raising are among the few businesses that patricians are allowed to practice, but nobody ever said you couldn't get rich that way. "If it weren't for the *lupercalia*, I'd be up in Gaul with my horses right now." The Fabian and Quintilian gens had charge of that very strange and ancient festival.

"But it is more than four months until *lupercalia*," I pointed out.

"But that would mean crossing the Alps or traveling by sea in January, and who wants to do that? Besides, some of my Gallic clients are here in the city and need my guidance." He looked out onto the track. "There are some of mine now." I looked to see a *quadriga* of four splendid Gallic bays thundering from the gates, cutting swiftly to the left to put the chariot in the best position next to the *spina*. It was beautifully done, but in a real race it was a dangerous maneuver, because all four charioteers would be trying for that position. More smash-ups happen during the initial scramble for the *spina* position than at any other time in a race. The charioteer was a handsome youth with long, yellow Gallic hair streaming from beneath his helmet. There was something familiar about him, but in the moment it took him to flash by us I could not pin it down. We all praised Sanga's horses and then Aurelia brought up her business with Crassus.

"Marcus Licinius, I belong to the college of priestesses of Ceres. Our temple"—she pointed at the beautiful structure on the hill—"is in need of repair. Will you undertake the needed restorations?" It was customary for rich men to do these things.

"Haven't the market fines been sufficient this year?"

he asked. The plebeian *aediles* had their offices in the temple, and the fines they collected in the markets were supposed to pay for its upkeep.

"I'm afraid not. The *mundus* shows signs of collapsing. It could bring down the whole temple."

"That does sound serious," he admitted. The *mundus* was very important to us because it was the only passageway into the underworld. There are others in Italy, but only one in Rome. All those offerings and messages had to reach the underworld gods and our dead somehow, so we couldn't just let our *mundus* collapse.

"Restorations are so tedious and complicated," Crassus said. "Perhaps I should just build you a new temple." He was not joking. Crassus used to say that a man could not claim to be rich unless he could raise, equip and pay an army out of his own purse. He was that rich.

"Absolutely not!" Aurelia exclaimed. "We want to keep our old temple. Restorations only, if you please, Marcus Licinius." In this I heartily concurred. I hated the way people were always tearing down our ancient temples so they could build something modern and carve their name all over the pediment in letters three feet high. Not that the Temple of Ceres was all that ancient. It was a bit under four and a half centuries old, making it respectably venerable. At least, when the great Temple of Jupiter had burned twenty years before, Sulla had had the good taste to restore it to its original design and condition. They don't make tyrants like Sulla anymore.

"Then it shall be done. Report to your sisters that I will send my architect and building manager to make a preliminary survey and report tomorrow."

She clapped her hands delightedly. "Thank you, Marcus Licinius! The goddess thanks you. Now, you must do me the further favor of accepting an invitation to a reception I am giving for the Parthian ambassador tomorrow evening."

"I accept with great pleasure," Crassus said.

"You must come too, Decius," she said. Attending any sort of event with Crassus was far from my idea of a

pleasant evening, but I was willing to endure it for a
chance to spend more time with Aurelia.

"You may depend on it," I told her. "I haven't met
the Parthian ambassador yet."

"He is a savage, but barbarians are far more amusing
than most Roman politicians," she said.

"I couldn't agree more," Crassus put in.

"Excellent. At my mother's house tomorrow, then."
Catilina and Orestilla had been married by the casual
practice of *usus*. Once, patricians had only married by
confarreatio, but marriage customs had broken down in
the previous generation. Divorce was far easier with *usus*
and it allowed the woman to keep her property.

I took my leave and hastened away, anxious to be out
of Crassus's sight. There was much that was puzzling
about this latest murder, and I did not want to go investigate one of the others just yet, so I walked down to
the to the great pound beyond the starting gates where
the horses were walked to cool them after running. I got
there just as the young Gaul was descending from his
chariot. The attendants loosened the reins from his waist
and he pulled off his leather helmet, letting his extravagant hair fly free. Except for his downy mustache, a
facial disfigurement I have always considered an abom-
ination, he was an extremely handsome youth, and now
I remembered where I had seen him before. He was one
of the party of Allobroges who had been hanging about
the city for months, complaining of Roman extortion
and rapacious *publicani* squeezing them for tax debt.

"That was splendid driving," I told him as he was
stripping off his leg-pads. He looked up and flashed a
big-toothed smile.

"Thank you. My patron's horses only understand Gallic. These Italians and Numidians and Greeks can never
get the best out of them. I saw you up on the *loggia*
speaking with my patron." Now I remembered that Fabius Sanga was of the branch of the Fabii who were
surnamed Allobrogicus. An ancestor of his had soundly
thrashed their ancestors and that family of Fabians had
thereby become the hereditary patrons of the Allobroges. The worse you beat Gauls and Germans, the more

loyal they are to you. At least they are sincere about it. Asiatics, once defeated, kiss your sandals and protest loyalty, then do something treacherous.

"Have you raced in Rome before?" I asked him.

"Not yet. I've raced in the circus of Massilia and the one at Cartago Nova. My name is Amnorix, but I race as Polydoxus."

"I expect to hear great things of you. How do you happen to be with the Allobrogian party?"

"My uncle was chosen by the tribe to come here with the grievance party, and I got him to bring me along for a chance to race in the Circus Maximus."

"What do you think of it?" I asked.

"I've never seen anything so big, but the circuses in Gaul and Spain are built better, and they aren't cluttered with all this gear for the wild beast fights. It's the track that counts, though, and this one is well kept. The African sand is the best. But it's the stables here that are greatest. It seems like half the horses in the world must be here."

"This is the first circus ever built," I told him. "The circus has grown as Rome has grown. That's why it seems rather ramshackle and unplanned. Wait until you see it on a race day."

"Oh, I've attended the races here, although not from the sand. I would not have believed that so many people could be assembled in a single place. The noise is incredible." He laughed. "They are well behaved compared to a Gallic crowd, I must admit."

"You've never seen a good circus riot, then. Pray you never do." Now that we had established a sort of friendship between us, I decided to take advantage of it. "When I arrived, your patron and Crassus were arguing about something. Any idea what that was about?"

He frowned. "I don't know. Crassus has called on the patron several times, lately. Last time he was with that man Valgius. I saw him up on the *loggia*, too. They meet privately, but the patron always looks upset after Crassus has left."

This startled me. "Valgius? Are you sure he was with Crassus?"

"He was last time. He stayed out in the *atrium* with the rest of the clients while Crassus and the patron conferred. He would only talk about the circus, so I held some conversation with him, but he could not hide how much he despises Gauls."

"I don't much like him myself. Did you recognize the other bearded man, or the lady who was with me?"

"Never saw either of them before," he admitted. "She was very beautiful, in the Roman fashion."

"You see a lot, for a man flashing by in a chariot. I would have thought the *quadriga* would require all your attention."

"It was not as if I was racing," he said. Then his eyes narrowed. "You ask a lot of questions, sir."

"It is my duty. I am the *Quaestor* Decius Caecilius Metellus and I am on official business."

"Oh, I see. Is there any other way I may be of service?" Barbarians think that all Roman officials have infinite authority. This is because the ones who show up in their lands seem to act like gods.

"Was there anyone else with Crassus and Valgius?"

He thought for a moment. "No. But later, I think it was a day or two after, a man came up to us in the Forum. He spoke to my uncle and the elders. Then they were taken to the house of Decimus Brutus and we younger men were told to return to the house where we are quartered. That seemed strange to me."

"Do you know the name of this man?" I asked.

"Umbrenus. Publius Umbrenus. I heard that he is some sort of businessman who has interests in Gaul. I don't like all this secrecy. We came here to petition the Senate openly, not to conspire."

"I am glad to hear it. The politics of Rome can get very rough, and you people should not try to get involved. Keep your eyes open and if you see anything suspicious, let me know. I am to be found at the Temple of Saturn, most days."

"I shall do as you say," he said. He seemed to be an intelligent and well-spoken youth, for a barbarian. His accent was quite tolerable.

I hurried off to the Forum, where I knew my father

was sure to be. He was already canvassing for the next year's censorship election. I found him standing in the *comitium,* just about equidistant between the *Curia* and the *Rostra* in the midst of a knot of men and speaking, no doubt, with nobility and rectitude. As I went closer I saw that most of the men were important officers of the centuriate assembly, men who would have great influence over the outcome of the upcoming elections. I saluted him as father and patron and he looked at me with his usual expression: annoyance.

"Why aren't you in the treasury?" he demanded.

"I've been out on official business," I said. "I need some advice involving your recent tenure of office in Gaul." The other men drew aside to let us speak privately.

"Well, what is it?" Father asked, impatiently. He never liked to be interrupted while politicking.

"What do you know of a man named Publius Umbrenus?"

"Umbrenus?" He glanced at me sharply. "That's not advice. That's information."

"It involves official business on behalf of the Urban *Praetor.*"

"Celer? What have you to do with him?" He looked disgusted, never much of an effort for him. "Don't tell me. You're out conspiracy-hunting again, aren't you?"

"I have done the state some small service in that capacity before, Father," I pointed out.

"And come close to being killed doing it."

"Now, Father," I chided, "a Roman is not supposed to fear death, only disgrace." His face grew red, so I appealed to his ever-dominant sense of duty. "There have been murders, Father."

"Eh? Of course there have been murders. What of it? When did a few *equites* more or less ever make any difference?"

"Quite aside from obvious criminal activity, I think a very real danger to the state is involved, and Celer concurs. Now, what do you know of Publius Umbrenus?"

"Well, you're a fool, but Celer isn't, so maybe there's something to this after all. Umbrenus is a publican who had sizable dealings in the Gallic communities: horses, slaves and other livestock, grain, that sort of thing. He belonged to a consortium of investors here in Rome and he was their traveling agent in Gaul. The last I heard, they were bankrupt. Like most, they were hurt when Lucullus cut the Asian debt, then they speculated heavily in grain and were wiped out when the Egyptian and African harvests were the best in years and the price of grain plunged. Served them right." Father detested capitalists. Like most aristocrats, he thought that only income from landed estate was honorable. As long as someone else is doing the farming it suits me too.

"Did he have dealings with the Allobroges?" I asked.

"He must have. They're the most powerful tribe in the North so he would have had to deal with them. What's this all about? No, don't tell me. Bring me hard evidence and keep your foolish suspicions to yourself. Now go be a nuisance somewhere else."

I visited the baths and returned to my house. There was to be little rest for me, though. Before long, I was interrupted in my letter writing when a delegation of my neighbors called on me. I received them in my *atrium* and feared the worst when I saw who it was: a collection of shopkeepers, guild officers and free artisans, the typical inhabitants of the extremely raffish district that was my home. Their spokesman was Quadratus Vibius, owner of a bronze foundry and president of a district funeral and burial society. By Subura standards, he was a pillar of the community.

"*Quaestor* Metellus," he said, "we your neighbors call upon you as the most distinguished resident of the Subura." It didn't take much to be the most distinguished resident of Rome's greatest slum.

"And I greet you as my friends and neighbors." This they were. I truly liked living in that slum.

"Sir, as you know, in a few days, on the ides of October, the whole city will be celebrating the festival of the October Horse. We would like for you to represent the Subura, as our leader in the contest after the race."

My heart sank. "Ah, gentlemen, my friends, I cannot

tell you how deeply appreciative I am of the honor you do me. However, the press of office—"

"The dwellers of the *Via Sacra* won last year, sir," said a baker who lived down the street. "As a result, no one in the Subura's had good luck all year. We need our luck back."

"Truly. But the Subura wins most years, does it not? Because we are better people, as everyone knows. However, my duties—"

"Nobody'll think much of us if our *quaestor* doesn't lead us," said my tailor, a man who could make my old tunics look almost new. "You're a man destined for the highest office and the great army commands, sir. Who else should be our representative?"

I could feel my thread being stretched tight on the loom of the Fates. "But surely—"

"Sir," said a burly water-carrier, "the *Via Sacra* people are to be led by Publius Clodius this year."

"Clodius?" I choked out.

The waterman grinned. "Yes, sir. Clodius."

They had me trapped. If I backed down from a meeting with Clodius, I might as well leave the city for good and go to Rhodes or some such place and study philosophy.

"I shall, of course, be most honored to be your leader on the ides, and we shall return with the *Subura*'s luck." At this they all cheered and pounded me on the back and dragged me out to a wineshop where we stuffed ourselves and I got drunk enough to look forward to the festival.

VI

Parthia was a problem for us, and it was sure to become a greater problem now that Mithridates and Tigranes were both out of the picture. One of several kingdoms squabbling over control of the old Persian empire, Parthia was in the happy position of sitting smack astride the silk route, and had grown rich thereby. Silk was a great mystery to us. It was the most prized of fabrics, indeed the most prized of substances, more valuable than gold. Light, strong, its dyes unfading, it was so esteemed that from time to time the Censors forbade its wear as an Oriental extravagance. Men and sometimes even women were subject to fine if caught wearing silk in public. Both sexes sometimes took to wearing a silk *subligaculum* beneath the garments. If one could not have the ostentation of flaunting silk publicly, one could at least enjoy the lubricity of wearing the sensuous fabric in a more intimate fashion.

The kingdom of Parthia was not a central monarchy in the old Egyptian or Persian sense. It was far too primitive for that. Rather, it was a loose confederation of quarreling chieftains, the strongest of whom called himself King of Kings, like the old Persian monarch, and lorded it over the others. In the usual Eastern fashion, the royal families indulged in mutual homicide. The kings bred innumerable sons, which they then felt compelled to murder. If one or more survived to manhood, one of them would sooner or later kill his father unless the old man managed to eliminate him first. At this time, the king was one Phraates III, who had not one but two grown sons in rebellion against him.

They were little more than primitive tribesmen recently arrived from the great eastern grasslands, and this was the source of their single strength, for they had a most unique method of waging war. Alone of all peoples in the world, the Parthians fought entirely from horseback, and their only weapon was the bow. Devoid of armor and swift as birds, they darted about the battlefield, raining shafts on enemies confined to the speed of a man on foot. They might have been truly formidable had they possessed any sort of organization. It was our own intent to supply them with good Roman organization, whether they wanted it or not. With the rest of the East pacified, Parthia remained as the only decent realm for further conquest.

Pompey had formed an alliance with Parthia when fighting Tigranes, but treaties were never more than a convenience for him, and he had offended Phraates by concluding a treaty with Tigranes without consulting the Parthian. Undoubtedly, this little problem would constitute the greater part of the ambassador's business in Rome. Much good would it do him.

It offended us that a contemptible pack of horse-eating savages should control so important a commodity as silk. It especially offended us that they should have grown so rich doing it. The answer to all this offense, naturally enough, was to conquer the place, and even now we were searching for an excuse. When we should have conquered Parthia, of course, it would only mean that the next nation to the east would become the one controlling the silk route. There seemed to be quite a lot of land between us and the land of the Seres, where the silk was made. But then, that was how we had built our empire: one nation at a time. Eventually, we would reach the land of the Seres and conquer them as well. We knew nothing about them except that they made silk, but being Asiatics they couldn't amount to much.

First, though, we would conquer Parthia. If only we had known at the time what a struggle that would entail.

But I was not thinking of these things when I presented myself at the door of Orestilla's house. I was thinking of Aurelia. I had been doing far too much of that lately. So much so that, when the *janitor* admitted me, I thought that it was Aurelia whom I saw coming to greet me, but I was mistaken. The woman crossing the *atrium* was her mother, Orestilla. She was still a great beauty, and with none of Aurelia's abstracted air. For the moment, I could well sympathize with Catilina. I might have murdered a son or two myself for such a woman.

"*Quaestor* Metellus, welcome to my house." Her smile was dazzling and she took my hands in both of her. She was constructed just like her daughter, with a few extra pounds that did nothing to distract from her beauty. "Did you bring any friends?"

I looked around to make sure. "No. Should I have?"

"It's just that everyone else this evening has shown up with someone in tow, so we're having to move the dining tables and couches out to the *peristylium*. Our little dinner reception has turned into a minor banquet. It will be a fine affair, but please forgive me if things don't happen exactly according to schedule." She was a woman of infectious gaiety, as her daughter was one of brooding melancholy.

"I promise only to be overwhelmed by your hospitality and your equally renowned beauty. Speaking of which, that is a most spectacular gown." She was wearing a sheer *stola* made of what appeared to be pure silk, emerald-green in color. The thought of its cost was unsettling.

"Isn't it amazing? It's a gift from our guest of honor. I never expected anything so splendid. He brought another for Aurelia. She's off somewhere trying hers on and admiring her reflection, no doubt. Come along, everybody's out in the *peristylium* and getting in the way while the house slaves are trying to set up." She took my hand and all but towed me out into the open colonnade. Her *peristylium* had an unusually large *compluvium*, transforming it into a virtual courtyard. Instead of the usual central pool, it had a grated drain running around the base of the columns, making it possible to use the enclosure for large parties such as this one. There were at least thirty people there already, and it

seemed that more were to arrive. They stood about on
a floor of exquisite mosaic. Mosaic floors in private
houses were still rather new in Rome, except for the
tessellated kind made of squares and rectangles of colored marble, making abstract designs. This was a gen-
uine picture-mosaic, made of tiny bits of colored stone,
glass and even fragments colored with gold or silver
leaf. It depicted a pastoral scene of gods and goddesses,
nymphs, satyrs, centaurs and such amid vines and cedar-
clad hills. Gods and fabulous creatures danced, feasted
and flirted among mortal shepherds and the occasional
hero. Quite aside from its breathtaking beauty and artistry, the design was perfect for an area intended for
entertainment and I strongly suspected that Orestilla
had deliberately arranged for the unexpected guests so
that she could get everyone out here to admire her mosaic.

The evening was wonderfully warm and clear for October, almost like a fine summer evening. There was still
plenty of light, because it was still considered disgraceful for an entertainment to run on after dark, so we
usually got started during the hours of daylight. As for
calling it quits with the onset of darkness, nobody paid
any attention to that nonsense anymore.

I saw that all the most beautiful, scandalous and best-
bred ladies were there: Sempronia, Fulvia, Orestilla herself, of course, Clodia and a few others who were quite
famous at the time but whose names have faded from
my memory. Aurelia had not made her appearance yet.

The men were as distinguished, by notoriety if not by
beauty. Catilina and Curius were there, and Lisas, the
Egyptian ambassador. Crassus had not arrived yet, but
Caesar was there, for *populares* and *optimates* mingled
freely at this sort of affair. He had won a praetorship
for the next year and was therefore a bit more aloof
than when actually standing for election. He was chat-
ting amiably with Catilina. They were both patricians,
after all, and that was a more binding connection than
mere political convenience. Indeed, except on the floor
of the Senate and on the public speaking platform, it
was very difficult to tell one party from the other. Poli-

ticians always denied belonging to any faction at all, claiming to act only from disinterested motives of statesmanship. It was their enemies who belonged to parties, they claimed.

There were three men dressed in exotic garb: short jackets with long sleeves, trousers and soft boots. These were the Parthians. As heirs to the Persian empire, they claimed to be civilized and we humored them, as if people who wore trousers could be considered anything but barbarians. They also wore headgear indoors, something done by no Roman except the *Flamen Dialis*.

I forgot about them when Aurelia appeared. She wore a gown like her mother's, but hers was of flame-colored silk. The material was so thin that it clung when she moved and floated free when she was still. To my great amazement and delight, she ignored the other guests and came to me first. We exchanged formal greetings and then got down to serious dalliance.

"The ambassador's gift is most becoming on you," I said.

"Isn't it wonderful?" she said, her eyes alight. "I'm so glad I got the red one. It suits my coloring much better than the green would have."

"I can only agree."

"Mother looks wonderful in hers, don't you think?"

"Yes, but not as stunning as you." I was enjoying this.

"That's because she hasn't yet realized the possibilities of the material." She smoothed the silk downward, drawing it taut. "For instance, she's wearing a *strophium* and *subligaculum* under hers. Well, I suppose when I'm her age I'll need a *strophium* too, but what's wonderful about a pure silk *stola* is that it combines the advantages of being decently clad with those of being naked."

I cleared my throat needlessly. "Truly, a marvelous fabric."

"I hear that you will be captain of the Suburrans the day after tomorrow. How exciting."

"Well, one must uphold the honor of the district. I am amazed that you've heard about it so soon. I only accepted the honor yesterday evening."

"It's all over the city. I think it's terribly brave." Her look of adoration almost made up for my fear.

"Oh, the danger is greatly exaggerated. I'm looking forward to it." I could lie with the best of them, in my youth.

"I'll be watching," she promised. "From a safe spot. Now, have you met our guests of honor? I suppose you haven't, the way Mother's been fluttering about. Come along with me." She took my hand and towed me to the group of Parthians. "Ambassador, this is the *Quaestor* Decius Caecilius Metellus the Younger. Decius, his Excellency, the ambassador Surena."

The Parthian smiled and bowed slightly, his fingertips extended and touching his chest, then his lips and brow. He wore a pointed chin-beard and his long hair was dressed in scented, oily ringlets. The Parthians followed the disgusting Oriental practice of wearing cosmetics. His face was dusted with white powder, with scarlet rouge on lips and cheeks. His eyebrows had been augmented by kohl into a single, black line, high-arched over the eyes and drawn down into a point over the bridge of the nose, so that they resembled a gull in flight, as seen from a distance. More kohl outlined his large, brown eyes. What a prize fop, I thought.

"I bring the greetings of King Phraates," he said. It was a practiced formula and his accent indicated that he was not comfortable with Latin.

"And the Senate and People of Rome extended their warmest greetings to his envoys," I said in Greek, which was spoken everywhere in the East and which, like all wellborn Romans, I was forced to learn in childhood. I longed for the day when we would be able to beat the Greek out of these barbarians and teach them a decent language.

"I think I hear Crassus arriving," Aurelia said. "Excuse me for a moment, gentlemen." I was grieved to see her go, but it gave me an opportunity to admire her shapely bottom as the silk gown performed exactly as she had indicated.

Surena did not seem to be as enthralled with the sight, but then easterners have strange tastes. "Wonderful stuff, silk," I muttered. Surena's eyes brightened within their rings of kohl. Apparently he liked silk better than what it contained.

"It is the gift of the gods. You must come to Parthia some time, and see the great silk bazaar at Ecbatana. It arrives by the camel-load from the Far East."

I was always intrigued by tales from far places. "Are the caravans manned by the Seres?"

He shook his head. "No one in the West has ever seen those people. The silk is many months, even years on the trails before it arrives in Ecbatana. It is traded from one caravan to another and as far as I know nobody has ever traveled the entire route. The Seres are said to be a small, yellow people with tilted eyes, but that could be fable."

"And what is the origin of silk?" I asked him. "One hears the most unlikely theories."

"Then you hear as much as we do," he admitted. "Some think it comes from a plant, like flax, others say that it is spun by giant, domesticated spiders. There is a belief that it is hair from the heads of women, which seems most unlikely, and some maintain that it is produced by tiny worms that eat the leaves of the mulberry bush. Whichever, it makes the lightest, the strongest, the most beautiful fabric in the world." He was wearing a good deal of it himself. "I delivered many bolts, a present from my king, to your General Pompey when we concluded our alliance against Mithridates and Tigranes."

"You were acting as envoy at that time?" I asked.

"No," he said, smiling, "as general of the Parthian forces."

The idea of this overdressed, bedaubed, effeminate foreigner leading an army seemed faintly ludicrous and I assumed that, as in so many monarchies, he received rank through his family relationship to the king. I did not know, of course, that I was speaking to the most powerful man in the Parthian empire. The kings of Parthia were just figureheads selected by the great families of Scythian descent, of which the house of Surena was the greatest. Ten years after this evening, he was to show

Crassus and Rome that silk and cosmetics had done nothing to soften Parthia's warlike ferocity.

Then Aurelia and Orestilla arrived, towing Crassus. He exchanged fulsome greetings with the ambassador and, as soon as he could, took me aside. The recent marriage alliance of our families had made him benevolent toward me. Temporarily, at any rate.

"Decius, assure your father that he has my support for next year's censorship election," he said.

"He will rejoice to know it," I told him. "Your support is as good as an assurance of election." This was not much of an exaggeration.

"Getting elected is only the half of it," he reminded me. "I hope he has better luck in his colleague than I did." Two years before, Crassus had had a notably unsuccessful censorship. He and his colleague, the great Catulus, could agree on nothing and each had undone the other's work. Finally, they had both abdicated without even completing the census of citizens, which was their primary duty in office.

"You know my father," I said. "He gets along with nearly everybody. He wants Hortalus to come out of retirement and stand for Censor. They would work well together, but Hortalus has lost his taste for public office since Cicero has risen so high."

"I'll speak with Hortalus," Crassus assured me. "He'll never be able to resist wearing the *toga praetexta* one more time, if he can be assured of working with a cooperative colleague."

"That would be a great favor, sir," I said.

He leaned close. "Can you believe these Parthians? They're more contemptible than the Egyptians! Mark me, Decius, as soon as they give us an excuse, I'm going to demand a command against that nation if I have to pay for the whole campaign myself. I'll be looking for legates then. It'll be a good place for a young man to make his military reputation."

"I'll keep it in mind, and I'm honored by the offer." Inwardly, I made a vow to have nothing to do with the East, nor any military adventure led by Crassus, a decision I have never regretted.

He clapped me on the shoulder. "Good lad. And good luck at the festival."

No sooner had Crassus left my side than Catilina sought me out. "Decius, I heard about your captainship of the Subura. Congratulations!"

"Lucius, these constant reminders of my fate are stealing the pleasure from my evening."

He grinned and chuckled. "Think it might get rough, eh? But that's the fun of it. Excitement and honor, that's what life is all about." And there you have Lucius Sergius Catilina: a big twelve-year-old boy who never grew up. Young Marcus Antonius was to become the same sort of man. The two had many qualities in common.

"Have you ever acted in that capacity?" I asked.

"Of course. I captained the *Via Sacra* when I was about your age. That was in the consulate of Carbo and Cinna. I was laid up in bed for a month afterward, but the glory was worth it."

"As it occurs, I have a special hazard this year," I pointed out.

"Right. Clodius represents the *Via Sacra* this year. That little—" He looked around. "Clodia's not within hearing, is she? I'll never understand how a woman like that could be sister to a slimy little reptile like Publius." He lowered his voice, conspiratorially. "Look, Decius, I'm going to assign a few of my lads to look out for you. Not all of them live in the Subura, but who's to know, eh?"

I was willing to trust in the protection of my neighbors, but anything that might get me closer to Catilina's doings would be welcome. "Thank you. Ordinarily, it would just be a roughhouse, but I suspect that Publius and his boys may take the opportunity to murder me."

"Just what I was thinking. Never fear, my men will watch out for you. And"—he paused dramatically— "after the festival, I am holding a little get-together here. Only the really important men to attend, if you get my meaning. It'll mean great things for your future, I can promise you."

This was what I had been hoping for. "If I am in any shape to go anywhere at all, I shall be here without fail."

"Good, good. And"—he all but nudged me in the

side—"Aurelia's quite taken with you. And that, in turn, pleases Orestilla no end." At that moment, the lady in question appeared at his side and he placed an arm around her shoulders, a sight that would have been shocking in a less sophisticated gathering. At this time, about the only thing that was still regarded as perverted was a public display of affection toward one's wife. It was not as if they were out on a street or in the Forum, but even at a gathering like this it was rather daring. Cato would have called for his exile. Somehow, I found this simple gesture almost ennobling. Even the worst of men have their little affections and redeeming loves, and Sergius Catilina was far from the worst of men, despite what was said about him later.

"We are finally set up," Orestilla told us, slipping an arm around his substantial waist. "Come and let's get dinner started, everyone is starving."

Through the meal, I wondered whether I was just kindly disposed toward Catilina because of what he had said about Aurelia. Could he just be dangling her before me as bait? I did not want to think so, but the very fact that I was willing his words to be true made my own judgment suspect. I could take little pleasure in the banquet. I was couched close enough to a Parthian to smell his perfume, which ruined my appetite, and I dared not drink any wine, since I had to be ready for the ordeal of the festival in two days' time. The conversation was uninspiring as well, for I remember little of it, even though I was sober.

When the dinner was over and the hired acrobats were performing their contortions, I rose from the table and took a walk in the garden, which was rather large for a house within the city walls. To take best advantage of the limited space, it was a labyrinth of hedges high enough to block the sight of nearby buildings, so that one could wander among the plantings and imagine that they were on the grounds of a country estate. Here and there, lamps and small torches provided illumination and fountains played musically in little fishponds.

For the moment, all was serene. Intrigues and horse festivals seemed far away. In the dark nooks and on the other sides of hedges, I could hear whisperings and other, more intimate sounds. I had not been the only one to steal away from the party for a bit of privacy. A voice called my name quietly and I turned to see a shadowy form with a dim light shining behind it.

"Aurelia?" I said, my mouth gone dry. She came closer until I could feel the warmth from her body.

"I'm so glad I found you here," she said, barely whispering. "I wasn't expecting such a crowd tonight and I thought we would have some time together. I have to go back in a few minutes, but you'll be here after the festival, won't you? Sergius said you would."

"Depending upon my condition," I said. I desperately wanted her to stay. "Surely, you don't have to—"

She came even closer. "Oh, I am sure you will come through it gloriously! Just stay behind after everyone else returns home two nights from now, and—then I can treat you as a hero should be treated."

"If I am going to emerge from the festival a hero," I said, "then perhaps you could lend me some more of your luck."

She came into my arms and pressed herself against me, her arms winding around my neck and pulling my head down, first kissing me, then drawing my face into the valley between her breasts. My hands slid over her and the silken gown was like a coating of oil. Voluptuous as she was, her flesh was as firm as that of a young racehorse. My hands tested the firmness of her thighs and buttocks, the rocklike points of her nipples as her tongue played with mine. Then, much too soon, she broke away.

"I must go back. Later, Decius. In two nights, we will have all the time we need." Then she turned and was gone.

I was trembling like a boy who has just had his first, inconclusive experiment with a slave girl. My pulse pounded in my ears and I was sure that my breathing could be heard on the other side of the hedges. I had to readjust my *subligaculum* before I could return to the house and take my leave. I must have looked a bit wild-eyed and disheveled, but everyone else was far the worse for the wine, so my condition was not remarked upon.

As I made my way home through the dark streets, I tried to analyze the things I had seen and heard in the last few days, but Aurelia kept intruding on my thoughts. I was sure that I was missing some terribly obvious things, but my mind never worked properly when I was obsessed with a woman. This may not have been solely a personal failing, as other men have reported similar afflictions.

Whatever my frailties may have been, when I got home I collapsed on my bed in a fever of lust and confusion.

VII

That year, we held the festival of the October Horse in the Forum. In other years, it was usually held in the *Campus Martius,* but the augurs had seen signs that were unfavorable to the *Campus Martius.* Mars wanted the festival held within the city walls this year. In earliest times, the festival had always been in the Forum, but in those days the Forum had been an open field. With its present clutter of public buildings, temples, monuments and speakers' platforms it was a rough place to hold a horse race. But by that time the city was spilling out onto the *Campus Martius* as well, since it had grown too crowded for the old walls to contain any longer. The old mustering-field for the army was quickly growing as urbanized as the rest of the city.

Holding the race in the Forum was favorable to me in one respect: If it had been in the *Campus Martius,* the race would have been run in chariots. I was a competent rider, but a wretched charioteer. The chariot has been obsolete for centuries, except for races and ceremonial processions, so I never saw any point in acquiring the skill, although I had taken some lessons out of curiosity. Clodius, on the other hand, was known to practice regularly at the stables of the Greens (he had switched from Red to Green upon becoming a man of the people). It would have been unthinkably disgraceful for any well-born man to race publicly, but many race-crazed young men practiced assiduously to learn a skill they would never be able to use.

To my further advantage was Clodius himself. He was a bit shorter than I, but of stocky build and he weighed

a good many pounds more. Much would depend on the
respective strength of the horses we drew. Since they
would have been chosen from among the best race-
horses of the stables, it was probable that their power
would be nearly equal, giving me the advantage.

With half the Subura behind me, I entered the Forum
amid thunderous cheers. The whole city seemed to be
packed into the ancient city center, or on the balconies
and atop the gates and rooftops overlooking it. People
had climbed onto the monuments for a better view. Beside me were two other men who would ride for the
Subura. They were both handlers for the Circus, expert
riders.

Mars in those days was still an extramural god, and
had no altar within the city except for a shrine in the
house of the *Pontifex Maximus,* so a temporary altar had
been erected in front of the *Rostra,* similar to the permanent altar on the *Campus Martius.* There stood the
Flamen Martialis and his attendants, ready to conduct
the ceremony. Behind the priest, on the *Rostra,* stood
the magistrates of state and the other *pontifices* and *flamines,* the augurs, and a few privileged foreigners.

Approaching from the other end of the Forum I saw
Publius Clodius and his two companions, backed by the
dwellers of the *Via Sacra.* Like mine, most of his followers were young men, excited and ready for a brawl. Clodius was still a rather handsome young man, despite
some marks I had put on his face and which were always
a great joy for me to look upon. I was pleased to note
that he had added a pound or two since I had last seen
him. In keeping with the solemnity of the occasion, we
didn't make faces at each other, but maintained an im-
passive, hieratic demeanor.

I stepped onto the low dais that had been erected for
the altar and stood there with the other five riders. My
father was there, along with the fathers of two of the
other men. Since, by the well-known Roman legal fiction, we were still our fathers' property, the three fathers
and the *flamen* had to go through a certain mummery
temporarily releasing us to the service of the god. When
that was done, my father came to me and said: "This is

a damnably risky business, but they'll remember it in the tribal assemblies when it comes time for you to stand for the aedileship. Just be careful and let the others take the risks, as much as possible." Then he left the dais. Father had a wonderfully political way of looking at everything. Anything short of death was acceptable to him, so long as it helped you get elected.

Then the *flamen*'s attendants stripped us of our tunics. This was an ancient practice, but the main reason for it was to ensure that we were not wearing armor or concealed weapons beneath our outer garments. Only a *subligaculum* was permitted, and even that was discreetly searched lest we be concealing some amulet or charm intended to put a curse on a rival. During this stage of the proceedings I was pleased to note that I looked far better thus unclad than Clodius, with his extra poundage. He was a powerful man, though, and not to be underestimated. I did not shine so well in comparison to the other four, all of whom were as well conditioned as any professional athlete.

As the others were being searched I looked out over the crowd. Besides the Suburans, I had other supporters. I saw Milo and a large group of his thugs. The enmity between Clodius and me was as the love of brothers compared to what lay between him and Milo. A number of Catilina's men were there as promised, including Valgius and Thorius, the bearded lovelies who had followed Aurelia. The sight of Valgius tickled something in my memory, but he also made me think of Aurelia, which was something I was doing too much of already. I looked up at the Capitol, where the new image of Jupiter was at last in place, and saw that the repairs to the wall where it had been moved in had been completed. The *haruspices* had said that the new Jupiter would warn us of dangers to the state. Then I heard the sound of trumpets and a reverent silence fell over the crowd. The ceremony had begun.

Down the *Via Sacra* came the Palatine *Salii*, the twelve young patricians who formed the brotherhood of the dancing priests of Mars. Dressed in scarlet tunics and wearing bronze helmets and breastplates of antique de-

sign, they performed a slow and solemn war dance to
the music of the holy trumpets and wailing flutes. Each
bore in his hand one of the sacred spears of Mars, and
on his other arm he carried one of the *ancilia*, the
strangely shaped bronze shields of Mars. This was their
last ceremony of the year, and they would dance in all
the holy places for four more days, at which time the
holy shields, spears and trumpets would be purified and
stored away in the *regia* and all worship of Mars would
cease for the duration of winter, barring the outbreak
of war.

Behind the *Salii* came the horses. These were spectacular beasts: three bays, a white, a black and a brown with
black stripes on his haunches. Each horse had had a
numeral painted on his brow, from one to six, in the
order they had been chosen by the *Flamen Martialis* according to criteria known only to the *pontifices*. The
horses halted before the altar, the handlers having their
hands full with the nervous, temperamental animals.
The *Salii* continued their dance, circling the horses three
times, singing a song so ancient that only a few words
of it were intelligible, even to the priests themselves.
Everyone watched breathlessly, concerned that the dance
should be performed properly. Above all it was important that the spears should not be allowed to clash
against the shields, for that was the signal to summon
Mars to aid us in battle. He would be very angry to find
that there was no war going on. But the dance was performed flawlessly and the *Salii* came to a halt before the
dais.

Now one of the Vestal virgins took a helmet from the
head of one of the dancers and gave it to the *flamen*.
One of the attendants placed five knucklebones inside
These were not real knucklebones, but bronze repli-
cas, each the size of a child's fist and brilliantly polished.
One by one, we riders took the helmet from the *flamen*,
shook it, and cast the knucklebones onto the dais. We
were assigned horses according to the score each of us
threw.

Mine was three, the white. This seemed lucky to me.
I had always liked white horses because, I suppose, ev-

eryone likes white horses. Clodius drew one of the bays. My two side-men got the black and another of the bays. Although the race was supposed to be between the horses, these men would actually be trying to prevent Clodius and his men from fouling me. Clodius's men would have the same task.

A handler boosted me onto my white. The horses wore no saddles and we could control them only with rope halters, for metal bits were forbidden. A vestal handed each of us a whip that had been plaited of new leather and horsehair within the *Atrium Vestae*, thus ensuring that none of them were envenomed.

The horses were lined up so closely that my knees touched the knees of the riders to either side. One of them was Clodius, who was on my left. This was a stroke of bad luck. He spoke to me, too quietly for anyone else to hear.

"I hope you have your mourners hired, Metellus. You'll be dead before nightfall."

I could tell that the years since our last serious encounter had done nothing to sweeten his disposition.

"You'd better not try anything," I warned him. "I have archers stationed on top of the *Curia*." The fool actually looked.

Then the handlers released our reins and darted out of the way. The horses trembled with eagerness to start, restrained only by a chalk-whitened rope stretched at breast height a few feet in front of them, held taut by two slaves. My nerves were stretched as tight by the wait and the silence. All eyes were on the *Flamen Martialis*. He nodded, and the attendants of the *Salii* blew a long blast on the sacred trumpets. The crowd erupted.

As our horses lunged forward, Clodius lashed at my eyes with his whip. I had been expecting it and I ducked, but the whip caught my brow and scalp, cutting deep. This was why I had been distressed to find Clodius on my immediate left. It gave him full freedom to use his whip against me with his right hand, while I would have to reach across my body to get at him.

Clodius pulled ahead as we pounded down the narrow track marked out by ropes, the screaming crowd

packed behind the ropes urging us on. My white was
infuriated at the bay for passing him and as we dashed
past the Basilica Aemilia, he snaked out his neck and
bit the bay's haunch. Clodius almost lost his seat as the
bay squealed and jerked. My white put on a burst of
speed and I slashed Clodius with my whip as I passed
him, leaning far over to do it. This was not a good thing
to do, because at that moment one of Clodius's men
gained my right rear and slashed me across the back.
The force of the blow and the sudden, unexpected pain
almost pitched me headforemost. If the fall to the hard
pavement did not kill me the trampling by the horses
behind surely would have. I squeezed with my knees and
clung to my horse's neck to stay on, and I could hear
Clodius's laugh as he dashed past.

One of my side-men got his whip around the neck of
the lout who had lashed me from behind and jerked
him from his mount. The crowd cheered frantically at
this adroit move. In this race, the riders were free to
attack each other, but not one another's horses. That
would have been sacrilege.

The horses themselves were under no such compul-
sion, and just as I regained my seat and dashed the blood
from my eyes, my side-man on the black and Clodius's
man on the striped horse drew up on my left. There was
not sufficient room for two horses there and the animals
attacked one another with teeth and hooves. Men and
horses went down in a tangle of thrashing limbs, flailing
hooves and hissing whips.

I caught up with Clodius as we rounded the monument to a Consul of four hundred years before. It was
greatly in need of repair and was demolished a few years
later because nobody would pay for its restoration. The
family was long extinct. As we made the turn he cut too
close and his horse's haunch caught the corner of the
monument, breaking loose some old repair work and
causing the beast to stumble. At this I surged past him,
striking out with my whip, but without success.

Now I was rushing back toward the altar. I looked
behind me just in time to cut in front of Clodius, who
was getting close. (The other remaining rider was be-

hind him.) The three riderless horses had regained their feet and rejoined the race like the spirited animals they were. My white was running his heart out, even though this was a far shorter race than he was used to. Once around the Forum is nothing like seven times around the *spina* at the Circus, pulling a chariot.

Foam from the white's mouth mixed with the blood on my face as we dashed back over the starting line. The crowd cheered frantically as I pulled up and dismounted. I patted the beast's flank as a handler took charge of him. All the cheering was for the horse, naturally. This was not an athletic contest and I would receive neither crown nor palm.

At least my Suburans cheered me. A woman tossed me a scarf and I bound it around my head to stop the blood from running into my eyes. My back burned as if someone had laid a hot iron across it. Handlers were catching the three riderless animals. I walked, somewhat stiffly, to the dais. Clodius was already there, having no serious injuries to be tended. He glared at me and I grinned back. He was not through yet, as I well knew. This had been only the first stage of the day's ordeal.

The crowd quieted somewhat as we assembled. The two riders who had taken the worst falls were not seriously injured and managed to hobble to the dais, bloodied but proud. Then the white horse I had ridden to victory was led up. The people sang the ancient chant to the October Horse and showered him with honey cakes and dried petals of the summer's flowers.

The handlers walked the October Horse onto the dais while the *flamen* and his attendants intoned their prayers. The *flamen* Stroked the horse's head from ears to muzzle and the beast ducked his head in a nod, a propitious sign. A vestal handed scarves to the riders and we covered our heads with these as the men in the crowd did the same with their togas and the women with their *pallas.*

When the *flamen*'s prayer was done he nodded to an attendant who struck the horse on the brow with a long-handled hammer. The beast stood planted to the spot, stunned, as the *flamen* cut his throat with the sacrificial knife that he must always carry with him. The blood was caught in two vessels, one of which would go to the Temple of Vesta to be used in the lustrations of the coming year, the other to be poured out over the hearth of the *Regia,* where once the kings of Rome had lived and where the *Pontifex Maximus* now dwelled.

I was saddened to see the great horse die, as I always was at these sacrifices, but especially this time, for he had borne me so magnificently. But then, if there is no sadness, of what value is the sacrifice? How could the god take pleasure in an offering for which the givers felt only indifference? I never saw much point in sacrificing pigeons and other such inferior victims, but the sacrifice of the October Horse has always marked for me one of the noblest links between the Roman people and their gods. And why should a fine racehorse want to grow old and feeble? Better to perish this way, and join the herd of the gods. Woe to the people when we forget these duties owed to our gods.

As the blood was collected, the *flamen* continued the prayer to Mars. An attendant held the written service before him so that he should not stumble over the archaic words and behind him a flute-player trilled so that no unseemly sound or word from the multitude should distract the *flamen.* Any slightest flaw in the performance of the ritual, and the entire ceremony would have to be repeated from the beginning.

When the blood collecting was done, the flamen went to the great corpse and with a few deft, well-practiced cuts of the sacrificial knife, he severed the head and held it aloft, still dripping. The assembled multitude clapped three times, cheered three times, and repeated the ritual laugh three times. Reverently, the *flamen* placed the head upon the altar, then sprinkled it with barley meal and poured over it fresh-pressed oil mixed with honey. Then, in a rite peculiar to the October Horse, the *flamen* and the vestals piled cakes baked that day from fine wheat around and atop the noble head. Then the *flamen* stepped back, clapped three times and laughed three times. A collective sigh went up from the multitude and they uncovered their heads, satisfied that all due honor had been paid the October Horse and that Mars must now be contented, ready to undertake his four-month absence from the city.

Now the tension began to rise again. The solemn ritual was done with. The final, climactic phase of the festival was at hand. The fun was about to begin. I was keyed up and ready for it, but I had seldom felt myself to be in so much danger.

The *flamen,* his attendants and the vestals left the dais and mounted the *Rostra.* A space was made for the *flamen* at the front of the platform. He stepped into the space and beside him stood the master of the herald's guild. The master herald, in his long, white robe and bearing his wand of office, stood ready to repeat the *flamen's* words so that all could hear. This master had earned his position by possessing the loudest voice ever heard in Rome.

The *Flamen Martialis* spoke the ritual formula and the herald repeated it: "MARS IS HAPPY!"

With that, we stormed the altar. Clodius got there first and snatched at the head, but I caught him in the back with my shoulder and he lunged across the altar and only got an armful of wheat cakes. Shoving his flailing legs aside, I wrapped my arms around the noble head and lifted it from the altar. Whirling, I made a dash in the direction of the Subura. Two men jumped in front of me but I swung the head to right and left, knocking them aside. I ran through the breach I had made. Now a dozen Suburans fought their way in front of me and struggled to clear my way to our home territory.

The Forum was in an uproar. The press was so great that only those closest to me could see where I was, but people on rooftops and balconies and monuments pointed me out for the benefit of those who thirsted for my blood.

We got across the pavement and into a street leading toward the Subura, but gained no security thereby. The Via Sacrans were on the rooftops and they began to shower us with roof tiles. One struck me on top of the head, almost knocking me to my knees. White light flashed in my eyes and I almost dropped the head. My

newly lacerated scalp began to bleed profusely, soaking
the scarf bound around my brow and running into my
eyes. My defenders snatched up boards and tore loose
shutters to use as shields from the ex tempore missiles.

I saw one tile make it through the rude shields and
drop the bearded Thorius to the pavement. So Catilina's
men were at my side, as promised. I wondered where
Titus Milo might be. It was his men I wanted with me
should things get rough.

As we passed an intersection of two *itenera,* a mob of
Via Sacrans bulled into us and my bodyguard dissolved
into a score of individual fights. Arms grabbed me from
behind and then Clodius was in front of me, trying to
wrestle the head from my grasp. His grip was uncertain,
because by this time I was covered with oil, honey, blood,
both my own and the horse's, along with other fluids, all
of them discouraging to a firm grasp. Besides these, I
was liberally dusted with crumbs and barley meal. I
kicked out mightily, catching him in the testicles most
satisfyingly. As he fell, I struck to the rear with an elbow,
heard an explosion of breath, and the arms around me
loosened. I broke free and dashed for an alley, kicking
Clodius in the face as I passed, just for good measure.

A few steps down the alley I turned into another. This
alley curved to the left, then turned into a flight of stairs
leading up to a shrine of Quirinus. I had lost pursuit,
but likewise I had lost my protection. In fact, I was lost
generally and I stopped to get my bearings. There was
a small fountain beside the shrine and I took the opportunity to wash some of the blood from my face. My
whole body screamed with pain but I maintained a stoic
silence. Any sound from me was sure to draw Clodius.

I knocked on the nearest door and, somewhat to my
surprise, it opened. The man who gaped at me was a
bearded foreigner in a long, striped robe. This was excellent luck. Any citizen would have been attending the
festival.

"Excuse me," I said, "I am the *Quaestor* Decius Caecilius Metellus the Younger. Could you direct me toward
the Subura?"

He gathered his composure and bowed. "Certainly,

my lord. If you will just go back down those stairs and turn right—"

"I am afraid I cannot. There are men back there who might kill me, or at least take this." I held up the head, which now seemed to weigh twice as much as it had when I lifted it from the altar. "Is there an alternative route?"

He thought for a moment. "If you will come into my poor house, there is a back door that opens on a street leading in that direction." He bowed again and gestured for me to enter.

"I would hate to drip on your floor," I said.

"It is nothing. Please, my lord, come in." I could scarcely refuse such hospitality and entered. As I did, I saw an interior door close softly, a veiled woman disappearing behind it. The room was humble but not shabby, and was scrupulously clean.

"If my lord will come this way." The man led me into another room containing a desk and a cabinet of scrolls, and then into a kitchen.

"Where do you hail from?" I asked. He seemed vaguely eastern.

"Jerusalem." I knew little of the place except that Pompey had sacked it a couple of years previously. Gesturing for me to stand back, he opened the kitchen door and looked out into the street on the other side, turning his head to see both ways. Then he turned to me. "The street is deserted. If you go to the right, uphill, you should reach the Subura in a few minutes' walk."

"This has been most kind of you," I said, stepping out into the street. "If I can ever do you a favor, please feel free to call upon me."

"My lord is too generous," he said, bowing again.

"And your name?" I inquired.

"Amos, son of Eleazar, a humble accountant for the House of Simon, importers."

"Well, perhaps I'll be able to do you a good turn someday. I might be elected *Praetor Peregrinus*. If, that is, I can reach the Subura alive."

"I wish my lord the best of fortune," he said, bowing

again and closing the door, a most polite and accom-
modating foreigner.

By now I had regained my breath and I set off up the
street at a fast trot. My arms were aching from holding
the horse's head, which must have weighed more than
thirty pounds. I had my bearings now, and knew that if
I could just avoid the *Via Sacra* mob for a few minutes
longer, I would be safe in the Subura. In the distance, I
could still hear the rampaging mobs in full uproar.

As I passed an intersecting street someone saw me
and pointed. "There he is!" I began to sprint. A few
paces behind me, my pursuers poured into the street,
screaming, cursing me and shouting encouragements to
one another. I caught a glitter from something metallic.
I had thought myself near exhaustion, but this caused
my heels to grow wings like the sandals of Mercury.
These were Clodius's personal followers, and they had
their daggers out.

The street abruptly narrowed and became a short
flight of steps. I climbed them, my breath sounding like
a blacksmith's bellows. At the top of the steps I turned
right into an *itenera* that I knew led directly into the
Square of Vulcan, which was firmly within the Subura.

Something hit my shoulder and I felt a burning pain
and saw something glittering fly past me to clatter on
the cobbles. One of my pursuers had thrown his knife
and managed to cut my shoulder. I dared not look back.
Then I saw men in front of me and was sure I was done
for. I clutched the horse's head tightly to my chest, lowered my own head, and charged directly toward them.
To my unutterable relief, they stood aside for me. They
were Milo's men.

When I was past them, I paused to look back. There
were only about ten of Milo's men, and they were armed
only with staves and short clubs, but they were all burly
ex-gladiators, unafraid of a little sharp steel. I was never
so happy to see a pack of thugs in my life. The sound
of skulls cracking beneath the hardwood clubs was as
the poetry of Homer to my ears. The street began to
grow littered with fallen men and dropped weapons.

I turned to trot toward the square when a scream from

above made me pause and look up. Something large was descending upon me from an overhead balcony. I had a quick impression of a face that was a mask of blood, a mouth twisted into a grimace of fury and demented eyes. Even in flight, Clodius was unmistakable.

He landed on me like a stone from a catapult, driving me to the ground and forcing the breath from my lungs. Clodius grabbed the horse's head and twisted it from my arms, standing and raising it aloft, screaming a victory cry like some Homeric hero who has slain an enemy and stripped him of his armor.

If Clodius had run then, he might have gotten away with it, but the fool had to pause and kick me for a while. The first few got through my dazed defense, but then he spun to run away and I lurched forward from my kneeling position and tried to tackle him. I did not manage to get both knees but my arms wrapped around one leg. As he tugged and stumbled to get away, my slimy coating made me slide down his leg until I held only his ankle. My hands and arms were terribly weary and I knew I could not hang on much longer, for he was kicking back at me violently. My jaw muscles, however, were quite unfatigued. As he tried to kick back at my face, I sank my teeth into his heel, which was unprotected by his sandal. He screeched and tried to twist away, but I held on grimly. At last I was able to grip his other ankle and brought him down.

The instant he hit the cobbles, I scrambled atop him, pummeling away. He raised his hands to defend his patrician face and I got both arms around the horse's head and stood, wrenching it away from him. He tried to get to his feet, but I raised the head and brought it down sharply on his skull, twice. Clodius collapsed into an inert heap. This time, I did not pause to kick him as I leapt over him. Look what that had done for Clodius.

I was running like a man made of half-melted wax when I reached the Square of Vulcan. Somebody saw me and raised the cry. Soon I was surrounded by my neighbors, enduring slaps on my back as we walked to the Guildsmen's Hall, the building where the neighborhood guilds held their meetings and banquets. There,

the still-beautiful head was washed in a trough and was
fastened to a spike atop the pediment over the portico
of the hall. The Subura had regained its luck and the
rejoicing was deafening. At least, that was what I was
told later. I passed out during the head washing.

I awoke looking up at a grave, bearded old gentlemen
who leaned on a staff. The staff was wound with a serpent and the old man was about twenty feet tall and
made of marble. I was in the Temple of Aesculapius, on
the island in the Tiber. Now a much smaller man appeared above me, one whose face I knew.

"Asklepiodes!" I said, or rather croaked. "I thought
you were in Capua."

"There will be no more games for a few months, so
my services were not much in demand. I took leave to
come here and work in the temple. You are not badly
hurt, and I took advantage of your unconscious state to
do most of the necessary stitching. Your face escaped
damage, but your scalp was not so lucky. You will not
appear comely to gods regarding you from above for
some time to come. The shoulder wound was nasty, but
the stitches took care of that. The whip injury is just the
sort of thing that most slaves have to put up with, and
they seldom complain. Can you sit?"

With a little help from one of his Egyptian slaves, I
was able to sit on my pallet. A wave of dizziness washed
over me, but it was quickly gone. There were many pal-
lets in the temple, but few patients. The beds would fill
in the evening, when the ill and injured would come to
the temple to sleep, in hopes that the god would send
them a dream to aid in their cure.

I found that I was naked, but I had been washed well
by the slaves. Except for numerous unsightly bruises, I
looked as if I had just returned from the baths. "I would
appreciate the loan of something to wear home."

"Certainly." He checked the bandaging of my scalp
and made sure that all was to his satisfaction. His slaves
were the most artistic bandagers who ever dressed my
wounds. "You have not consulted me on a murder in a
long time," the physician chided.

"It is not for lack of homicides," I assured him. "It's just that the latest string of killings have been damnably crude and unimaginative, with no subtlety about them." I found myself relating to him the story of the murders since I had encountered the body of Oppius.

Asklepiodes was a very eccentric physician, who actually did his own cutting and stitching. As physician to the gladiators of the Statilian and other schools, he had acquired a knowledge of every sort of weapon-inflicted wound, and I had consulted him on murders before. He could glance at a wound and say what sort of weapon had made it, whether a blade's edge had been straight or curved, whether the killer was right- or left-handed, whether he was taller or shorter than the victim, whether the victim had been standing, sitting or lying down when he received his deathblow. Asklepiodes had developed this sophistry into a sort of sub-branch of medical philosophy that had no name. He was named for the Greek god of medicine, Asklepios, which is how the Greeks name Aesculapius. Greeks can never pronounce anything correctly.

"The art of murder in Rome seems to have reached a new low of amateurism," Asklepiodes commented.

"Cheer up," I said. "Somebody may die interestingly yet. If so, I shall not hesitate to call upon you."

A slave brought a tunic that was almost my size and I drew it over my head, wincing at the stiffness of all my movements. I tried out all my limbs and they all seemed to work. The pain was so diffuse that I seemed to hurt everywhere equally.

"What time of day is it?" I asked. It seemed like several days since I had mounted the October Horse.

"About midafternoon," Asklepiodes said.

"Good. I have a dinner engagement and I need to get home to change clothes."

"In your condition," the physician said, "I should devote the evening to repose."

"A matter of duty," I said. "It is connected with the murders. At least, so runs my theory. There is also a lady of high birth and great beauty involved." I have found that one can discuss these things with a physician.

"After a day of such exertion your mind is still fixed not only upon duty and danger, but upon love. This is truly heroic, my friend! Incredibly foolish, of course, but much to be admired."

VIII

I descended the steps of the temple, wincing at the pains that enveloped my body like a cloud. I might have persuaded Asklepiodes to lend me a litter and some slaves, but I was determined to walk lest I grow too stiff to move at all. I crossed the bridge to the riverbank. This was the old wooden bridge. The fine stone bridge that now stands there was built the next year by the Tribune Fabricius. In the city, the celebration was still in full roar. Applause greeted me wherever I showed my bandaged head, and red-dripping wineskins were held out to me by the score, but I only sipped at a few, just enough to ease my way to my house. I wanted a clear head that evening. It took a great effort of will, because I desired nothing more than to drink until my pains were forgotten and lose all my cares in the city's festal mood. I was weary of murders and intrigues and scheming politicians and generals.

Ladies wearing the brief tunic and feminine toga of the courtesan offered themselves to me freely, but my mind was so fixed upon a single woman that I was not even tempted. Infatuation is a terrible thing. Musicians wound through the streets playing flutes and cymbals, and behind them danced women in the fashion of Bacchantes; their hair unbound and dressed only in animal skins or flimsy chitons open down one side. This was a Greek custom frequently forbidden by the *aediles* or the Censors, but it had been a few years since the last censorship and the *aediles* had more important concerns, anyway.

A vendor handed me a flat loaf wrapped around a

heap of thin-sliced lamb, fried onions and olives, all of
a delightful greasiness. This I devoured hungrily, for I
had had nothing since breakfast and I knew I would
have to drink with Catilina and his cronies or else be
suspect. It was so good that, when another vendor offered me a broad fig-leaf heaped with grilled sausages,
I accepted that too. These needed something to wash
them down, so I next took a cup of unfermented apple
juice at a stall, along with a handful of figs and dates.

Women rubbed themselves against me for luck and I
did not complain. Men tried to do the same and I did
complain. I was hero for a day, but for a day only. The
Roman people are infinitely distractable, and I would
be forgotten by the next day.

I reached home pleasantly stuffed and let my elderly
house slaves fuss over me for a while. They might treat
me like a hero for as much as two days, or perhaps even
three, if I did nothing to offend them in the meantime.
Cassandra wanted to strip the fine bandages from my
head and try her favorite poultice on me, but I preferred to trust Asklepiodes's more professional treatment.

When the sun drew low to the west, I donned a decent
tunic and opened my arms chest. Inside were my swords,
my field armor and my parade armor, my daggers and
my *caesti*. I took a sheathed *pugio* and thrust it beneath my
tunic, under the girdle. Then I took up a *caestus*. I had
won the boxing gloves in a long-ago game and I had
stripped one of its complicated straps, leaving only the
thick, bronze bar that went over the knuckles. With its
half-inch, pyramidal spikes it was just the thing to give
an assailant a truly memorable punch. I tested it to make
sure the single strap was still snug against my palm and
then tucked it beneath my tunic on the other side, where
I could reach it easily with my left hand.

I did not fear trouble from Catilina or his men, but it
was likely that Clodius and his men might be prowling
the city and he was unstable enough to attack me on
sight. I would have to watch out for Clodius until someone else should enrage him. That would not be long.

Clodius acquired enemies the way Caesar picked up votes.

Leaving word that I would return late, I left my house and entered the darkened streets. The revelry had quieted some, but not entirely, by any means. It is seldom truly quiet in the Subura, but by this time most of the roistering had moved indoors, although in the open squares and courts of some neighborhoods, tables had been erected and the dwellers of the local *insulae* sat back, picking their teeth contentedly. The day's sacrifices had provided plenty of meat and the harvest was in, so fruits and vegetables were plentiful and cheap. Fall was usually a good time in Rome, unless the harvest had been bad. Then it would become necessary to squeeze the provinces.

I reached Orestilla's house without encountering Publius or his myrmidons. The *janitor* let me in and I went into the *atrium.* A cheer went up at my arrival. Catilina rose and took my hand.

"Well done, Decius, well done!" His arm around my shoulders, he turned to face the others and gestured grandly. "Here is our hero, at last. We've been awaiting your arrival, Decius."

There were a dozen men present, and all of them rose from their seats to congratulate me. Some of them I knew already: Curius, Cethegus Sura, Laeca, the twin beards, Thorius and Valgius. The latter two showed the trophies of their vigorous efforts on my behalf that morning. Thorius sported a bandage around his head, although it was not as artistic as my own. Valgius had a pair of black eyes, nearly swollen shut. There was a bulky, balding man in the *tunica laticlavia* with the narrow red stripe; an *eques.* The rest bore no marks of distinction.

"Decius," Catilina said when the balding man approached, "this is Publius Umbrenus, a prominent businessman with interests throughout Gaul." So this was the mysterious financier who had been speaking with the Allobroges.

"I knew your father in Gaul," Umbrenus said. He had the false heartiness of an auctioneer.

The others were introduced, but I had little opportunity to absorb more than their names: Publius Gabinius Capito, Lucius Bestia, Marcus Fulvius Nobilior and Lucius Statilius were all of the equestrian order, although they had purposely attended in common tunics. They were living proof that not every *eques* was a wealthy businessman, for these were as ragged and hungry a pack of ne'er-do-wells as one could ask for. Some were ruined entrepreneurs like Umbrenus, others had never reach high enough to achieve ruin.

There were others, but the rest were not from Rome. They were minor nobles from various Italian *municipia* and *coloniae*. I no longer remember their names, although they are to be found in the court records. I remembered what Milo had said about malcontents. It gave me cause to reassess the fairly rosy picture I had of the empire's condition. In truth, only the city of Rome itself was relatively tranquil. Everywhere else there was discontent and unrest.

Amid the backslapping and embracing, Catilina's brows went up at a faint clink from under my tunic. I displayed my weapons for their admiration.

"I wasn't taking any chances on encountering Clodius this evening," I told them. Several of them grinned and exposed the grips of daggers or short swords beneath their tunics.

"You won't find anyone here who's squeamish about carrying arms," Catilina chuckled. "But you needn't have bothered yourself about Clodius. He's safe at home, being nursed by his beloved sister and complaining piteously of his wounds. He says that only serpents are in the habit of biting men on the heel."

"Hence your new name around town," Cethegus said, "Metellus the Viper."

"I like the sound of that," I said.

"I heard one of his sycophants at the baths this evening," said Laeca, toadying it up superbly. "He was declaiming some new verse he'd cobbled together, likening Clodius to Achilles, wounded in the heel by a coward." He laughed loudly and falsely. "As if the man who carried the head of the October Horse from the Forum to the Subura single-handed could be accused of cowardice!"

"You'll be the talk of Rome for some time to come, Decius," Catilina said.

"And forgotten next time I stand for office," I said, remembering my role.

"But then, that's why we're all here," Catilina said. "We are all fed up with the fickleness of the electorate. They were spoiled by the Gracchi and have been growing worse ever since." He paused while the others made grumbles of agreement. "Now, I would never want to see us return to monarchy, but things were best when decisions were made by the Senate and the Centuriate Assembly, all solid men of property and military experience, patrician and plebeian both. Now they hand out citizenship to anyone, even freedmen." Then he remembered the non-Romans present and added, hastily, "And on top of that, our demagogues have robbed the *municipia* and *coloniae* of their old rights of self-government without giving them a commensurate place in the government." That was the sort of mistake Caesar never would have made. Catilina just wasn't a born politician.

"Very true," said one of the strangers. "We Italian allies supposedly have citizenship, but we must come here to Rome for the voting if we want to be represented. We crowd into tents and tenements at a miserable time of year." The man was glowering, his words bitter. "Then, as often as not, we are cheated of our vote. Whenever an issue that might favor us comes up for a vote, the speakers carry on endlessly, or the augurs suddenly see omens decreeing that the vote must be delayed. Then they wait until we must return home before voting." This was indeed a common abuse of the day, and the allies had much just cause for grievance.

I put on a stern face. "Such injustice is intolerable!"

"And we will see it corrected," Catilina said. "Gentlemen, take your seats and let us get down to business."

We seated ourselves and slaves came in to set a table with pitchers of wine and platters of fruit, nuts, olives and the like. This was not a dinner party, but Romans cannot talk seriously without refreshment save in the

Senate and the courts, and there we are just pretending to be dignified. The slaves withdrew. Like most such homes, this one had no internal doors in that part of the house, so we could see into the *peristylium* and the adjoining rooms and be sure that no one was lurking in them.

"Orestilla has locked the domestic slaves in the rear of the house," Catilina said. "We may all speak openly, without fear of being overheard." He looked around the room with the eagle-eyed gaze of a general proudly surveying a veteran legion. "I will make no speeches. The time for that is past and the time for action is at hand. Let us hear your reports. Publius Umbrenus, let us hear yours first."

Umbrenus rose as if addressing the Senate, his left hand going up as if to grasp that fold of the toga just below the collarbone that is so beloved by orators. Remembering that he was not wearing his toga, he grasped a handful of tunic instead.

"My agents in Gaul have been successful and the tribes will rise upon our signal. Roman government in the Transalpine Province is weak. When Lucius Murena came back to Rome to stand for the consulship, he left his brother Caius to rule in his stead as *legatus*. To Gauls, that's like a king leaving his idiot son in charge while he goes raiding in someone else's territory. It is an invitation to rebellion.

"My negotiations here in Rome with the envoys of the Allobroges have been most successful. Their support consolidates our grasp on the northern part of the province. They were hesitant at first, but when I demonstrated to them the extent of our preparations, our power, our backers, then they were eager to cooperate. They stand in readiness to receive our orders."

"Excellent," Catilina said. "Marcus Fulvius, speak to us."

Nobilior stood. He was a thin, nervous man who was of some kinship to Fulvia, the mistress of Curius. "My preparations in Bruttium are now complete," he reported. "When you give the signal, Consul"—he addressed this title to Catilina—"they will rise. You may be assured of the complete loyalty and support of the Bruttians."

I solemnly raised my cup and took a long drink in order to avoid bursting into laughter. If ever there was an assurance of disaster, it was to have the Bruttians on your side. They succumbed to every enemy of Rome who ever marched against us from the south. They harbored Pyrrhus and they harbored Hannibal and even Spartacus tarried there for a while, since the Bruttians weren't up to fighting a pack of runaway slaves. They weren't even proper Latins, speaking as much Greek and Oscan as Latin. In truth, nobody knew exactly what they were, and nobody cared. Nobilior sat.

"Lucius Calpurnius?" Catilina said. Bestia stood. That year he had been elected one of the tribunes of the plebs for the coming year. Since Sulla, the lowest of the tribunes had little more authority than a low-ranking *quaestor* like me. About all that was left to them was the power to summon the plebs to vote on a proposed law and submit the decision to the Senate for ratification.

"Unlike you men of action"—Bestia smiled around at his listeners—"I have had little part in the preparations for this epoch-making revolution, which will return men of birth and nobility to their rightful place." His words were the proper ones for a gathering like this, but something seemed wrong about him. Despite his raggedness, there was a steely resolve in his stance. Beneath his words and behind his eyes I saw a sort of mockery, as if he were amused by all this.

"My time will come after you have all sprung to arms," Bestia went on. "When the uprising is in full roar throughout Italy, from the tip of Bruttium to Cisalpine Gaul, and in Transalpine Gaul, when our new Consul is at the head of his army and marching upon Rome, then, as Tribune-elect, I shall call upon the people to rise up and oust the usurper Cicero. With me at their head, they will throw open the gates and welcome our new Consul to his curule chair in the *Curia.*"

"Decius Caecilius," Catilina said, "you seem skeptical." Apparently, I had not been guarding my expression.

"Cicero is contemptible," I said, "but what of his colleague, Caius Antonius?"

"He will already be out of Rome," Catilina said. "He is so anxious to get to Macedonia and start looting that Cicero is all but threatening him with arrest to make him stay in Rome long enough to make a show of finishing his year in office." Catilina leaned back in his seat and laughed richly. The others quickly joined him. "He'll be summoned back to Rome, of course, but by that time we will be firmly in control, and he'll have no more luck than his brother Marcus had in Crete." He nodded toward Valgius. "Quintus, of our two youngest colleagues, you seem to be marginally better able to speak this evening. Tell us how you have fared among the laureled youth of Rome."

Valgius rubbed his bearded jaw ruefully. "If that flunky of Clodius's had kicked a little harder, I'd not be speaking until next *Saturnalia*. Marcus and I"—he nodded toward the bandaged Thorius—"have been untiring in our work among the young men of senatorial families. All of those who have spurned our Consul in the past, those who have sought to prosecute him and those who are sure to resist us when the uprising begins, have been marked out. Their sons will kill them in their beds as soon as they hear the trumpets sound."

Catilina caught my expression. "Oh, don't worry, Decius. We won't make you kill old Cut-Nose. He's never offended me and he'll come around as soon as he sees how the wind is blowing."

"That's a relief," I said to cover my confusion. "We have our differences, but things between us haven't deteriorated to that point yet."

"But then," said Cethegus, "you really must kill someone, Decius."

"I must?"

"Oh, but of course." Cethegus's tone was as sarcastic and insinuating as ever. "All of us have."

"It's a sort of initiation," Laeca said. "Rather like joining one of the mystery cults. Each of us proves his sincerity and loyalty to our cause by killing someone."

"You have to admit it's an effective and unquestionable

display of solidarity." Still with that hint of inner amusement.

"I see. Anyone in particular?" I inquired.

"That's the easy and agreeable part," Catilina said. "You recall that once before, several of us discussed how we were all but ruined by the moneylenders?"

"I recall it," I said.

"Well, then, there you are. What can be more pleasant than to kill a creditor? You mentioned that you have had to borrow heavily to support your current office and against your future aedileship. To whom are you so deeply in debt?" He sat back, smiling.

I lifted my cup and drank slowly, frowning into the depths of the excellent Massic. It swirled red as blood in the lamplight reflected from the silver bottom. I was pretending to be pondering my answer. Actually, I was frantically trying to find a way out of this. If I couldn't come up with a credible answer, I might not walk from this place alive. Actually, it was almost pleasant not to have Aurelia on my mind.

Then inspiration struck. It was one of those moments of blinding insight that are sometimes granted by our guardian *genii*. Of course, there are philosophers who insist that each of us has two *genii*, one good and one evil, and it was from the latter that I had most of my near-suicidal inspirations, but they all seemed brilliant at the time. In any case, I was in no position to discriminate. I lowered my cup.

"Asklepiodes, the Greek physician," I said.

Everyone looked puzzled. "The doctor to the gladiators?" Curius said.

"Do you think that's all he is?" I said. "That's just for surgery. For medicine, he doctors the rich, like all Greek physicians. Why, people come from as far away as Antioch and Alexandria for his treatment." I looked around at them, as if we were all men of the world and understood these things. "Discreetly, of course. He specializes in those condition people prefer not to talk about. Lisas the Egyptian alone keeps him on a retainer of a million *sesterces* a year just to treat him for those diseases he's always picking up from his incessant perversions."

"I never would have guessed it," Umbrenus said.

"And," I said, leaning forward and speaking conspiratorially, an excellent way to speak in such a gathering, "do you think that being physician and surgeon to the gladiators is not a way to grow rich?" I paused and drank, letting the implications sink in. "He knows who is in top form and who isn't. And who better than their own physician to make sure that a champion isn't quite up to his next fight? That's the time to make the long-odds bets, my friends. And he doesn't give that information away, he sells it, or passes it along in return for favors."

"So that's why you win so often at the fights," Bestia said.

"It seems almost a shame to waste a resource like that," Laeca added.

"But I'm up to here in debt to the wretched Greekling," I said, raising a hand level with my bandaged scalp. "He only gives me tips in hope that I'll be able to pay him back a little of what I owe him."

"Yes," Catilina said, "let's not cheat Decius Caecilius out of his just revenge. A true Roman shouldn't bet on the *munera* anyway. They are supposed to be funeral games, after all. Races are the proper contests for gambling." He turned to me and smiled. "Very well, it's settled, then. Decius, you can kill Asklepiodes. But we have little time, so you must act soon—within two days. Is that agreeable?"

"Oh, decidedly," I assured him. "The sooner the better."

"Excellent. Now, Valgius, what about the fires?"

"Our teams have been assigned their sites," said the bearded one. "On the appointed night, the fires will begin all over the city. The authorities will have a busy time of it, I assure you all."

He resumed his seat and I drank, deeply this time. It was far worse than I had thought. Thus far, they had plotted treason, murder and parricide, serious crimes but not exactly uncommon. This was arson. Fire-raising was the most hated and feared crime in Roman law.

Arsonists taken in the act had reason to envy men who were merely crucified.

And yet, horrible as it all was, I had difficulty in crediting any of what I was hearing. I knew with certainty that these men had committed murder, I had seen the evidence. But revolution? This was like boys playing at war, naming themselves general, each pretending to be a cohort or century. Surely, this pack of strutting posers and babbling loons could not possibly hope to overthrow the majesty of the Roman government? And yet I had witnessed the effectiveness of some of their acts. It left me with one conviction: there was somebody else behind all this, somebody who was not about to appear personally before these lunatics.

I had questions to ask, but I wanted to ask them of Catilina, not these madmen. He was not without his own strain of insanity, but most of the great men of that day were mad to some extent or other. He was far more intelligent than the others, I was sure, although I had my suspicions about Bestia. But I was sure that Catilina was not going to risk everything with only the support of such as these.

A few others tendered their reports, each of them as vaporous and self-deceiving as the others. It was like a dream, except that I knew they were shedding real blood in their ramblings, the blood of citizens.

And I have never taken kindly to the murder of citizens, nor even of resident foreigners under Rome's protection. Some of the victims may not have been particularly savory, but others had been upright members of the community. At any rate, people who do not die in the natural course of things have a right to die by their own hand, or else be put to death only after the proper deliberations of state. That is why we have crosses and arenas. They should not die violently at the hands of malefactors and I have never been able to tolerate such criminal behavior.

If ambitious men wanted to kill one another in the pursuit of power, they had my full blessing to do so. Every such demise made the world a better place. But in doing so they had no right to kill ordinary citizens guilty of no more than going about their everyday lives. If their armies wished to follow their generals and slaughter one another in furthering the ambitions of those men, I was satisfied. I yield to none in my admiration of the Roman legionary, but soldiers are men who bear arms, kill and die as a profession. That does not constitute a right to victimize those who merely go about their lawful occupations.

The truth was that I was not a man of greatness as that age, which now seems almost as remote as the days of Homer, judged such things. I had no ambition to lead armies, to conquer new provinces, to come home a *triumphator*. I was a Roman in the old sense of the word. I was a citizen of a hill town on the Tiber that had, through an astonishing set of circumstances, found itself to be master of the world. I wanted to live with my neighbors, govern over them as my birth and education gave me competence, and, when necessity dictated, fight in their defense to the extent that my less than heroic capabilities allowed.

I enjoyed parties at the Egyptian embassy where the mighty of the world gorged and connived, but I also enjoyed the celebrations of Subura workmen where a whole guild had to pool their dues to buy an amphora of decent Falernian and the loaves were the only white bread those men ate all year. The corner temple of Jupiter near my house, where I attended sacrifices on most mornings, had only five priests. One of these was freeborn, two were freedmen and two were slaves. That was the Rome I loved, not the imperial fantasy that the likes of Crassus and Pompey and so many other fought over. It was men like these who had destroyed the old Rome. Now Catilina wanted to be one of them.

And yet, for all his foolishness and brutality, I could not help liking Catilina, in a grudging sort of way. He was like an importunate puppy, or a rambunctious boy who insists upon barging in on the debates and solemnities of his elders, waving his wooden sword and shouting his shrill battle cries, annoying everybody and impossible to ignore. He had *hubris* in plenty, as the Greeks define such things, but he had little meanness and even less pretentiousness. I sincerely hoped that, after all his murders and treasons, he would be given a quick, easy and dignified death.

The drinking went on for some time after the serious talk was over. We walked out into the street and made our farewells as personal slaves were released from the rear of the house to accompany their masters home. Thorius, bandaged head and all, crawled into a litter borne by a matched team of Nubians, which I assumed must be borrowed. Since he had come by his wounds in my ostensible defense, I felt it incumbent upon me to be solicitous.

"Fine rig, Thorius," I said, winking. "Who is she? Rich man's wife?"

He managed to smile, despite what was probably a broken jaw. "Not this time. Bought the litter and the slaves myself." Then he sagged back into the cushions and was carried away. I noticed other such anomalies. Bestia walked away with a new toga, its hem not merely dyed with the murex purple, but embroidered in the Scythian fashion with interlacing animal and vegetative designs. Granted, he had been promised a curule position, worthy of the toga *praetexta* when Catilina should come to power, but a purple stripe was all that was necessary. That toga was worth the loot of a medium-sized municipality. These things, I was sure, were the gifts of Catilina, a notably penurious man. Where was he getting the money?

As we saw them off, Lucius kept a hand on my shoulder, a plain sign that he wished me to remain behind. I was nothing loath, for more than one reason. When they were all departed, we returned to the *atrium* and were given wine by the slaves. We sipped and sat in silence for a while.

"Go ahead, Decius Caecilius," Catilina said after a while. "Ask the questions that have been burning you all evening."

"Not just this evening, Lucius," I said. "But for a long time, at least since the dinner at Sempronia's house."

He sat back in his chair, in that disarming manner he had. "Let me see, what questions might you have? Could it be this: Why is Sergius Catilina involved with this pack of half-baked imbeciles? How does he think that he stands a chance of snatching power when his followers are such trash?" He slid his eyes sideways, arching his brows and fixing me with his gaze. "Confess it. Isn't that what you were thinking?"

I knew what a sacrificial ox feels like when the *flamen*'s assistant brings the hammer down between its brows. Still, we Metelli have always been quick on our feet.

"I saw what nonentities they were when I came in, such of them as I had not already dismissed on earlier acquaintance. I take it that you are using them for whatever service they may render."

He leaned forward and laced his fingers before him. "Exactly. Decius, you are a man of experience, descended from one of the greatest of the Roman families. You are obviously not going to be taken in by those buffoons we saw tonight. May I be candid with you?"

I leaned forward likewise. "Please do." I wondered how many of the others had been offered this heart-to-heart. Had the bearded Valgius been flattered thus, told he was honored above the others by the master's confidence?

He leaned back. So did I. "But tell me," he said. "What is missing? What struck you wrong? I would like to know how perceptive you are." This is an excellent way for a man to pretend to omniscience in a puzzling situation, causing another to reveal unseen ramifications while giving away nothing himself. I have used it myself on a number of occasions.

"Lucius," I said, "nobody does a thing like this without the connivance of highly placed men. Who is it? Who backs you? There are no more than ten men who could be working with us." Nice bit of phrasing, that, I thought. "Who are they?"

Catilina smiled smugly. It was the look of a man who is sure of his position. At least, it was the look of a man who wanted to give that impression.

"There are a good many," he said, "all of them well fixed, but all of them cautious. You don't get to be great and rich without being cautious." He paused for effect. "Lucullus is one of them."

I frowned deliberately. "He has retired from public life. He has riches and glory enough already. What has he to gain from an adventure like this?"

"He hates Pompey. You will find that to be true of all our supporters, Decius. They all hate Pompey and they fear, rightly, that the man wants to make himself king of Rome."

This, for once, had great credibility. Pompey had robbed many worthier men of their rightfully won glory. Throughout his career he had specialized in letting others do most of the fighting and then bullying the Senate into giving him their commands so that his men were only in on the kill. The anti-Pompeian faction in the Senate might well contemplate desperate action to forestall a coup by Pompey. Everyone remembered Sulla's infamous proscription lists.

"What Lucullus spends on a single banquet could finance a war," I admitted, "and the moneylenders are always howling for his blood in the Senate and the assemblies."

"And there are others," Catilina went on. "Quintus Hortensius Hortalus, for instance. He has the best legal mind of this generation, and will be able to convince everyone that all shall have been done by correct constitutional form. And he is your own father's patron. He will be looking out for your career, as will I."

"I confess these sound far better than the likes of Valgius and Cethegus. Who else?"

"Don't despise those men too readily. Can a general fight a war by himself? No, he must have loyal legionaries and *auxilia*. He must have expert centurions to provide leadership at the lower levels. Valgius and the other bearded young ones provide the street-level violence. They have nothing to lose."

"And are therefore eminently expendable," I said.

"Exactly. It's not a bad way for a young man to start out in politics. Plenty of action and excitement, and none of the tedium of grubbing for votes in the Popular

Assemblies, eh? I did much the same work myself, for Sulla."

"I hadn't thought of it that way," I admitted.

"You must learn to think this way, Decius," he said earnestly. "Aristocratic attitudes are all very well when one thinks only of ruling, but you have to retain the common touch when you are organizing. Even fools and louts have their uses."

"I must remember that."

"Do. Umbrenus is a failed money-grubber, but he has done excellent service in organizing the Gauls for us. And Bestia will be truly valuable as tribune. Of course, I plan to do the same thing Sulla did when I am Consul: I will put the tribunes firmly back in their place. It was a disgrace giving them the power of veto in the first place."

"I couldn't agree more," I said. I wanted to urge him back to the original point. "Now, you mentioned that there were others?"

"Oh yes. There is Publius Cornelius Lentulus Sura, the *praetor,* and Caius Julius Caesar."

"Caesar? I can well believe he wants to kill off moneylenders and as *pontifex maximus* he will lend a certain dignity to our revolution, but is he dependable?"

Catilina shrugged. "He can be depended upon to look out for his own interests. Nobody can sway the Popular Assemblies like Caius Julius. Granted, he's worthless as a leader of men. His military experience is negligible for a man his age and his priestly office forbids him to see human blood, but you can bet that all the omens will favor us and the gods will be on our side. And, as *pontifex maximus,* Caesar is in charge of the calendar. He can make the Consul's year in office much, much longer than the conventional twelve months."

"Ahh," I said, the light dawning. "That will give you plenty of time to make the, shall we say, adjustments necessary."

"To include making certain that the next year's Consuls are the two men of my choice. Now, even with Caesar's manipulation of the calendar, it may be that I shall require more time to complete my work."

"But these Consuls will be your men," I said, "and on commission of the Senate, the Consuls can name a Dictator."

A broad grin split his face. "I knew you were quick, Decius. *That* is the office worth having! Six months as Dictator and I will reform the state and give Rome a decent government once more. It will be a government of the best men, and you shall be among them. And it will be perfectly legal, according to our ancient constitution. Hortalus will see to that."

Rome had not had a Dictator in 139 years. A true dictator, anyway. The dictatorship of Sulla had been unconstitutional. The thought of Catilina with six months of total *imperium,* answerable for none of his acts when his term of office was done, was chilling. Yet, it was conceivable that there were men in Rome who would rather see that than a virtual kingship for Pompey. This brought us to the prime question.

"Lucius, all of this sounds excellent. Your consulship and subsequent dictatorship will be the salvation of Rome. But what of Pompey? Even choosing the best season, when travel for him will be difficult, he could be outside Rome, with his army, within six weeks of learning about our revolution. What then?"

"It takes no time to raise an army in Italy," Catilina said. "Sulla's discharged veterans are everywhere, and there are others. Have no fear on that account. And we have been caching arms all over the peninsula. Even," he chuckled, "within the Temple of Saturn itself."

I let my jaw drop and my eyes go wide. "The Temple of Saturn?"

"Yes. Can you think of a better place? It is right in the middle of the Forum, where my men, once armed, shall control the center of the city. And they will be in control of the treasury. Our greatest cache is in the house of Cethegus. After arming themselves there, my men will go to seize the city gates." This was valuable information.

"Then," I announced, "my mind is at ease. Oh, one more thing: There are always two Consuls, if we are to follow strict constitutional form. Who is to be your colleague?"

Now he smiled and patted me on the shoulder. "Let me keep *some* secrets, eh, Decius? Rest assured that you will have no qualms about my choice." Now he rose from his chair and stretched. "It seems to have gotten late. You don't want to be wandering these streets on such a night, Decius. Stay here. We've plenty of guest rooms."

I rose, feigning more stiffness than I felt, which was still considerable. "I thank you. I may need a few days to recover from the festival."

He called for a slave and, after much comradely leavetaking and backslapping, I followed the slave to one of the guest rooms that opened off the *peristylium*. It had a bed of generous size and a marble table that bore a three-wicked lamp supported by a bronze statuette of a satyr who sported the shameless erection common to those carefree mythical creatures.

The slave left and I sat on the bed, thinking hard. I knew that I had little time left for thinking. Too much was missing from Catilina's story, and I had no idea how much to believe of what he had said. I was sure that some of the names he had given me were included only to impress me. Hortalus, for instance. I certainly had no reason to believe in the man's integrity, but I knew Hortalus was far too intelligent to be mixed up in anything as harebrained as this conspiracy. He was a veteran conspirator himself, and he had always played a cautious role. Caesar? Then, as always, that man was impossible to fathom. Lucullus? This I doubted, but his detestation of Pompey just might have led him into something rash.

What troubled me most was the one name Catilina had *not* brought up. Where was Crassus in all this? He coveted Pompey's military glory. He was the man who was rich enough to raise and pay his own legions. And Catilina was getting money from somewhere, if his lavish gifts to his followers were anything to go by.

The talk of Sulla's discharged veterans was nonsense. They hadn't fought in seventeen years and would be no match for Pompey's men, fresh from the Asian campaigns. Crassus, though, had veterans spotted in enclaves all over Italy who would make a much more credible fighting force. Plus, he could buy up *auxilia* from Gaul or Africa as needed. But was he foolish enough to back Catilina?

There came a scratching at the door curtain and I stopped thinking. The blood left my head and traveled to regions of more immediate utility. I tried to speak but did not even manage to clear my throat. The curtain swept aside and there stood Aurelia, dressed in her flame-colored silken gown. As she entered, I saw that she wore pearls, but I could not tell whether they were part of the huge rope she had worn when I met her, for they disappeared beneath the gown.

"Decius, that bandage is most becoming. You look like a soldier home from the wars."

She held out her hands and I took them, drawing her close. "I think my greatest fear at the festival was that I might be in no condition to be with you tonight," I said.

"I knew you would be here," she whispered. "Didn't I say you were a hero?" She came into my arms and pressed her lips to mine, her tongue sliding enticingly into my mouth to play with mine. I was not sure of my heroism, but I now shared much in common with that bronze satyr on the table.

Our lips parted for a moment and with hands suddenly grown clumsy I fumbled with the clasps that fastened her gown at the shoulders. She smiled maliciously and gave me no help, merely running her hands over my body, her smile widening when her fingers found and judged the state of my excitement. Then the gown slithered down her body in that impossibly sensual manner peculiar to pure silk. It paused as if it could not make its way past the rich swell of her breasts and hung for a moment on their hardened tips, then it was past them and slid down the swell of her belly and over the rondure of her hips, down her thighs and calves to pool on the floor around her feet. She stepped back for a moment to let me admire her.

I had seen the little statues that the Red Sea sailors bring back from India. These depict the handmaidens of the gods, called *yakshi*. They have huge hemispherical breasts that have no sag like mortal flesh, and waists small enough to span with both hands. Their hips and buttocks are likewise round and everything about them is a supernatural exaggeration of the feminine, yet they are as graceful as gazelles. They are more sensuous than the attendants of Venus and I had always regarded them as mythical, yet now I saw a living *yakshi* before me.

The lamplight played on flesh the color of palest amber wine, except for delicate, brown nipples that graced her breasts more beautifully than the finest jewels. She had adopted the fashion among highborn ladies of having her body plucked clean of hair and smoothed with pumice, and I found myself envying her *depilator*. Below the dimple of her navel the swell of her belly blossomed into a more richly curved mound, divided at its bottom by that vertical cleft which Greek sculptors always modestly omit, but in which the Indian and Etruscan artists take delight.

I sat on the bed and drew her to me with my hands at her impossibly small waist just above the hips. I tongued her navel and savored her musk, feeling the shivers that rippled her spine. Her hands delicately caressed the back of my head, then began tugging urgently at my clothes. I stood again and began to pull off my tunic, and now she stood back to watch. She still wore her pearls, the amazing rope looping behind her neck and crossing between her breasts to wrap thrice around her waist. It offset her nakedness to an incredibly provocative degree.

At last my *subligaculum* fell away and she began to caress me lasciviously, but a frown of concern creased her smooth brow.

"Decius, you've been hurt worse than I thought! How can you bear the pain?" I was covered with cuts and bruises, although the worst of the cuts were bandaged. There was nothing to be done about the long whip-stripe that divided my back diagonally.

"Pain is the least of my sensations just now," I assured her.

"But we must see to it that you suffer as little as possible," she said. "Let me guide you." Slowly, we fell back on the wide bed. With incredible delicacy, she arranged our bodies so that I was enveloped by the richness of her flesh while she never pressed against my many sore spots hard enough to cause agony. She used her mouth with a precision I had thought possible only to the hands of an artist. When at last neither of us could stand more delay, she gently pushed my shoulders back against the bolster and sank down upon me as lightly as a cloud, yet with a thick, furry cry that might have been wrenched from the throat of a maenad. Slowly, and then with mounting urgency, she began to ride me as I had ridden the October Horse that morning.

IX

"**A**sklepiodes, you must let me kill you," I said. The physician looked up from his desk, where he was writing on one of his innumerable medical texts. He was always his own scribe when he worked on his first draft.

"That is a bit much to ask, even of your physician."

"It will only be temporary," I assured him.

"Temporary death, while a relative commonplace in mythology, is seldom met with in the mundane world." He set down his reed pen and frowned at me. "Just what is it you are suggesting?"

We were in the Temple of Aesculapius, on the island. The back of the temple was devoted to quarters, libraries and offices for the priests and physicians, along with lecture halls and gardens for growing medicinal plants.

"It won't be real at all," I insisted. "We just have to fake your death. It will only be for a few days."

"Never fear, Decius," he said soothingly. "It is quite common for wounds such as you have recently experienced to cause delirium."

"I am not delirious, and I feel excellent, except for being in agony."

"Then perhaps some explanation is in order. First, though, I must examine your wounds and re-dress them. Get out of your clothes and one of my servants will remove your bandages." I complied and Asklepiodes looked me over in great detail. You would have thought he intended to buy me.

"You are coming along nicely," he said when he was finished and the slave was renewing the bandages.

"There is no sign of infection in the wounds. Your skin and muscle tone are as healthy as ever, although I detect the signs left by venereal labors of some magnitude. It seems you were serious about finishing your strenuous day with a lady."

"It was the longest day of my life," I said, sinking upon a chair, now back in my clothes. "It began with a horse race and then a battle and it ended rapturously with the most beautiful woman in Rome, but in between there was plotting with men of evil intent. Murder, treason and arson were among the subjects discussed."

His eyes brightened. "Criminal doings! At last, you become interesting. Tell me all about it." The man absolutely thrived on skulduggery. I told him most of what I knew and suspected, because it is not wise to withhold information from one's physician. He nodded and chuckled at every horrible revelation. Well, he was a Greek.

"Oh, this is exciting!" he said when I was done. "I cannot tell you how bored I have been here, treating a lot of sick people. This will give me a chance to exercise some ingenuity. Let me see, how shall we go about it? Might you fling me from the Tarpeian Rock, leaving my shattered body covered in blood and bruises? No," he answered himself, "that would call for jagged shards of bone thrusting out through the skin, a difficult thing for me to simulate. Perhaps you could strangle me. The facial discolorations will be challenging and I can construct a swollen wax tongue of great verisimilitude to protrude between my dead, blue lips."

"I am known as a rather direct man," I told him, "of traditional Roman pugnacity. My fellow conspirators will expect a simple stabbing or throat-cutting."

"I shall concoct convincing lacerations and become a most realistic corpse. Shall I be found murdered tomorrow morning?"

"That would be convenient," I said. "Are you sure you can carry it off?"

"No one will ever suspect. By combining my own talents with the Roman fear of touching dead bodies, the illusion will be complete. My patron, Statilius Taurus, is in Capua, so my funeral obsequies can be delayed for days while my servants summon him, supposedly." He looked around him with satisfaction. "I'll hide out here in my quarters for a few days. It should be very restful and I can catch up on my writing. My servants are utterly discreet. You are sure this is quite legal?" he asked with some anxiety.

"Sanctioned by the *Praetor* Metellus himself. And I shall be calling on the Consul Cicero soon to apprise him of my findings."

"I would suggest you do that very soon," Asklepiodes advised. "It will do little good if you delay until the conspirators kill him." That seemed to be most reasonable advice.

I rose. "I'll leave you now. I look forward to news of your death."

"Try not to grieve," he said.

I went to the Temple of Saturn without attracting notice. My celebrity had already staled. Such is the nature of glory. I spent a profoundly boring but restful day amid the wealth of the empire. I attended the baths, bandages and all, and pondered my next move. I resolved to call upon Cicero that evening.

As I was leaving the bath, I encountered my father entering amid a knot of his cronies. I greeted them all and received their congratulations for my performance at the festival, then steered my father aside for a private talk. We went to one of the niches that lined the walls of the *atrium* and stood beneath a statue of Bellona.

"What do you want? Be brief," he said in his usual solicitous fashion.

"How is the situation with Hortalus?" I asked.

"He is enjoying his retirement too much, but I think he'll decide to stand for Censor. He knows there is no rush and I suppose he's waiting for half the Senate to go out to his country house in a mass and beg him to come out and save the Republic or some such." I told him what Crassus had said and he nodded, pleased. "I knew that this marriage-tie with the Crassi would be wise. I wish my niece Caecilia would hurry up and produce a grandchild for Marcus. He's not so bad, you know, despite his obscene obsession with accumulating money." The only way in which Marcus Crassus differed from most of his contemporaries in regard to money was his expertise in acquiring it. That, and his extraordinary honesty about it. There was supposed to be something unaristocratic about money. It was beneath the dignity of a wellborn man. What it meant in practice was that you robbed provinces when you could and left the money-grubbing to your freedmen.

"Has Hortalus had ... oh, visitors, that you know of?" This was incredibly lame, but I could not think of a good way to phrase it. Father and Hortalus were great friends and Father would probably know if any of Catilina's men had approached the old fraud.

"What? Visitors?" He fixed me with a withering glare and I knew I had misstepped. "What sort of man does not have visitors? Quintus Hortensius Hortalus is one of the most distinguished men of his generation. Of course he has visitors! What are you getting at?"

I decided to get off that subject and ask something that had been troubling me but that I had not thought to ask him about.

"Father, were my mother and Orestilla close friends?"

He was startled by the change of subject, but years of legal practice had made him nimble on his mental feet, if I may use an awkward metaphor.

"You mean the wife of Sergius Catilina? Not that I know of. They must have known each other, attended the rites of Bona Dea, that sort of thing. All Senators' wives know one another, but I never heard that Servilia was especially close to Orestilla, as she was with Antonia the Younger and Hortensia. Orestilla's a scandalous woman, anyway. Why do you ask? What are you up to, you young reprobate?"

"All shall be made clear in time, Father," I assured him. "I am working on a delicate matter of crucial importance to the state."

He was utterly unimpressed. "I shall be pleasantly surprised to learn that you have been working on anything at all. Have you any further excuse for detaining me?" I had none and he left. It would never have occurred to

him to inquire about my injuries. He probably thought
that bandages were effeminate. No doubt I should have
just left my wounds open and dripped on the pavement,
in manly Old Roman fashion.

It was still early in the afternoon and I did not want
to be seen going to Cicero's house. As I descended the
steps of the public bath I noticed one of the monuments
that seem to spring up overnight in Rome, like mush-
rooms. It was one of several that Crassus had erected to
himself. To Crassus, modesty was for men who had good
reason to be modest. This one commemorated his victory over Spartacus. Monuments to that event were considered by most Romans to be in extremely poor taste.
Everyone loved commemorations of a foreign victory,
but a slave rebellion was best forgotten. His real monument had been the six thousand crosses he had erected
along the Via Appia between Rome and Capua, where
the rebellion had begun. Gawkers from Rome and the
towns along the road had gone out for days to witness
the mass execution. The record for longevity was held
by a burly Gaul who had taken eight days to die.

Now, thinking of Crassus in connection with Catilina
and his boneheaded conspiracy, I saw the monument
differently. Crassus was reminding the Romans that he
had saved them from what they feared the most and
would never admit to. Old Mithridates might have been
fearsome, but he didn't live in your own house, in a
position to cut your throat while you slept, should he
take the fancy to.

Like many of the great men of that time, like Catilina
himself, for that matter, Crassus had grown rich in the
Sullan proscriptions. He had hunted down and killed
men whose names Sulla had published in the Forum
and had collected their estates as reward. Before the
proscriptions, at the end of the civil war between the
adherents of Marius and those of Sulla, it had been
Crassus who had led a Sullan army that smashed the
rebel Samnites outside Rome's Colline gate, a fight that
Romans had witnessed from atop the wall as if it were
being staged in the Circus for their edification. Crassus
had won the battle, but Sulla had taken the glory. Ten

years later, he had defeated Spartacus. That time, it had been Pompey who had stolen the glory.

Crassus was a man badly in need of glory. He had held the highest offices and seemed to own half the money in the world, so glory was all that was left. Did he want it badly enough to take Rome by coup? Rome itself was the one thing Pompey had not yet taken. If so, it meant that Crassus had finally gone mad, as had Marius in his later years, yet I did not think so. He might be playing some deeper game, one that was as hidden from Catilina as it was from me.

I was thinking about Crassus because I did not want to think about Aurelia. Was she no more than bait, a form of bond to keep me attached to Catilina and his cause? If so, he had discerned my weakness with an astuteness I would not have given him credit for. She bedazzled my mind and senses like no woman since—well, since Clodia. Was my susceptibility to women now common knowledge?

Asklepiodes had once said to me: "Young men are easily led about by the masculine member. You are one of the few I have known who are intelligent enough to know when it is being done to him yet susceptible enough to allow the process to continue regardless."

Had someone—Clodia, perhaps—told Catilina that nothing was necessary to secure my participation except to dangle a beautiful woman before my aristocratic nose? That I would then become the most malleable of clay, as my lower organs seized control from my brain? I did not know. I did know that I wanted Aurelia again, and felt that I could never get enough of her.

Cicero's house was near the Forum, a small but elegant dwelling that he maintained to be close to the seat of government. He had other houses both in the city and in the countryside, but during the fall and winter he was usually to be found in this one. Many Romans retired with the onset of darkness, but I knew that Cicero always worked late into the night. The *janitor* asked my business when I called at the front door.

"The *Quaestor* Metellus," I said, in a low voice, "to see the Consul on an urgent matter." The *janitor* said something to a slave boy who ran off into the interior of the house. A few minutes later Tiro appeared and admitted me. Tiro was Cicero's secretary and close companion, so indispensable that he was almost as famous as Cicero himself.

"Please come with me, *Quaestor,*" Tiro said. "My master is with another visitor at the moment, but he wishes to see you and will come as soon as he has a few free minutes." He led me to a small room off the *atrium* where a table had already been set with refreshments. As a lawyer and now as Consul, Cicero was accustomed to receiving late visitors, who did not wish to be seen approaching him in the daytime.

"Thank you, Tiro," I said. "I hope you will inform the Consul that this is a matter of danger to the state. I would not call upon him at such an hour, unannounced, for anything less serious."

"He is well aware of that, sir. He will not be long. In the meantime, please refresh yourself while you wait."

I did as advised. The wine was a fine, mellow old Setinian, far better than I could afford. From nervousness and perplexity I had forgone dinner that evening, so I attacked the snack tray with appetite. Besides boiled quail's eggs there were pastries stuffed with chopped pork and others with honey and nuts. I was finishing off one of the latter when Cicero arrived. I fear I made a poor impression, as I was sucking honey from my fingertips as he came in. I sprang to my feet and made the expected apologies for disturbing him, but he waved them off and indicated I should resume my seat. He sat opposite me, ignoring the table and its temptations.

"People are always coming to me with tales of danger to the state, Decius Caecilius, but you have rendered loyal service in the past on matters touching state security. Please tell me what you have uncovered."

So I told him. I spoke of the murders, and of my discovery that the victims were moneylenders, and of Milo's advice that I contact the indebted malcontents who infested Rome. When I get to Catilina, I could see the look of distaste that crossed Cicero's face. All I left out was the part about Aurelia. A man should be allowed a few secrets.

"Lucius Sergius Catilina!" Cicero said, almost spitting the name. "So it has come to this? He wants a return to the evil days, when Romans killed Romans in the very streets of Rome? I always knew he was pernicious, now I know that he is mad." He looked at me with a frosty smile. "This has been most sagacious, Decius. I know of no other man whose mind works like yours, sifting evidence and placing seemingly disparate facts together to construct a—how shall I put it?—a *model* of how things might have happened. You should have been a philosopher."

"I'll accept that as a compliment, Consul," I told him. "Yes, I was stymied when the banker Caius Rabirius told me, at the Egyptian ambassador's, that the mere death of the lender did not cancel the debt. But when I found out that the murders were a show of earnestness, things began to make sense again."

"But the *eques* Decimus Flavius, the director of the Reds, was not a moneylender and seems to have no connection with the conspirators. How do you explain his demise?"

"I have a theory about that, Consul, but I need more proof." Actually, I was almost certain of why Flavius had died, but I also had a terrible feeling that Aurelia was directly involved and I did not want to bring her into it, still hoping to find proof of her innocence.

"And you intend to go through with this charade of murdering the physician?" He laughed, something one rarely heard from Cicero. "It is the most insane thing I have ever heard, but then you are dealing with madmen and I suppose mad measures are called for."

"About Crassus—" I began, but he cut me off.

"That is mere speculation, Decius. You have incontrovertible evidence of the machinations of Catilina and his cronies, but none at all that Crassus might be involved."

"But they can have no hope of succeeding unless they are supported by real wealth and a credible army," I pointed out.

"Decius, these men are mad and desperate enough to think they can get away with it," Cicero insisted. "Their heads are full of airy fantasies and they are totally detached from reality. They are the sort who believe that they deserve high office because of some innate quality apparent only to themselves. They have never faced the fact that the only path to the highest honors is through education, hard soldiering and long, rigorous service. They hope, through desperate action, to have it all in a few days through the mere risk of their worthless lives." He shook his head. "No, Decius, Crassus has everything now. Why would he throw in with such men?"

"You have said nothing that has not occurred to me," I told him, "but I fear that you misread Crassus."

"Then bring me proof, Decius. If I had a single shred of evidence, preferably in writing, I would stand before the Senate tomorrow, denouncing Crassus and calling for his exile. But I must have more than your suspicions."

I was silent. He leaned back in his chair and went on, less severely. "Continue your investigation, Decius. You have rendered invaluable service already, and I must know all you can find out about this conspiracy. Knowing where their two largest arsenals are in the city will be worth half a legion to us when they make their move."

"I don't yet know when that will be," I said.

"We have a while yet. Let's get every name we can before I take this to the Senate. In the meantime I will speak to the *Praetor* Metellus and ensure that your legal position in this will be unassailable."

"Speaking of *praetores*," I said, "do you think there is any likelihood that the *Praetor* Lentulus Sura is really involved?"

Cicero pondered. "Lentulus Sura is a man of ignoble character. He is one of the few men ever to be elected Consul only to be expelled from the Senate the next year by the Censors. If any man of such rank is involved with the conspirators, it would be Lentulus, but I will not believe it until I see proof."

Now I remembered something else. It had been Crassus, during his abortive censorship, who had reinstated

Lentulus as a member in good standing of the Senate, allowing him to stand for the praetorship elections held the next year. He owed Crassus much. I said nothing of this.

"You are right to be wary of the names Catilina gave you. Hortalus and Lucullus have become a pair of slothful gardeners, but they would have nothing to do with this nonsense. If those two and others like them would stay in Rome and help out in the Senate more often, instead of fish-raising, we would not have so much trouble with mediocrities such as fall in with the likes of Catilina." Both Hortalus and Lucullus were inordinately proud of their fishponds, in which they experimented with new types of foreign fish for domestication in Italy. Cicero considered this frivolous and said so, before the Senate.

"Yet you and Hortalus and Lucullus have been at odds before," I commented.

"What have my personal likes and dislikes to do with it?" he snapped. "They are both enormously capable men and ought to be here, serving the state, not playing the retired gentleman out in the country."

"And Julius Caesar?" I asked.

"There's more to him than most people think, even if he did get elected *Pontifex Maximus* through the most shameless campaign of bribery I have ever witnessed. He could be involved, but once again I would have to see proof."

"If you will pardon me, Consul," I said, "you do not seem terribly surprised or shaken by my revelations, which I had thought to be dramatic in the extreme." I was rather disappointed that he had not ordered an emergency meeting of the Senate to denounce the traitors.

Again that frosty smile. "I have known of Catilina's plottings for two or more years now. Oh, don't look so surprised. A man doesn't reach my position without having a great many sources of information. You are the first to bring me such detailed information, gleaned from Catilina himself, but my secondhand knowledge has been rather good."

"Who? Or would you rather not say?" I was stunned and a bit crestfallen.

"No, I know that you would not betray my sources. Fulvia is one."

"Fulvia!" In the midst of all the male plotting and strutting, I had all but forgotten the women involved, save for Aurelia.

"Yes, Fulvia. That cretin Curius loves her insanely, and when he isn't threatening her life from jealousy he tells her everything, including two plots by Catilina to murder me. Fulvia is a wild and shameless woman, but she draws the line at murder and she has informed me when I was in danger. She has told me a bit about this scheme of Catilina's, hoping that I will spare Curius when the coup is inevitably crushed."

"And will you?" I asked.

He shrugged. "That is not up to me, is it? It will be up to the Senate to decide."

At the time, I was so agitated that I did not notice that Cicero had said "the Senate," not "the courts." It was a slip weighted with much trouble in days to come.

"Consul," I said, "granted that this coup has no chance of succeeding, yet even a few men, if they are desperate enough, can wreak fearful carnage in a city as crowded as Rome, and they have supporters in the countryside."

"That is true. As soon as possible, I want you to go to your kinsman, Metellus Creticus, and alert him. Can you do that without arousing suspicion?" Poor Creticus still waited outside the walls of Rome for permission to celebrate his triumph.

"Next week the *gens* Caecilii hold a yearly family religious observance. Since Creticus can't enter the city, it will be held this year at his villa on the Janiculum. I can speak privily with him then."

"Excellent. Tell him of a planned coup, but no specifics. Tell him to await my summons and be ready to rally his men from wherever they are dispersed awaiting his triumph. I shall have Tiro take the same message to Marcius Rex. Between them, they should be able to summon a full-strength legion on short notice."

"And your colleague?" I asked.

"Hibrida is chafing to get away to Macedonia. I'll tell him to go ahead and assemble his men, but march no farther than Picenum. Have no fear, Decius, we'll take care of this sorry business handily."

I wished that I could be so sanguine. I greatly feared that there would be far more travail out of Catilina's mad plan than he foresaw. "But, Consul, what of Gaul? The Roman authorities and citizens there must be alerted! The Allobroges can spark a tremendous blood-bath there. Our hold on Gaul is not so firm that we cannot be expelled by a mass tribal uprising."

"Oh, that." Now the smile was frostier than ever. "Fulvia is not my only informant, Decius. I want you to meet the other gentleman with whom I have met this evening."

I sat mystified while he summoned a slave and sent him to bring this other guest. A few minutes later a tall, bold-faced man entered, a man I recognized.

"*Quaestor* Decius Caecilius Metellus," Cicero said formally, "greet the patrician Quintus Fabius Sanga, of Rome and Gaul."

"We've met," I said. "At the Circus, a few days ago."

"Then you understand that Fabius Sanga is the patron of the Allobroges?"

"Yes," I said. Then, to Sanga, "I spoke to your charioteer that day, the boy Dumnorix."

"Amnorix," Sanga corrected me.

"Amnorix, then. He races as Polydoxus. He mentioned that you were the patron of his tribe and I remembered that your family surname was Allobrogicus."

"Fabius came to me a few days ago with alarming news," Cicero said. "This evening, he came by to bring me up to date."

"That detestable rogue Umbrenus approached the Allobrogian envoys some time past," Fabius said. "He's the worst sort of *publicanus*, but he was careful to keep on the good side of the tribes, in Gaul. He knew of the grievances the Allobroges had suffered, and were in Rome to protest. It was just the sort of thing that the malcontents who follow Catilina were looking for. Umbrenus approached them in the Forum and took them to the house of Decimus Brutus. Brutus is away from Rome, but Sempronia entertained them and provided an imposing setting for his proposition. They felt the Gauls would be impressed by one of Rome's great houses, and so they were."

"He claims to have received their firm support," I said.

Fabius laced his fingers and leaned forward. "Let me tell you something about Gauls. Like all *Keltoi*"—he used the Greek word for that race—"they are excitable and they love to boast, but they are not the comic figures we see in the theater. One must never accept their first, emotional reaction to anything as their final feeling on the matter. Given time for reflection, they are usually as sensible and levelheaded as anyone else.

"When Umbrenus pretended sympathy with their plight, they went into their usual extravagant lamentations of how they have suffered. When he told them that true men will always fight rather than surrender their liberties, they shouted that they would gladly follow any man who promised them the restoration of their ancient freedoms. He told them of Catilina and they declared themselves for him."

Fabius took a cup from the table and drank. "Of course," he went on, "that was just Gaul talk, but Umbrenus took them at their word. Once they had had a little time to think it over, they grew afraid that they had gotten themselves into something serious. When I returned to Rome, they very sensibly came to me to ask what they should do. I came here, to speak with the Consul."

"And I advised him to tell the Gauls to play along, to find out who the conspirators are. They told Umbrenus that they would be happier to know that there were important men involved. That turned out to be a mistake, because then the conspirators began to throw in names purely to impress, as they did with you. Your own father's name was one they gave the Gauls."

I all but choked on my wine. "Father? Well, I suppose barbarians might believe such a thing."

"They used the name because the Allobroges would know it," Fabius said. "Your father was their recent governor, and a proconsul is the next thing to a god in barbarian lands."

"I have instructed them," Cicero said, "through Fabius, to demand this: that their kinsmen in Gaul will not rise in support of the rebellion unless they have the signatures and seals of the leading men of the conspiracy on a document that guarantees their own rewards upon success of the revolution."

I stared at him, aghast. "They absolutely cannot be that stupid!" I protested. "Granted they are unrealistic to the point of dwelling in the midst of fantasy, but even the most amateur of conspirators knows that you never put your name to anything in writing!"

"And yet they have promised to deliver this document," Cicero said. "It even makes sense, in a way. They feel that they must have the Gaulish support to succeed, and they know that if they do not succeed, they shall all die. Besides, like most such fools they don't think of themselves as conspirators. They fancy themselves to be patriots. They are going to restore the Republic to its rightful condition."

"By the time this document reaches Gaul," Fabius said, "the operations in Italy shall have commenced, so what is a bit of written evidence then? The letter is to be delivered in the next few days."

An awful though occurred to me. "I suppose I will be expected to sign it."

"What of it?" Cicero said. "I will attest that you acted under my orders."

"Your pardon, Consul, but if they act before we expect, your assassination will be the signal that the war has commenced."

"Oh, well, you'll still have Celer to vouch for you, if he lives, and Fabius here. To be safe, the sooner you talk to Creticus, the better. And now, gentlemen, I have much work to do. Please report to me as soon as you have important evidence. When I have that document in my hands, with the names of the leading conspirators upon it, I shall denounce Catilina in the Senate and we shall crush this rebellion before it has a chance to start."

We took our leave of the Consul and Tiro conducted us to the door. Outside, I spoke to Fabius.

"I would like a few words with you, Quintus Fabius, if it is convenient."

"And I with you. Let's walk to the Forum. The moonlight is adequate tonight, and there we can see for a good distance in all directions." I was glad to see that he was being cautious. A full moon made the streets navigable, and once we were in the Forum, it was reflected from the white marble that was everywhere, bathing the whole place in a ghostly luminescence. The Forum is like a place seen in a dream on such nights. We paused before the Rostra.

"You first, Decius Caecilius," Fabius said.

"When I met you a few days ago, you were speaking with Crassus. More accurately, you were arguing with him. When I approached, you broke off your argument. Then Crassus said something strange. There were two men with me, Valgius and Thorius, both involved in the conspiracy. Crassus said that he had not met them. Yet when I spoke to your charioteer, he said that Valgius had accompanied Crassus to your house."

"That is so. I believe that, just now, Crassus is trying to put distance between himself and anyone involved in the conspiracy."

"And the nature of your argument?" I asked.

"He wants me to surrender my patronage of the Allobroges. He claims it is for business purposes, involving his many Gaulish interests." He snorted disgust. "He offered to buy my patronship, as if such a thing could be subleased! Crassus thinks of everything in terms of money. Of course, he simply wants to manipulate the Gauls in Catilina's behalf. He does not yet know that they have already revealed everything to me."

"And you told Cicero of this?" I asked.

"I did. By now, you know that he is afraid to prosecute Crassus."

"So I have found, and I cannot understand why. I thought that Marcus Cicero was afraid of nothing. Why is he so fixed on Catilina when he knows that there must be someone more powerful behind him?"

He brooded over the expanse of moonlit marble around us. "Decius Caecilius, you and I are of ancient senatorial families, mine patrician, yours plebeian, families almost synonymous with the Roman state. Cicero is a good man, but he is *novus homo,* and can never forget it. No matter how high he climbs, he will never be secure." This was a sorrowful thing to hear about a man I greatly admired, but in later years I was to find it an accurate assessment of Cicero. "He will pursue Catilina, and that ruthlessly, precisely because he is the *least* of the leading traitors. He wants to smash the rebellion before it has a chance to become fully organized, in hopes that the great men will then back away from a lost cause."

"But won't Catilina implicate them?" I asked.

He shrugged. "Who will believe him? We have already heard the names of wholly innocent men he and his followers have thrown around to appear stronger than they are. If he should accuse Crassus of backing him, why should Crassus not claim to be as innocent as your father?"

"Why, indeed?" I said. "And we can be sure that Crassus will put his name to no foolish letter to the Gauls."

"Of that you can be certain," Fabius agreed.

"Quintus Fabius," I said, "one more question. You went to Cicero with your report of treason. Why not to Antonius Hibrida?"

He laughed, a flat, humorless sound. "The same reason as you. Hibrida is no more to be trusted than any other man bearing the name of Antonius. They are a reckless, unreliable breed, and I've no doubt that Catilina has already approached him."

I had not thought of that. "Any chance that he is with them, do you think?"

He shook his head. "You recall how the proconsular provinces were assigned, after the election?"

"Certainly. Cicero drew Macedonia, Anotonius drew Cisalpine Gaul. But for some reason Cicero refused Macedonia and Antonius got it by default. Catilina thinks Cicero is afraid of the command because there is fighting in Macedonia."

"Wrong. Catilina wanted to be Consul this year with Antonius as his colleague, but Antonius threw in with Cicero instead. Too much dirt has clung to Catilina from past corruptions. Anyway, Cicero made him a better offer."

"A better offer?"

"He *gave* Antonius Macedonia because Antonius wanted it. Antonius wanted a foreign war and the loot that a foreign war brings. And thus he bought Antonius's loyalty. I don't doubt that Antonius is toying with Catilina even now, but not seriously."

He was uncommonly well informed for a man who spent little time in Rome, but patricians have their ways of passing information among themselves. Another imponderable occurred to me.

"I am greatly troubled by the position of tribune-elect Bestia in all this," I said. "He is more intelligent than the others, and I think he's playing some game of his own."

"When are tribunes ever anything but troublemakers?" he said, in true patrician fashion. "Somehow, over the centuries they've bypassed the Senate and the courts and come to be the most crucial members of the government, and *anybody* can get elected to the tribunate."

"Anybody but a patrician," I reminded him. "Clodius has given up his patrician status just to become a tribune."

"It's about what you'd expect from a Claudian," Sanga all but growled. "I know very little about Bestia, but he seems to be a friend of your kinsman, Metellus Nepos."

"Pompey's *legatus*? That makes little sense."

"Things seldom make much sense in politics until you get a closer look. Sometimes not even then."

"How true. For all I know, Nepos and Bestia are old school friends, studied philosophy at Rhodes or some such. Pompey is the one man we can be certain has nothing to do with this conspiracy."

"Nothing is certain," Sanga reminded me. "Good night, Decius Caecilius Metellus."

I bade him good night and we went our ways. Before returning home, I trudged the long climb to the Capitol and entered the Temple of Jupiter Capitolinus. At that hour there was no one in the temple but a slave who, every hour or so, would check the oil level in the lamps and trim their wicks.

The new statue of Jupiter was a beautiful thing, much like the old one but nearly double its size. It was in the traditional mode, modeled after the legendary Olympian Zeus of Phidias. This statue had been paid for by the great Catulus and the god's body was sculpted of the whitest alabaster, his robes of porphyry. His hair and beard were covered with gold leaf and his eyes were inlaid with lapis lazuli. In the flickering lamplight, he almost seemed to breathe.

I took a handful of powdered incense from a chased bronze bowl and tossed it onto the brazier of coals that glowed at the feet of the god. The *haruspices* had said that this new Jupiter would warn us of dangers to the state, but as the smoke ascended he said nothing. As I left the temple, I paused on the steps, but I saw no mysterious flights of birds, no lightning from the clear sky, no falling stars or thunders from inauspicious directions. As I walked home, I decided that the gods probably had little interest in the petty schemings of the degenerate dwarfs men had become. In the days of heroes, when Achilles and Hector, Aeneas and Agamemnon had contended, the gods themselves had taken an active part in the struggle. Those heroes were near to being gods in their own right. The gods were not likely to bestir themselves for anyone like Catilina, Crassus or Pompey, and least of all for Decius Caecilius Metellus the Younger.

X

The next morning Asklepiodes was found murdered on the bridge connecting the island to the riverbank. Since I was investigating these murderous doings, I made my way to the Temple of Aesculapius to view the body. Anything to get out of the Temple of Saturn. Forum gossip was full of speculation about this latest wrinkle in the wave of murders that had swept the city. Most of the other victims had been wealthy *equites*. This one, while wealthy, was not even a citizen. For once, I had the satisfaction of knowing what it was all about.

Asklepiodes had a fair number of friends and many professional colleagues, but the city was being swept by one of its frequent gusts of superstition, and the rumor had gotten around that, with so many murders in the city, it might be bad luck to attend the obsequies of the slain. As a result, poor Asklepiodes was laid out in an *atrium* of the temple with few attendants except for his own slaves. Among the few visitors I recognized Thorius, his jaw still in a sling, sent there to confirm that I had indeed murdered my creditor. As he left he winked at me, the little swine.

Asklepiodes had been washed and laid out on his bier, with lamps burning at its four quarters. His skin was gray and there was a shocking wound in his throat. This was carrying fakery to an amazing extreme. Surreptitiously, I touched his face. His skin was cold. I took a wrist. There was no pulse. He was really dead.

I was shaken more thoroughly than at any time since this whole insane business had begun. Who had murdered him? For a few disordered moments I entertained the thought that I had done it myself. Perhaps I was as crazy as the rest of them. One of the physician's slaves came up to me and handed me a note. I unfolded the papyrus and read.

The Quaestor *Metellus is requested to attend the office of the physician Asklepiodes on the sixth hour on a matter touching the physician's will.*

"Who wrote this?" I asked. The slave shrugged. None of his assistants spoke Latin, or so he claimed.

I passed the day in a state of agitation. In fact, that had been my invariable state for some time. I kept checking the sundials as the shadows crept slowly across them. When it looked as if the sixth hour might be approaching, I hurried off to the island.

When I arrived the *atrium* was vacant, the body having been removed to await the arrival of the Greek's city patron, who would have the duty of seeing to his burial. A slave conducted me into Asklepiodes's office, which was empty. As I sat the slave shut the door behind me and, far too late, it occurred to me that this was a trap. Somebody had murdered Asklepiodes, and I was next. I leapt to my feet, my hand going to my dagger, as another door opened. I would sell my life dearly if need be.

"Please, Decius, you needn't stand for me," Asklepiodes said. "I pray you resume your seat."

I sat, or rather collapsed into the chair. "I saw you this morning," I said. "You were irrefutably dead."

"And if you thought so, knowing that we were planning to perpetrate a fraud, how much more convincing must it have looked to those who suspected no such thing?"

I knew what he wanted me to ask and I struggled against the temptation while he sat there, smiling smugly, all bland Greek superiority. At last I could stand it no longer.

"How did you do it?"

"Through skill, artistry, and, I doubt not, some aid from the god who is my patron. A decoction of hemlock, belladonna and wormwood, taken in a minutely measured quantity, brings on a near-cessation of the vital signs, convincing to any but the most astute of physicians, of which I must say in all modesty I am the only specimen in Rome."

"It could bring about a complete cessation, I would think. Wasn't it hemlock that Socrates was executed with?"

"It is a matter for delicate judgment, but it has been used in the past to simulate death when such a subterfuge seemed desirable. I tested it first on a slave, a man of my own age, physique and general state of health. The results were wholly satisfactory; three hours of deathlike coma followed by a quick recovery and no aftereffects."

"And the wound?" I asked, searching his neck for marks.

"A most excellent effect, was it not? I obtained the skin of an unborn lamb, such as is used to make the finest parchment. This I trimmed to proper shape and used to cover my neck. The skin is all but transparent, and the cosmetic I applied to exposed areas to simulate a deathlike pallor contributed to the illusion. I had the skin stitched up at the back of my neck, and the edges where it met with my actual flesh were covered by my hair, my beard or my clothes. The slit over my throat I packed with thin strips of calf's liver to simulate a most ghastly wound. Was it not convincing?"

"It was a masterpiece," I said sincerely. I had gotten over my fright and now was all admiration. "How did you manage an illusion so elaborate on such short notice?"

Asklepiodes preened. Like all Greeks, he throve on praise. "I have been called upon before this, to simulate wounds. Your Italian mimes, who perform on the stage without masks, sometimes wish to add an extra note of realism. And certain gentlemen of high rank who must remain nameless, who wished to avoid military service, have called upon this particular skill of mine."

"Asklepiodes, you shock me!" I said.

"Mine is but the skill," he said, "and theirs the guilty conscience. Just remember me when your superiors plan your participation in some particularly suicidal military adventure."

"A man dedicated as I am to serving the Senate and People of Rome could never stoop to such perfidy," I said piously. He just sat there, smiling his superior Greek smile, knowing that I would do exactly as he advised should it come to that. I was not about to get killed winning glory for the likes of Crassus or Pompey.

"In any case," he said, "you may now rest assured that you are as respectable a murderer as any in the conspiracy. My congratulations."

"I thank you," I said, rising. "Within a few days this business should be over and you will be able to reveal yourself and enjoy the looks on everyone's faces."

"That I look forward to with great anticipation."

"In the meantime, enjoy your solitude, catch up on your writing, and I hope you will suffer no disagreeable aftereffects from your brush with the fatal hemlock."

"It was quite refreshing, really. I may employ it in therapy." He rose to see me to the door.

"Then don't tell anyone what's in it," I advised.

"I seldom do. Good day, Decius Caecilius, and good luck."

I left the island feeling better than I had in many days. With the shadow of Asklepiodes's ostensible murder lifted, everything else looked much better as well. I was well in with the conspirators, and I felt that my official backing was far more secure now that I had conferred with Cicero. And the political situation was not quite so murky. I was still not certain exactly who was involved, but it was clear that Catilina actually had a halfway credible plan of action and was backed by one or more of the great players of the day. The rest of us were, to use my cousin Felicia's metaphor, knucklebones.

In my happy mood I extended the metaphor. Not all knucklebones are honest. They may look like the others but, like dice, they may be loaded. I knew that I was one of the loaded knucklebones. Were there others? Some had at least had their corners shaved. Fulvia was an informer, and by extension Curius had become Cicero's tool.

And what of Bestia, the tribune-elect? In those days, the tribunes were elected by the *Consilium Plebis,* a profoundly undiscriminating body of citizens. Of the elective bodies, it was the most fertile field for a demagogue and far too many of our tribunes were uncultivated, self-seeking knaves and scoundrels. It had become the quickest route to real power and was thus avidly sought by men such as Clodius and Milo. Cato had sought the tribunate as a way to frustrate the activities of political enemies. My kinsman Nepos, recently seen in the company of Bestia, had won a tribunate to use as a platform from which to push Pompey's fortunes and career, as if such a thing was needed. It made sense that a tribune would be in league with Catilina. A tribune was in an excellent position to whip up the urban mob into a rage against the current government, something a haughty patrician like Catilina could scarcely do. Yet, I had been disturbed by the tone of insinuation I had detected in Bestia. He had not seemed mad or self-deluded like the others, merely amused and superior.

My improved mood even lightened my fears about Aurelia. If she was being used by Catilina as bait, surely it was not through her own connivance. Surely, I thought, she could not be a part of the conspiracy. Catilina and his men were not the only self-deluded fools in Rome that day.

The next days were filled with elation and anxiety. There were no more meetings with the conspirators, although from time to time I would encounter one or more of them in the Forum or at the baths, at which times they could not help giving me adolescent signs of complicity, as if we were fellow initiates of one of the mystery cults.

I sought excuses to call on Aurelia, but the slaves at Orestilla's house told me that both ladies were away, although they were vague about the destination and duration of this absence. Naturally enough, once I was cut off from contact with Aurelia, I was able to think of nothing else. Memories of our night together ran through my mind like the most salacious of those mimes frowned upon by the Censors, each fantasy more heated and fevered than the last.

I neglected my duties at the treasury, but the slaves and freedmen there took no notice, since I customarily neglected them at the best of times. Dinner companions noticed my fidgeting and abstraction and plied me, successfully, with wine. It may be taken as a matter for wonder that a man embroiled in an incredibly dangerous mesh of intrigue, treachery and murder should be distracted by the charms of one young woman, however voluptuous. It is simply that young men are like that. I was, at any rate. The Greeks and Trojans once fought a war over a woman, so I was not alone in this fixation, although there seemed to be something un-Roman about it.

The day of the gathering of the Caecilii arrived, and with the others I crossed the river and climbed the Janiculum to the expansive villa where Quintus Caecilius Metellus Creticus awaited permission to celebrate his triumph. Every great family has one or more of these yearly gatherings, where special family rites are observed, marriages are arranged and decisions concerning the whole *gens* are made.

Of course, not every Roman bearing the name Caecilius attended, for then several thousand persons would have had to crowd into the villa. Every *paterfamilias* who was not on foreign military service was there, and their adult male offspring. These would pass on the decisions and celebrate the rites at home for their own Caecilian freedmen and clients.

The villa and its grounds were cluttered with the loot of Crete, kept there in anticipation of the coming triumph and guarded by hard-eyed veterans of Creticus's legions. I was glad to see that there were so many of them, since they would be needed soon.

Among those present were my father, the *Praetor* Metellus Celer, the *pontifex* and Caecilian by adoption Metellus Pius Scipio, and Pompey's *legatus* Metellus Nepos. I feared that my major problem would be finding a few minutes to speak privately with Creticus.

After the opening invocation of the gods, the *genius*

of the family and the *lares* and *penates* of the house, the serious business of the meeting began. Among the questions brought up was, of all things, my name. Some of the older and more traditional members of the family wanted the name Decius banned from future generations. Decius, they said, was not properly a *praenomen* at all, but a *nomen*. My father argued, eloquently, that a name decreed by a god must be deemed just and fitting and we had won the fight with the Samnites the next day and so Decius must be a fitting *praenomen* for *gens* Caecilii. The anti-Decian faction were not impressed. Apparently, they thought that the family simply could not have enough Quintuses. I think this gives some indication of how slack and complacent all of Rome had become during the easy years. Never once was the family's political stand brought up. The business about my name was never decided, and remains undecided to this day.

After the rites and business were taken care of, Creticus entertained us at a splendid banquet where we drank nothing but the very best Cretan wines. Creticus was an undistinguished, mild-looking man. He had been an easygoing, plodding politician and had eventually worked his way up the ladder until he won the office of Consul, which he held with Quintus Hortensius Hortalus, my father's patron. As his proconsular command, he had been given the war against Crete and the pirates based there. He was as undistinguished a general as he had been a politician, and fought a long, desultory campaign. But then, unexpectedly, he displayed courage and stubbornness when Pompey, as was his wont, tried to usurp his command when the campaign was all but over.

Pompey's supporter, the tribune Gabinius, had passed a law giving Crete to Pompey. A number of the Cretan cities, knowing that the war was lost, hastened to surrender to Pompey. Everyone was in the habit of surrendering to Pompey at that time, while surrendering to a third-rate general like Metellus Creticus would be a disgrace. Metellus had refused to recognize Pompey's right to accept their surrenders and threatened to attack Pompey's officers. For a while, it almost looked as if civil war would break out, but Pompey backed down. The next year the tribune Manilius passed a law giving Pompey command of the entire Mediterranean in order to crush the pirates, but by that time Creticus had Crete conquered and reorganized as a province. Pompey still held a grudge and his flunkies resisted Creticus's right to celebrate a triumph.

In justice to Pompey, I must say that his campaign against the pirates was brilliant, crushing them completely and almost without bloodshed. It was a masterpiece of organization rather than tactics, and causes me to believe that had Pompey concentrated on administration rather than conquest he might have been one of Rome's great benefactors, instead of being a mere military adventurer, who plunged the Republic into the most destructive of its civil wars.

I finally managed to get Creticus aside after the banquet. Many of the family had already gone home, and the rest of us were walking our dinner off in the formal gardens or admiring the loot from Crete. Crete is not Asia, and Creticus had brought back no such treasure as had Lucullus, but the pirate strongholds had yielded some respectable loot and the cities had possessed some very fine Greek statues, which he had appropriated. His proudest display was a trophy in the form of a Cretan column, studded with the bronze rams of pirate galleys. He had a slave who did nothing all day except polish the bronze.

I found Creticus on the broad portico of his house overlooking the gardens. I made one of those half-unconscious gestures that indicates a desire for a private audience. I had decided that I would arouse no suspicion thereby. Everyone would just assume that I was hitting him up for a loan.

"Good to see you, Decius," he said. "I am happy that your father stood up to those idiots on the matter of your name. Have you any idea what it was like, growing up in this family with the name Quintus? At a family gathering like this, somebody yells 'Quintus!' and three quarters of the males turn to see who is calling them."

"I never thought of it that way," I admitted. "Actually,

sir, I am here to speak with you on behalf of the Consul Cicero. It's a matter of urgent danger to the state."

He was understandably startled. "Speak on."

Very briefly, I sketched the conspiracy for him, and Cicero's instructions to him. His expression went from incredulity to concern to calculation. I knew exactly what he was calculating: how long would it take Pompey to reach Rome once he had word?

"Sergius Catilina planning a coup?" He gave a laugh that was half snort. "The man's an embarrassment to the Republican system. It was presumptuous enough that he dared to stand for election as Consul, but this! Mark me, Decius, someone else is behind this, and I suspect Pompey."

"That I doubt, sir," I said. "Personally, I suspect Crassus."

"Even if he isn't behind it, Pompey will try to take advantage of the situation." I gave him no argument on that point. "We'll have to smash it hard and fast. You think he'll make his move this winter?"

"Assuredly. His bunglers couldn't keep their activities secret for longer than that. I think he plans to strike very soon."

"All to the good, then. It's the worst sailing weather of the year and the overland route would take Pompey far too long to do him any good. Who else is being informed?"

"The Consul will personally inform Marcius Rex," I told him.

"Excellent. Marcius is a good man and he's kept a strong cadre of his legionaries close to him. His bandits are an even meaner lot than mine. If we can keep things pacified here in Rome and the surrounding countryside, the *praetores* should be able to raise enough men from the *municipia* to control Italy handily. Tell Cicero I am at his orders, at least until the end of the year."

"I shall do so," I promised. "Meantime, Antonius Hibrida is assembling a force to accompany him to Macedonia, but they will stay in Picenum."

Again, the snort-laugh. "Cicero had better not put too

much trust in that Antonine lout. He's as likely to be a party of the plot as he is to crush it."

"I doubt that," I told him. "He's too anxious to loot Macedonia."

"That could be. I hope you are right." Then we were joined by a party of family elders and I slipped away.

As I prepared to leave the villa of Creticus, it occurred to me that Cicero was being characteristically astute in dividing up the defense among so many commanders. He saw little danger to the state from Catilina and his featherbrained followers, but a great danger indeed from a possible "savior" of the Republic. Any general who found himself near Rome, in possession of a large army after a quick, victorious campaign, might well feel entitled to take advantage of the situation. It had been done before.

I took my leave and as I left the villa I was joined by the one man I least expected to seek me out: Quintus Caecilius Metellus Nepos, the tribune-elect and Pompey's *legatus*. I knew him only slightly and had not spoken with him in a number of years. He was only a year or two older than I, a tall, erect man who looked as if he was still in armor. He was as fair as I was dark and where I was compact, he was lanky. Only our mutual possession of the long Metellan nose proclaimed our kinship.

"Decius," he said as we wended our way down the Janiculum, "I have been meaning for some time to speak with you."

"I am always easy to find," I said. "My door is always open, both for official visits or social ones." We passed the Egyptian embassy. The Janiculum was covered with very fine villas, most of them owned by rich men who wanted to be near the seat of power but away from the crowding and squalor of the city.

"I had no desire to trouble you at home, and what I have to tell you I wished to deliver in privacy and strict confidentiality. The family gathering seemed like a good opportunity."

"And what requires such mystery?" I asked. "Surely your patron Pompey doesn't require my services to conquer the rest of the world?" His fair face flushed and I regretted my sharp words. I had no reason to dislike Nepos. "Forgive me," I said. "It's just that I detest Pompey, but everyone knows that. Please, tell me what you wished me to hear."

He stopped and we stood facing one another. It was a still day, and the only sounds came from the odd fauna on the other side of the wall surrounding the Egyptian embassy.

"Decius, I have heard, never mind how, that you are involved in something that is not merely ignoble and disgraceful, but deadly. I beg you to desist. If you go on as you have, you'll be dragged to the Tiber on a hook and the family will suffer ignominy. As a kinsman, I urge you to cease."

This shook me. If Nepos knew, then who else? And if Nepos knew, then Pompey would know about it within days. He could have his men and ships assembled in anticipation of word from the Capitol that an insurrection had begun. It could save him precious weeks at a time when travel was difficult.

"I won't ask you how you came by your information," I said, "but I accept your warning as a gesture of family loyalty. Now hear mine. Do not interfere with me. I think you know that I will do nothing to harm Rome or our constitution."

"Then what game are you playing, Decius?" I thought about that for a moment.

"Knucklebones," I answered him.

"What?"

"Quintus, is there anyone left in Rome who isn't playing some sort of game? The proceedings of the Senate and the popular assemblies have become the screen behind which we play our games. It's beginning to look as if Rome will be the prize of the best game-player."

He just looked at me, stolid and soldierly. "I think you have gone mad, Decius."

"Then I've fallen victim to the national affliction. Don't stand too close, Quintus, it's contagious."

"Good day to you then," he said and strode away stiffly.

My mind raced in a dozen different directions at once. It seemed as if Catilina's conspiracy held its secrets about as well as a basket holds water. Who had betrayed me to Nepos? Then I remembered that tribune-elect Bestia had been seen with Nepos. I stopped where I was and cursed myself for a fool. Bestia was Pompey's spy within the conspiracy.

That meant that Pompey had probably known about the plot from its conception. When Catilina should begin his insurrection in earnest, the tribunes Bestia and Nepos would pass a law for the Senate to recall Pompey from Asia, with emergency powers. That would give Pompey proconsular *imperium* within Italy itself, a virtual dictatorship in all but name.

And that, I realized in a sweat, would be a very bad time to be known as the enemy of Gnaeus Pompeius Magnus.

XI

I decided to blame it all on Aurelia. After all, if she had not ensnared me with her feminine wiles, my mind would have functioned normally. What man can plot and scheme rationally, when he has surrendered all his higher faculties and functions to woman-induced lust? Thus I salved my pride, as young men have done since remotest antiquity. This however did not bring about the slightest abatement of my feelings toward that woman. I dreamt of her constantly and held to my perverse hope that she was entirely innocent.

For two days after the family gathering I fretted thus, having no new word from Catilina and no idea of how to proceed on my own. Then, as I left the temple and made my way to the baths, Valgius accosted me, being elaborately casual about it, as if anyone were paying the slightest attention.

"We meet tonight at the house of Laeca," he said, almost hissing the words. "Be there as soon as it is dark. The time is near. Good job on Asklepiodes, by the way." He spoke as one craftsman to another.

At last. Surely, Catilina had to move soon, if this conspiracy were to be anything but talk. And there had already been too many murders for these men to confine themselves to mere words. I proceeded to the baths as if nothing was amiss. In fact, I took my time and luxuriated in the best bathhouse in Rome, using the cold, tepid and hot pools followed by the steam room, then back into the cold pool and finishing off on the masseur's table. I knew that it might be a very long time before I should be able to enjoy this homely, tranquil pleasure again.

At home I made out my will, something I used to do frequently in times of disorder, uncertainty and stress. Having made disposition of my negligible property, I armed myself and went out into the darkening streets. It is one of the most annoying aspects of conspiracy that it compels one to blunder about the streets at night. I got lost several times trying to find the house of Laeca, and it is always embarrassing to have to pound on doors and ask directions.

I found the house about an hour after sunset. It was Thorius who let me in. Apparently, the slaves had been confined for the duration of the meeting. That seemed to be about the only elementary precaution these people bothered with. Inside, about fifteen men were crowded into the *atrium.* All wore strained looks, as if the seriousness of what they were doing had at last become real to them. They spoke among themselves in tense mutters, as if each had a strangling hand at his throat. All fell silent when Catilina appeared from the rear of the house.

"My friends!" he began. "Comrades! Fellow patriots! The time has come for us to act!" His mood was one of barely suppressed hilarity. He was trying to speak past a grin that split his face like a sword-cut. His excitement put a quaver into his voice and I could see, appallingly, how much time, hatred, disappointment and bitterness had gone into the plan that was at last to bear fruit. I had the horrifying feeling that he was about to break into a dance.

"Today," Catilina declared, "I have sent word to my lieutenant Gaius Manlius in Fiesole. He is to call his men together and raise the rebellion immediately." The assembled men gave a hoarse cheer.

"The same message," he said when they were quiet, "has gone to Nobilior in Bruttium." A more restrained cheer greeted this announcement. The others probably shared my opinion of the people of Bruttium. "When word reaches Rome that there is insurrection in Bruttium and Etruria, there will be panic in the Senate.

That"–he shouted the word—"will be the time for us to rise here in the city. We will kill, and burn, and rouse the people against their oppressors, the moneylenders and the decadent aristocrats who have sequestered the high offices of state to themselves. We shall sweep over Rome like a cleansing fire, and restore the Republic to its ancient purity!" This, from the man who proposed to destroy the Republic utterly.

And something rang terribly false in Catilina's rant. His near-hysterical elation was desperate in its joy. Before, his confidence, however unjustified, had been real. Now it was forced. What could have happened? Had he suffered a sudden attack of reality? I doubted it.

"As soon as we have shown our hand here in the city," Catilina went on, "then I shall ride out to join our troops in the field. For it will be through fighting outside the walls that Rome shall be won. I will take with me those men who wish to win glory on the field of battle, while others remain here, to hold the city for me, a post equally honorable." I saw all around me men who wore a look of great relief. Street fighting was something they knew, and they had no stomach for hazarding their lives on an open battlefield.

Catilina seemed to be gaining confidence, as if it was something he absorbed from the worshipful devotion of his followers. He began to point out individuals and assign them their duties.

"Valgius, Thorius, have your bands of fire-raisers ready. Cethegus, be sure that the weaponry is in good order to be handed out to our supporters here in the city. Junius, put your street spies on alert." Then he turned toward me. "Metellus . . ."

"Yes, Consul?" I said, all my innards quaking.

"Remain here for a while after the others have left. I have duties for you to attend to."

"As my Consul commands!" I said dutifully. I felt a slight relief. Surely, if he had detected my true nature, he would have taken that moment to have his followers kill me.

"This is a momentous day in the fortunes of the Republic," Catilina proclaimed. "As momentous as that day almost seven centuries ago when we cast out the Tarquins, foreigners who had presumed to be kings of the Romans!" More cheering. "In years to come, whenever Roman schoolchildren are asked by their schoolmasters, 'When was the Republic restored?' they will answer, 'Upon the night that the supporters of the Consul Catilina met at the house of Laeca.' " At this the cheering and applause were deafening. This lust for the adulation of unborn generations of schoolboys has always eluded me, but it was very real to the men gathered in that *atrium*.

"Go, then!" Catilina cried. "Go to your stations of action. Now is not the time for talk, but for action. Do your duty now, by your rightful Consul, and future generations will bless and exalt your names. Monuments to the men present here this night will grace the Forum, for all to admire, and your names shall be as the names of our founding fathers." A hoarse and ragged cheer greeted this, as if even this group could not believe that they would ever enjoy such esteem.

When they were gone, I stood in the suddenly large room, fingering my dagger hilt and *caestus*.

After a few minutes, Catilina returned to the room alone. He carried a scroll of papyrus. This he unrolled on a table, weighting its corners. He dipped a reed pen in a pot of ink and turned to me.

"Decius, I want you to sign this. It's a message to the Gauls, committing ourselves to the rebellion and promising to uphold their demands, restore their liberties and cancel their debts."

I looked at the papyrus. They had actually taken the bait. "Lucius, isn't it unwise to commit something like this to writing?" Quickly, I looked over the document, which was as Catilina had described it. Foremost among the names, I saw the *Praetor* Publius Lentulus Sura, but none of the other high-ranking men whose names the conspirators had been so free with. Crassus, Hortalus, Lucullus and Caesar were conspicuously absent.

"The war has begun, Decius," Catilina said. "We are all as good as declared public enemies now. Our names on a paper will mean nothing ... Unless you feel you have some reason for refusing to sign."

"Not at all," I said, snatching up the reed pen and signing my name. I carefully used my title and my formal name, signing as *Quaestor* Decius Caecilius son of Decius grandson of Lucius great-grandson of Lucius Metellus. I wanted to ensure that no one could alter my name to implicate my father. Catilina glanced at my signature and made a satisfied sound. He scattered sand on the wet ink and shook it off, then rerolled the scroll.

"Lucius," I said, "you must sent Orestilla and Aurelia away to someplace safe until this is over." He just looked at me absently, as if he had his mind on more important things.

"Orestilla?" he said, coming back from wherever his mind had wandered. "I've sent them both to a house in the country. They'll be safe until I can send for them."

"What will you do now?" I asked, relieved.

"I intend to watch the excitement," he said, grinning. Now he sounded like the old Catilina. Whatever had unnerved him, he was shaking it off. "I will make some public speeches, pointing out the advantages of a change in government. Never fear, there will be plenty of popular support for me when the swords are drawn." This was the first I heard that he counted on much popular support.

I thought of this as I walked home that night. It was not only dark but chill, rainy and suitably miserable. As I splashed through puddles and dodged disgruntled dogs, I reflected on the fickleness of the Roman electorate. Although Rome and the empire as a whole were richer than ever, the body of poor citizens was also unprecedentedly great. There were many crushed by debt, with little hope of relief. The labor market was flooded with cheap slaves and even skilled craftsmen could only manage a living wage. The situation was worse in some rural areas, where slave-worked *latifundia* had crowded out and impoverished the free farmers, and the people had no access to a public dole.

Under such circumstances, many might grasp at a chance for a better condition. The rabble could easily be swayed by demagogues and opportunists, never thinking far enough ahead to see what they were being led into.

And there was the simple fact of boredom. Times had been quiet, Rome was victorious, life was a pallid round of work, games, public holidays, religious festivals and sacrifices. In a word: dull. There were many, and not just among the urban poor, who missed the bad old days, when the mobs and private armies of Marius and Cinna, of Sulla and all the others had fought in the streets, when a common city-dweller might kill a Senator with impunity, when the houses of the rich were sacked and torched in the name of one tyrannical warlord or other. They had been heady times until their great harvest of misery brought people to their senses.

But the temptation was always there, to revel in the swinishness of civil rapine and butchery, the mob glutting itself on blood and loot, heedless of the hangover that follows every great debauch. And what did they care? Civic participation in government had become little more than a hollow shell, now that a professional army did all the fighting and a few dozen families supplied most of the statesmen and slaves did most of the work. What did the people care whether a Cicero or a Catilina lorded it over them? Even a temporary respite from their misery would be desirable. That, and a little excitement.

Cato opened my door with his usual sour looks and words. "Late again. Not only that, but this woman came calling for you this evening, and she insisted on waiting. She's in the *atrium.*"

Puzzled and dripping, I went in. A heavily veiled woman rose at my entrance. No quantity of veils could hide that shape. "Aurelia!" I gasped.

She threw back the veils that covered her face. I would have embraced her but Cato made a scandalized sound. "Go to bed, Cato," I ordered. Grumbling, he left the *atrium.* Then I could hear his voice and his wife's coming from their quarters.

"Decius," Aurelia said, "don't you think you should dry yourself?"

I looked down at myself. Every fiber I wore dripped water onto my tiled floor. More water dripped from my hair. My dagger, I decided, was probably getting rusty.

"I think there are some towels in my bedroom," I said. "Wait here."

I went to my room and stripped off my clothing, snatched up a towel and began drying myself vigorously. As I rubbed at my hair I discovered that there was an extra pair of hands working the towel.

"Do you mind if I help?" Aurelia asked.

"Your impatience is flattering," I told her. I turned and saw that she had already loosened her clothing. I needed only a few moments to finish the task, then she wore only her pearls. I was baffled by her presence there on that particular night, but my need for her drove all questions from my mind. She covered my lips with hers and we sank onto my narrow, bachelor's bed. Our ingenuity made up for the inadequacy of the furniture and the oil in my lamp was as exhausted as I was before I had breath to spare for questions.

"Catilina said that you and your mother were safe in the country," I said. I lay on my back and she lay half-across me, her cheek and both hands on my chest.

"I came back," she said. "I could not stay away from you."

As deeply as I wished to believe this, I could not but note that she had successfully stayed away from me for quite a while. Had she been sent to spy on me? To make sure that I reported to no one tonight? But Catilina and his followers acted with such desperate recklessness that such a precaution seemed alien to them.

"The city is too dangerous for you now," I insisted. "How much do you know of your stepfather's plans?"

She stretched. "Enough to know that he will soon be the ruler of Rome. What of it?"

"Within a few days he will be declared a public enemy by the Senate," I said. "When that happens, no member of his family will be safe. There will be blood in the streets again, Aurelia."

She stifled a yawn. "There is always blood in the

streets. Usually it's common blood. A little noble blood is about to flow. Is that something to get excited about?"

"It is if the blood is yours," I said, then added "or mine."

"You mean you aren't anxious to throw your life away for your new Consul?" She snuggled closer against me and slid a leg over my hip.

"The whole idea behind a coup," I told her, "is to get someone else to sacrifice himself for your own advantage. That's what we are all in this for, after all. I could die heroically serving in some foreign war, without risking disgrace. I joined your stepfather's cause in order to reach high office without having to wait for fifty elder Metellans to die first."

"That's my Decius," she said. "The others are fools, just cattle to be sacrificed, but you know what this rebellion is truly about. Of all my stepfather's followers, only you have real intelligence."

"Followers are there to be used," I said. "But what of the men even Catilina must defer to?" Even here I could not stop probing for information. With my left hand I stroked her spine, but this was not merely a caress. I was feeling for the involuntary tension that would precede a lie.

"What do you mean?" she asked sleepily.

"He told me that Crassus supported him." It was a wild try, but I was desperate for any sort of confirmation of my suspicions.

"He told you that?" she said, waking up. "Then you truly stand high in his estimation. I thought he had kept that secret from his closest companions."

It was true. I had it at last but not, as Cicero demanded it, in writing. And there was admiration in her voice. I was an even more important man than she had thought. I knew about Crassus.

She yawned again. "He told you about meeting with Crassus last night?"

"No," I said, my scalp tingling. "The others were present."

"Crassus came to my mother's house last night, after dark. They went into one of the rooms and closed the

door. It sounded like they were arguing." Her voice
drifted off.

So another knucklebone had taken an unexpected
hop on the game board. Had Crassus reneged, after
leading Catilina on? That would explain the shaken
confidence Catilina had shown. If so, why? Had Crassus
given up on the plot as misconceived or incompetently
implemented? Or had he never been serious about his
support in the first place? As I pondered it, I decided
that this was the most likely explanation.

With Pompey in the East and Lucullus in retirement,
with at least one of the *praetores* involved in the conspiracy, Crassus was the most distinguished general left
near the Capitol, with many veterans ready to come at
his call and rally to the eagles. He expected that the
Senate, in a panic, would call upon him to crush the
rebellion, perhaps even name him *Dictator* for the duration of the emergency.

But Cicero had already taken steps to prevent that.
He might not take direct action to impeach Crassus, but
he would make sure that the military command against
Catilina was spread among as many commanders as possible. And in this he was undoubtedly wise and prudent.
The enemy here would be no Pyrrhus, Hannibal, Jugurtha or Mithridates, nor even a Spartacus. No unified
command would be necessary against what was essen-
tially several packs of bandits raising insurrection in
various parts of Italy.

All of this was a fascinating puzzle to work out, but it
was not my main concern. What was happening in
Rome, all over Italy and in far-flung parts of the empire
that night was a splendid example of the chicanery,
treachery, double-dealing and conspiracy that had become the lifeblood of Roman politics. And very little of
it was my concern, now that I had notified Cicero of my
findings.

What had concerned me from the beginning had been
the murders. I do not like murders in my city, especially
those involving peaceable citizens. I now had all but one
accounted for. They were creditors murdered as part of
an initiation rite by Catilina's followers.

The one that did not fit the pattern was the murder of Decimus Flavius, at the Circus. He was not a moneylender and he had died in a strange place, killed with an uncommon weapon. I had a question to ask, and it was one I had wanted to avoid since seeing her at the Circus that morning. Gently, I shook Aurelia to wakefulness, keeping my fingers against her spine.

"Aurelia, wake up."

She blinked. "What?"

"I need to know something. Were you with Valgius and Thorius when they killed Decimus Flavius?" My fingertips felt the tension that crawled along her spine.

"No. Why do you ask, anyway? He was just another *eques.*" She came wide awake with indignation. "Was his death any worse than that of the Greek physician you killed?"

"When I encountered the three of you that morning," I said, "you were not just passing by. You were actually *entering* that tunnel when I ran into the bearded twins."

"And what does that signify?" she asked, pouting.

I stared at my ceiling, barely visible in the flickering lamplight. "It made no sense at first, but then I learned more of what Catilina planned. You've been assigned to supervise those two, haven't you?"

She yawned again. "They aren't very bright. From the beginning, my stepfather has been plagued by the incompetence of his supporters. I've had to check everything they did to make sure they didn't bungle it."

"Why you?" I asked.

"I am trusted. They are near my age, and who would question a patrician lady accompanied by a pair of flunkies? Who would even notice who the flunkies were?"

"Who but I?" I said. "And Valgius is in charge of fireraising in the city. He is intimately familiar with the Circus Maximus, and everyone knows that it is the most dangerous firetrap in Rome. As I figured it later, he and Thorius had found that great heap of trash and decided that it would be a good place to start their fire. In their usual bungling fashion, they spoke out loud and sound carries in those galleries. Flavius was passing by on his way home and overheard them. He came too close when he tried to hear more, and they caught him."

"You have spent all this time reconstructing what might have happened from what you knew?" She sounded annoyed. "You're a man of strange tastes."

"I would have figured it out sooner had I not been so besotted with you, Aurelia."

"Oh, Decius," she said, pleased, patting me intimately.

"Anyway," I went on, "the two bearded wonders were at a loss what to do. Since they were merely scouting for arson, they had not come armed for murder. But Valgius is a race fanatic. Like many other superstitious race fans, he carries a charioteer's knife for luck. Its shape was inappropriate, but in their emergency it had to do and they cut Flavius's throat with it."

"I think this sophistry of yours is a waste of imagination," she said. "What does all this matter?"

"It matters to me," I said. "Were you the one who got them to catch Flavius before he could get away and then to murder him?"

"Why do you want to know these things?"

"Don't worry. I will think no less of you. I know you were involved. Why are you so reluctant to admit it?"

She squirmed a little and I could almost feel her blush heating my skin like a distant fire. "Well, it was not something—not something I wanted to be associated with."

I knew what she meant. It was not the murder. Murder is all too common and Roman citizens are rarely put to death for murder, unless it is done with poison. It was the arson, the one unforgivable crime on the Roman law tables. The citizenry would take terrible vengeance on anyone caught fire-raising. If this were known of her, she could find herself bound to a stake in the arena, soaked with tar and awaiting the executioner's torch.

I stroked her back. "It doesn't matter," I said. "Go back to sleep." Within minutes she was faintly snoring.

Indeed, it did not matter. The situation had moved far beyond a few killings. And one way or another justice would be done. Within a matter of days or at most weeks, Catilina and all of his followers would be dead or in exile. The shades of the murdered *equites* would not haunt the city. Perhaps they would not even haunt my dreams.

At first light the next morning I walked Aurelia through the awakening streets of Rome. She wore her veils, but no one sought her. I looked around for some sign of change, but there was none. The war had commenced, but Rome was blissfully ignorant of the fact. All that would change soon enough. I wanted Aurelia out of it when it happened.

She had left her litter and slaves at a friend's house, and I took her there. We made our goodbyes at the gate of the house, a respectable mansion near the Colline gate.

"Leave the city, Aurelia," I said. "Go as far as you can and as quickly as you can."

She smiled at me. "Decius, you are too nervous. Within a few days my stepfather will be Consul and I can return."

"It will not be as quick or as easy as that," I promised, "and for a while no member of the family of Catilina will be safe anywhere near Rome."

"Well, until then." She leaned forward and kissed me, as if we were being separated for the afternoon, then she turned and went into the mansion.

Despondently, I turned and walked toward the Forum. I knew that I would never see her again, unless she were hauled back to Rome in chains, for execution. I prayed that she, at least, would get out of this alive. I had ceased to care about her guilt. I no longer saw innocence anywhere I looked.

There was an eerie tranquility in Rome for the next two days. The city lay in its usual late-fall somnolence, the inhabitants lazing through the short days, waiting for the return of spring, the *Floralia* and all the ritual assurances that Proserpina had left the bed of Pluto and returned to the world of mortals. Thus, the news that arrived on the morning of the third day was doubly shocking.

There is some near-magical process, which I have never fathomed, by which news and rumor reaches every part of Rome simultaneously. When I walked into the Forum in the early morning, there was pandemonium. A half dozen self-appointed orators harangued the citizenry with impromptu speeches delivered from the bases of the various monuments and everyone shouted the latest rumors at one another. Women wailed and tore their garments in terror, although the immediate danger seemed rather slight, and hawkers of charms and amulets were doing an unprecedented business.

I decided that the Temple of Saturn could do without me for a while and shoved my way through the crowd to the *Curia*. At the foot of the steps I encountered the *Praetor* Cosconius, preceded by his lictors.

"What is this all about?" I asked him.

He surveyed the mob contemptuously. "You know how crowds are. There have been rebellious uprisings here and there in Italy. A few bandits sack some villas in Bruttium and Etruria and by the time the news reaches Rome you'd think it was old Mithridates come back to life, invading Rome with his whole army. For days Cicero has been warning that Catilina was up to something. This is probably it."

All morning long the Senators streamed in, many of them having been summoned from villas near the city. The lictors and heralds restored order in the Forum while the Senate debated. I forced my way into the Curia, but it was so packed that I had to stand on an urn at the very back of the chamber to see or hear anything. Reports from various parts of Italy were read out by heralds. From the younger Senators there were shouts for action.

Quintus Hortensius Hortalus, despite his semiretirement, was still *Princeps* of the Senate and thus had the right to speak first. In his matchlessly beautiful voice, he protested that his distance from affairs of state made him unfit to speak on this matter, but that in recognition of the emergency, the usual protocol should be bypassed and the Consul should be allowed to address the Senate first. This, I was sure, had been arranged beforehand between them. They had been bitter political rivals, but with lawyerly objectivity they could cooperate closely on important matters. Cicero stood from his *sella curulis* and all was silent.

I will not reproduce here his speech, which was the first of the three anti-Catilinarian speeches that are now among the most famous speeches since Demosthenes denounced Philip of Macedon to the Athenians. In later years Cicero wrote these speeches down (with embellishments), and published them. Now they are studied by every schoolboy and emulated by every would-be lawyer wherever Rome holds sway, which is the whole civilized world, these days.

Catilina was there, and he tried to brazen it out, proclaiming his innocence and protesting the malicious machinations of his enemies.

But Catilina was never the orator Cicero was, and he had few friends in the Senate. He began to rage, and the Senators jeered at him and demanded that he resign and leave Rome. The whole plot was not out yet, but there was enough known that Catilina had become like a diseased dog, snarling in the midst of a pack that has turned on him. I do not use the image without reason, for many of the men in the Senate were as bad as Catilina, or worse. He was just bolder than most.

At last, hurling curses and imprecations, Catilina stormed out, shouting something about "bringing it all down on your heads" or something of the sort. I heard many versions of his parting words. I do not think anyone heard him clearly.

When he was gone, Cicero, for reasons that seemed best to him, probably oratorical ones, waited for calm to return to the Senate chamber. It also gave Catilina time to get away, a calculated move on Cicero's part, I think. When he rose to speak, he held high a piece of papyrus that looked familiar to me.

Amid the stunned silence, he explained what it was, and how it had come into his hands. He cleared the Allobrogian envoys of wrongdoing and explained the role of Fabius Sanga. It restored the shaken spirit of the Senate to hear the ancient name of Fabius mentioned as a preserver of the state. Then he began to read the names. Shouts of rage and indignation greeted the recital of each name. Then I heard my own name read out. The men to either side of me stepped away as if I had some rare new disease. With unutterable relief I heard Cicero's next words:

"The *Quaestor* Decius Caecilius Metellus attended the meetings of the conspirators with my knowledge. He acted under authority granted him by the *Praetor* Metellus Celer. He is innocent of any wrongdoing." Now the men to either side took my sweaty hand and clapped me on the back. Then I was instantly forgotten as the speech continued. When Bestia's name was read out my cousin Nepos stood.

"The tribune-elect Bestia was never a part of the conspiracy!" he shouted. "He acted on behalf of General Pompey to ferret out this plot to endanger Rome and put the empire under the yoke of tyranny."

Cicero's face went scarlet, but his voice dripped with the sort of sarcasm only Cicero could muster. "How convenient. And since when has our esteemed and illustrious General Pompey had the authority to assign spies within the city of Rome? The last time I consulted the tables of the law, a *proconsul* wields *imperium* only within the borders of his assigned province. Is this some new interpretation of the Sibylline Books I have not been informed of?" It was no use. Pompey was just too popular, especially among the commons, who had little respect for the legal niceties. Bestia would be safe. I was galled by the knowledge. I wondered which of the *equites* he had killed to retain credibility with the conspirators. I determined to look into it, when all this was over.

And it would not be over for some time. Before the Senate session was done, Catilina and his followers were declared public enemies. This was only the beginning. Lamps were brought in as the daylight dimmed and messengers ran to and fro. Senators sent their slaves to their homes or to the taverns and stalls of the food sellers. They ate standing, on the steps of the Curia, talking among themselves in small groups.

State scribes scribbled frantically as commands were authorized, drafted and sent out. Mobilization orders flew about like so many birds. Magistrates were appointed to arrest the conspirators wherever they might be found. We junior magistrates were given orders to organize night watches to guard against arson. At last, we thought, something to *do!*

The next day, a number of the conspirators were apprehended. In this day of the First Citizen, with his reorganization of the *vigiles* into a true, and very efficient, police force, it may be wondered that so many public enemies moved about at will during a state of emergency, and that Catilina and a number of his followers escaped from the city without difficulty.

The fact was that Rome in those days had no police, and no mechanism for apprehending and incarcerating large numbers of felons. Ordinarily, when an arrest order was handed down, a *praetor* or curule *aedile*, accompanied by lictors, would approach the subject and summon him to court. The actual arrest was carried out by the lictors, using an ancient formula. If there was resistance, the magistrate would call upon any citizens nearby to aid him and they would haul the arrestee to court by force, if need be. This procedure was clearly inadequate when dealing with the conspirators.

At first, there was support for Catilina, especially among the ruined and the destitute. You will earn few enemies in Rome by attacking moneylenders and promising to cancel debts. For a while, Catilina's thugs roamed freely, made streetcorner speeches, and in general made life precarious for anyone in public office or belonging to a distinguished family.

The tide began to turn irrevocably against them on the third day after Catilina's flight, when all the stories about planned arson came out and several fire-raisers were caught in the act. After that, there was no sympathy for the Catilinarians in Rome, and a good deal of summary justice instead.

During this time, I was kept too busy to brood over Catilina or Aurelia. I organized a band of *vigiles* and we patrolled the streets during the hours of darkness, carrying torches and lanterns, occasionally running into other such bands, and avoiding brawls by shouting out watchwords at one another. Occasionally we encountered drunken bands of Catilina's supporters and then we brawled in earnest. It was deadly serious, but everyone seemed to enjoy it immensely. In years to come we were to get a bellyful of such activity, but at the time it was a welcome relief after the boring years of peace and prosperity.

The young *equites*, remembering their military tradition, armed themselves and formed self-appointed guard units around the homes of magistrates and distinguished men, foiling any planned assassination attempts. Seeing all of this half-organized, half-military activity, Cicero gave in to the inevitable and on the afternoon of the day following Catilina's flight the chief herald ascended the *Rostra*. For the first time since the sacrifice of the October Horse, his huge voice boomed through the Forum.

"OFF WITH THE TOGA AND ON WITH THE *SAGUM!*" At this a tremendous cheer erupted. This was another of those ancient formulae, and its meaning was that the Roman people, as a whole, were under military discipline. All citizens were to take off the garment of peace and assume the red cloak of war. It was the last time this formula was ever to be used in Rome.

And so I clattered importantly about in my red cloak and hobnailed *caligae*, although I did not wear sword or armor within the *pomerium*. With my old retainer Burrus acting as centurion, I commanded a light century of fifty *vigiles* and had all the fun of soldiering without having to leave the city and live in a leaky tent. My father and his formidable pack of retainers guarded the Ostian Gate, and he grumbled because he wasn't given one of the field commands.

During this time, I had one moment of great satisfaction. Under rigorous questioning, a captured Catalinarian revealed that word had reached the city that full-scale arson was to begin. That night, with a half score of my men, I waited in hiding outside the Circus Maximus until I saw two shadowy figures dash beneath the arcades. I waited a few minutes longer, then signaled my men to dash into the tunnel where I knew we would find them. We had slung our *caligae* around our necks and ran barefoot to make no sound. We covered our lanterns with our cloaks and were like ghosts as we crossed the pave.

Within the tunnel, I whipped my cloak from my lantern and others did the same. The sudden light revealed the white, bearded and terrified faces of Valgius and Thorius. The two were crouched over a smoking, low-flaming fire at the base of the great trash heap.

"Quintus Valgius and Marcus Thorius," I shouted as one of my men doused the fire with a bucket of water, "in the name of the Senate and People of Rome, I arrest you! Come with me to the *praetor*." I had hoped they would resist, but they broke down in tears and supplications. Disgusted, I turned to my centurion.

"Burrus, don't let the men kill them. They must be tried."

"Damned shame, that," the gray old soldier grumbled. "My boy's with the Tenth in Gaul, and these traitors want to stir up trouble there, getting the barbarians to murder Romans in their sleep."

"Nevertheless," I said, "they are citizens and must be tried first."

Burrus brightened. "Well, they ought to make a good public show, anyway, perhaps something with leopards." As we walked to the basilica where arrestees were being kept, the *vigiles* argued over the best way to put the fire-raisers to death. Every groan of terror from the bearded ones came to my ears as the songs of Orpheus.

But amid all of this exhilaration, there was a darker side. Catilina had joined Manlius in the area of Picenum, and he had gathered a credible military force, mostly Sullan veterans and other discontented soldiers left over from various wars, along with people from the *municipia* and a surprising number of wellborn young men who left Rome to join him, scenting an opportunity for quick advancement.

Darkest of all were certain events in Rome. I have mentioned the lack of provision for arresting numbers of felons. There was a similar problem when it came to putting highborn men or holders of high office into custody. In the past, when serious perfidy was detected in

such a person, he was given opportunity to slink from
the city in disgrace and go into exile. This was different.
Men who planned the violent overthrow of the state
could not be allowed to leave and join their leader. The
highest of the conspirators were delivered to the *praetors*, who kept them under guard in their own homes.

Since Publius Cornelius Lentulus Sura was a *praetor*
himself, Cicero personally arrested him and led him by
the hand to the Temple of Concord, where he and the
other leaders were to be tried. There Cicero argued that
the leaders of the insurrection should be put to death
immediately. There were some who protested that the
Senate had no authority to try citizens, and that this
could only be done by a duly constituted court. Cicero
argued that the state of emergency forbade this, and
that the sooner they were killed, the sooner the rebellion would collapse.

Caesar rose and spoke forcefully against any such
course of action. He said that it ill-befitted Roman
statesmen to act in the heat of passion. These were excellent sentiments, but they caused word to spread that
he was involved with the conspiracy, or was at least a
sympathizer. He was threatened by the mob as he left
the temple.

Cato, naturally enough, called for execution. That was
just the sort of action that appealed to him: simple, bru-
tal and direct. Many men, especially Cato himself, believed that because he led an upright life of virtue and
austerity, he must be right. In any case he spoke eloquently, and it may have been his speech that swayed
the Senate to its final decision. Before sunset on that
day, Lentulus, Cethegus and several others were taken
to the prison beneath the Capitol and there were strangled by the public executioner. Richly as they deserved
this fate, these executions were not constitutional and
when the excitement and hysteria were over, people understood that they had set a fearsome precedent. Then
men who had called for the blood of the conspirators
called as loudly for Cicero's exile.

Other ugly incidents abounded. Men saw a chance to
implicate their enemies, and did so forthwith. Luckily,

except for his haste to dispose of the high-ranking conspirators, Cicero stayed calm and disposed of most of these spurious accusations with his withering sarcasm. A man named Tarquinius, captured on his way to join Catilina, claimed that he had been given a message of encouragement by Crassus to deliver to Catilina. Cicero refused to countenance the accusation, although he was happy enough that some doubt was cast upon Crassus's loyalty. In later times, Crassus claimed that Cicero had put Tarquinius up to this accusation, but I never believed it.

Catulus and Piso, bitter enemies of Caesar, tried to bribe the Allobroges and others to implicate Caesar in the conspiracy. Caesar's eloquent speech in protest of the death sentence for the conspirators lent credence to this accusation, but once again Cicero refused to recognize mere word-of-mouth accusations.

Was Caesar involved? He was certainly capable of it, but I do not think that his defense of the conspirators was evidence. Throughout his career, Caesar was happy to kill droves of barbarians, but he was always reluctant to execute citizens. His clemency was a byword, sometimes used in derision by enemies who at first thought him to be softhearted. In the end, it was his undoing. When a later conspiracy ended in his assassination, many of the conspirators were men he had spared when they were within his power and he had good reason to execute them. I do not think that Caesar was especially merciful. It was just his way of showing contempt for his enemies and confidence in his own powers. He was always a vain man.

Various of the magistrates with *imperium* were directed to deal with the enemy outside of Rome. Complications were added by the fact that it was the end of the year and some magistrates would be stepping down while others would be assuming office. Cicero's brother Quintus, for instance, was a *praetor*-elect, and he was sent to deal with the Catilinarians in Bruttium. By the time he got there, he would have his full powers. Caius Antonius Hibrida, waiting near Picenum, still had *imperium* as Consul, and he was alerted to the Catilinarian

menace. The *Praetor* Metellus Celer was to march north
with an army. Since Antonius was taking Macedonia,
and Cicero had refused proconsular command, Celer
had been given Cisalpine Gaul. The campaign would be
merely part of his march to his province. The *Praetor*
Pompeius Rufus was sent to Capua, to watch for Catilinarian subversion among the gladiator's schools there.
Ever since Spartacus we have been nervous about a rebellion of gladiators, and in those days most of the
schools were in Capua. Campania was the home of the
gladiatorial cult. Actually, except when discharging their
duties in the amphitheater or when hired as bullies for
politicians, gladiators are usually the mildest of men.
The fear was constant, though.

The *Praetor*-elect Bibulus was sent to smash the Catilinarians among the Paeligni, which required only a small
force of men. The Paeligni had not amounted to much
for quite some time, although they made a show of in-
dependence up in their mountains.

Much of this, you understand, I heard secondhand or
read about later. As a mere *quaestor,* I was not yet a full
member of the Senate, and so I did not hear all these
speeches nor take part in the debates. I was kept too
busy with my city patrols to do more than catch up on
proceedings at the bathhouses frequented by Senators.

Even then, I think, I was half-aware that I was seeing
the death throes of the old Republic.

XII

I was in at the kill, although I had no desire to be. It was the next year, and the new Consuls were in power. Cicero was already in trouble, with his opponents calling for his impeachment for condemning the Catilinarians to death. Nobody questioned the justice of his action, only its legality.

The tribunes Nepos and Bestia had introduced a law calling for the Senate to summon Pompey from Asia to deal with Catilina, but that was a vain hope. Cicero had laid his groundwork too well. It was obvious to everyone that the various magistrates authorized to deal with the Catilinarians piecemeal would settle the problem long before Pompey could make an appearance.

I was assigned to the army of Metellus Celer. When I was given the assignment, the panic in the city was over. The citizens had redonned the toga, although the red flag still flew atop the Janiculum, in token of the state of war. As I packed to go and join the army, I somehow knew that it would be for a long time. I put my military gear in order and gave my slaves orders to keep my house well, against my return. Then I mounted my horse and rode through the winter drizzle, leading a packhorse bearing my comforts and personal belongings.

I have never left Rome happily. I always felt a wrench when duty forced me to leave the city, and this time was no exception. There was no one to see me off, and I rode out through the gate as desolate as any stranger leaving Rome.

After a long, cold ride I joined Celer's army near Picenum. Dreams of glory are wonderful, but as *quaestor* my position in the army was paymaster, scarcely the most heroic of ranks. Even so, I was able to throw myself into the supply and logistics apparatus of the army with some energy. As hastily thrown together as the force was, there was much work to be done.

The fortunes of Catilina had ebbed and flowed according to events in Rome. He had started with a fairly large and enthusiastic force of men, raised first by Manlius and then reinforced by the men who followed Catilina from Rome. They had gathered veterans, deserters, runaway slaves and other malcontents in good numbers for a while. Then, when news of the execution of his supporters in Rome reached them, his followers deserted in great numbers. Thus, one might say that the executions, however illegal, were of benefit to Rome.

What we had facing us at the end was a force of two understrength legions. Just north of the Arno, near Pistoia, we brought him to battle. He had been campaigning in the mountains, retreating toward Gaul. From deserters, Celer had determined Catilina's route of march and had made a sweep around him and placed his legions right across it. With Antonius pushing slowly north with a far larger force, Catilina was being squeezed into a trap.

On the final day, I sat in my saddle next to Celer, uncomfortable in my armor. Before us we could see the rebel force: two understrength legions, a pitiful army with which to conquer the world. They were determined soldiers, though, and we were not going to get through the day without a hard fight. Celer signaled, the trumpets sounded, and the armies rushed together.

The Catilinarians fought with desperate courage, even though their cause was plainly lost. It was a painful thing, to see so many Romans and Italians behaving so heroically, without a chance of victory. There were no mounted troops. Catilina had sent his horse with the others to the rear, in order to fight on foot among his supporters. This was the act of a fine general.

The spears flew, the swords flashed and weapon rattled on shield and armor. It was a long, hard, grinding fight for there were no surrenders from the enemy. Not a single prisoner was taken that day, and none of the defeated sought mercy. It was as if they had all caught the disease of insanity and desperation from Catilina, although I am certain that Celer would have readily granted quarter, had it been asked.

In the end, I saw Catilina's last gesture. We had been taking bad casualties, so hard was the fight. With Celer, I had ridden to a position just behind the center. Over the helmets of several ranks of men, I could see Catilina next to his eagle, waving his sword and urging on his men. As he saw his flanks crumple inward and his forward ranks disintegrate, he came charging through his own ranks, stabbing and slashing. He pushed past his own front rank and plunged into ours, apparently trying to carve a path all the way through our ranks and cut down our commander. It was a Homeric act, and one belonging to the realm of legend, not to the real world.

Just before he went down in a welter of blood, cutting down foes right and left, I thought his eyes locked with mine. I thought I saw a look of reproach in them, before he fell for the last time. It was probably just my disordered mind that saw this. I hope so, at any rate.

There was an uncertain lull for a while, then the men realized that the fight was over. A cheer was raised and the soldiers began a chant, hailing Celer as *imperator*. He cut this off instantly, berating them for hailing him thus, after a fight in which only fellow-citizens had died. Shamefacedly, the soldiers set about collecting the loot of the battlefield. A centurion came to us and held up two objects. One was Catilina's head. The other was his sword.

I took the sword while Celer directed that the head be sent back to Rome. When that was done Celer turned to me. I was turning the sword over in my hands. It was a fine one, its ivory hilt carved with a serpent wrapped spirally around it. The eyes were tiny rubies.

"It ends as it began," I said.

"What's that you say?" Celer asked.

"Nothing," I said.

"That's an African sword, isn't it?" Celer commented.

"He must have picked it up when he was *propraetor* there a few years ago."

"He picked up quite a few of them," I muttered.

"Keep it," Celer said. "You ought to have a souvenir out of this miserable business." I kept it. I have it still.

"What now?" I asked after a while.

"Why don't you come with me?" Celer said. "I've spoken with your father. Rome's a bad place for you just now. Pompey will be back in a few months and there's bad blood between you. Crassus has reason to dislike you as well. Be my *proquaestor* in Gaul. You can use the experience and when you get back those two will have forgotten about you."

I thought about it, but not for long. "I'm with you."

Thus perished Lucius Sergius Catilina, a man who could never acknowledge his own lack of greatness, and who was never more than a tool in the hands of greater men.

These things occurred during the years 691 and 692 of the City of Rome, in the Consulates of Marcus Tullius Cicero and Caius Antonius Hibrida, and that of Decimus Junius Silanus and Lucius Licinius Murena.

GLOSSARY

(Definitions apply to the last century of the Republic.)

Acta: Streets wide enough for one-way wheeled traffic.

Aedile: Elected officials in charge of upkeep of the city and the grain dole, regulation of public morals, management of the markets and the public Games. There were two types: the plebeian aediles, who had no insignia of office, and the curule aediles, who wore the toga praetexta and sat in the sella curulis. The curule aediles could sit in judgment on civil cases involving markets and currency, while the plebeian aediles could only levy fines. Otherwise, their duties were the same. Since the magnificence of the Games one exhibited as aedile often determined election to higher office, it was an important stepping-stone in a political career. The office of aedile did not carry the imperium.

Ancile: (pl. ancilia) A small, oval sacred shield which fell from heaven in the reign of King Numa. Since there was a prophecy that it was tied to the stability of Rome, Numa had eleven exact copies made so nobody would know which one to steal. Their care was entrusted to a college of priests, the *Salii* (q.v.) and figured in a number of ceremonies each year.

Atrium: Once a word for house, in Republican times it was the entry hall of a house, opening off the street and used as a general reception area.

Atrium Vestae: The Palace of the Vestal and one of the most splendid buildings in Rome.

Augur: An official who observed omens for state purposes. He could forbid business and assemblies if he saw unfavorable omens.

Basilica: A building where courts met in inclement weather.

Caestus: The Classical boxing glove, made of leather straps and reinforced by bands, plates or spikes of bronze.

Caliga: The Roman military boot. Actually, a heavy sandal with hobnailed sole.

Campus Martius: A field outside the old city wall, formerly the assembly area and drill field for the army. It was where the popular assemblies met. By late Republican times, buildings were encroaching on the field.

Censor: Magistrates elected usually every fifth year to oversee the census of the citizens and purge the roll of Senators of unworthy members. They could forbid certain religious practices or luxuries deemed bad for public morals or generally "un-Roman." There were two Censors, and each could overrule the other. They wore the toga praetexta and sat in the sella curulis, but since they had no executive powers they were not accompanied by lictors. The office did not carry the imperium. Censors were usually elected from among the ex-Consuls, and the censorship was regarded as the capstone of a political career.

Centuriate Assembly: (comitia centuriata) Originally, the annual military assembly of the citizens where they joined their army units ("centuries"). There were one hundred ninety-three centuries divided into five classes by property qualification. They elected the highest magistrates: Censors, Consuls and Praetors. By the middle Republic, the centuriate assembly was strictly a voting body, having lost all military character.

Centurion: "Commander of 100"; i.e., a century, which, in practice, numbered around sixty men. Centurions were promoted from the ranks and were the backbone of the professional army.

Circus: The Roman racecourse and the stadium which enclosed it. The original, and always the largest, was the Circus Maximus, which lay between the Palatine and Aventine hills. A later, smaller circus, the Circus Flaminius, lay outside the walls on the Campus Martius.

Client: One attached in a subordinate relationship to a patron, whom he was bound to support in war and in the courts. Freedmen became clients of their former masters. The relationship was hereditary.

Coemptio: Marriage by symbolic sale. Before five witnesses and a *libripens* who held a balance, the bridegroom struck the balance with a bronze coin and handed it to the father or guardian of the bride. Unlike conferreatio, coemptio was easily dissolved by divorce.

Cognomen: The family name, denoting any of the stirpes of a gens; i.e., Caius Julius *Caesar:* Caius of the stirps Caesar of gens Julii. Some plebeian families never adopted a cognomen, notably the Marii and the Antonii.

Coitio: A political alliance between two men, uniting their voting blocs. Usually it was an agreement between politicians who were otherwise antagonists, in order to edge out mutual rivals.

Colonia: Towns which had been conquered by Rome, where Roman citizens were settled. Later, settlements founded by discharged veterans of the legions. After 89 B.C. all Italian colonia had full rights of citizenship. Those in the provinces had limited citizenship.

Compluvium: An opening in a roof to admit light.

Conferreatio: The most sacred and binding of Roman forms of marriage. The bride and groom offered a cake of spelt to Jupiter in the presence of a pontifex and the flamen Dialis. It was the ancient patrician form of marriage. By the late Republic it was obsolete except for some priesthoods in which the priest was required to be married by conferreatio.

Consul: Supreme magistrate of the Republic. Two were elected each year. Insignia were the toga praetexta and the sella curulis. Each Consul was attended by twelve lictors. The office carried full imperium. On the expiration of his year in office, the ex-Consul was usually assigned a district outside Rome to rule as proconsul. As proconsul, he had the same insignia and the same number of lictors. His power was absolute within his province.

Curia: The meetinghouse of the Senate, located in the Forum.

Dictator: An absolute ruler chosen by the Senate and the Consuls to deal with a specific emergency. For a limited period, never more than six months, he was given unlimited imperium, which he was to lay down upon resolution of the emergency. Unlike the Consuls, he had no colleague to overrule him and he was not accountable for his actions performed during office

when he stepped down. His insignia were the toga praetexta and the sella curulis and he was accompanied by
twenty-four lictors, the number of both Consuls. Dictatorships were extremely rare and the last was held in
202 B.C. The dictatorships of Sulla and Caesar were unconstitutional.

Dioscuri: Castor and Pollux, the twin sons of Zeus and
Leda. The Romans revered them as protectors of the
city.

Eques: (pl. equites) Formerly, citizens wealthy enough to
supply their own horses and fight in the cavalry, they
came to hold their status by meeting a property qualification. They formed the moneyed upper-middle class.
In the centuriate assembly they formed eighteen centuries and once had the right of voting first, but they
lost this as their military function disappeared. The
publicans, financiers, bankers, moneylenders and tax-
farmers came from the equestrian class.

Faction: In the Circus, the supporters of the four racing
companies: Red, White, Blue and Green. Most Romans
were fanatically loyal to one of these.

Fasces: A bundle of rods bound around an ax with a
red strap, symbolizing a Roman magistrate's power of
corporal and capital punishment. They were carried by
the lictors who accompanied the curule magistrates, the
Flamen Dialis, and the proconsuls and propraetors who
governed provinces. When a lower magistrate met a
higher, his lictors lowered their fasces in salute.

Flamen: A high priest of a specific god of the state. The
college of flamines had fifteen members: three patrician
and twelve plebeian. The three highest were the Flamen
Dialis, the Flamen Martialis and the Flamen Quirinalis.
They had charge of the daily sacrifices and wore dis-
tinctive headgear and were surrounded by many ritual
taboos. The Flamen Dialis, high priest of Jupiter, was
entitled to the toga praetexta, which had to be woven
by his wife, the sella curulis and a single lictor, and he
could sit in the Senate. It became difficult to fill the
college of flamines because they had to be prominent
men, the appointment was for life and they could take
no part in politics.

Forum: An open meeting and market area. The premier forum was the Forum Romanum, located on the low ground surrounded by the Capitoline, Palatine and Caelian hills. It was surrounded by the most important temples and public buildings. Roman citizens spent much of their day there. The courts met outdoors in the Forum when the weather was good. When it was paved and devoted solely to public business, the Forum Romanum's market functions were transferred to the Forum Boarium, the cattle market, near the Circus Maximus. Small shops and stalls remained along the northern and southern peripheries, however.

Freedman: A manumitted slave. Formal emancipation conferred full rights of citizenship except for the right to hold office. Informal emancipation conferred freedom without voting rights. In the second or at latest third generation, a freedman's descendants became full citizens.

Genius: The guiding and guardian spirit of a person or place. The genius of a place was called genius loci.

Gens: A clan, all of whose members were descended from a single ancestor. The nomen of a patrician gens always ended with -ius. Thus, Caius *Julius* Caesar was Caius, of the Caesarian stirps of gens Julii.

Gladiator: Literally, "swordsman." A slave, prisoner of war, condemned criminal or free volunteer who fought, often to the death, in the munera. All were called swordsmen, even if they fought with other weapons.

Gladius: The short, broad, double-edged sword borne by Roman soldiers. It was designed primarily for stabbing. A smaller, more antiquated design of gladius was used by gladiators.

Gravitas: The quality of seriousness.

Haruspex: A member of a college of Etruscan professionals who examined the entrails of sacrificial animals for omens.

Hospitium: An arrangement of reciprocal hospitality. When visiting the other's city, each hospes (pl. hospites) was entitled to food and shelter, protection in court, care when ill or injured and honorable burial, should he die during the visit. The obligation was binding on both families and was passed on to descendants.

Ides: The 15th of March, May, July and October. The 13th of other months.

Imperium: The ancient power of kings to summon and lead armies, to order and forbid and to inflict corporal and capital punishment. Under the Republic, the imperium was divided among the Consuls and Praetors, but they were subject to appeal and intervention by the tribunes in their civil decisions and were answerable for their acts after leaving office. Only a dictator had unlimited imperium.

Insula: Literally, "island." A large, multistory tenement block.

Itinera: Streets wide enough for only foot traffic. The majority of Roman streets were itinera.

Janitor: A slave-doorkeeper, so called for Janus, god of gateways.

Kalends: The first of any month.

Latifundium: A large landed estate or plantation worked by slaves. During the late Republic these expanded tremendously, all but destroying the Italian peasant class.

Legates: Subordinate commanders chosen by the Senate to accompany generals and governors. Also, ambassadors appointed by the Senate.

Legion: Basic unit of the Roman army. Paper strength was six thousand, but usually closer to four thousand. All were armed as heavy infantry with a large shield, cuirass, helmet, gladius and light and heavy javelins. Each legion had attached to it an equal number of non-citizen auxiliaries consisting of light and heavy infantry, cavalry, archers, slingers, etc. Auxilia were never organized as legions, only as cohorts.

Lictor: Attendants, usually freedmen, who accompanied magistrates and the Flamen Dialis, bearing the fasces. They summoned assemblies, attended public sacrifices and carried out sentences of punishment. Twenty-four lictors accompanied a dictator, twelve for a Consul, six for a propraetor, two for a Praetor and one for the Flamen Dialis.

Liquamen: Also called garum, it was the ubiquitous fermented fish sauce used in Roman cooking.

Ludus: (pl. ludi) The official public Games, races, theatricals, etc. Also, a training school for gladiators, although the gladiatorial exhibitions were not ludi.

Munera: Special Games, not part of the official calendar, at which gladiators were exhibited. They were originally funeral Games and were always dedicated to the dead. In munera sine missione, all the defeated were killed and sometimes were made to fight sequentially or all at once until only one was left standing. Munera sine missione were periodically forbidden by law.

Municipia: Towns originally with varying degrees of Roman citizenship, but by the late Republic with full citizenship. A citizen from a municipium was qualified to hold any public office. An example is Cicero, who was not from Rome but from the municipium of Arpinum.

Nobiles: Those families, both patrician and plebeian, in which members had held the Consulate.

Nomen: The name of the clan or gens; i.e., Caius *Julius* Caesar.

Nones: The 7th of March, May, July and October. The 5th of other months.

Novus Homo: Literally, "new man." A man who is the first of his family to hold the Consulate, giving his family the status of nobiles.

Optimates: The party of the "best men"; i.e., aristocrats and their supporters.

Patria Potestas: The absolute authority of the pater familias over the children of his household, who could neither legally own property while their father was alive nor marry without his permission. Technically, he had the right to sell or put to death any of his children, but by Republican times this was a legal fiction.

Patrician: A descendant of one of the founding others of Rome. Once, only patricians could hold offices and priesthoods and sit in the Senate, but these privileges were gradually eroded until only certain priesthoods were strictly patrician. By the late Republic, only about fourteen gens remained.

Patron: A man with one or more clients whom he was bound to protect, advise and otherwise aid. The relationship was hereditary.

Peculium: Roman slaves could not own property, but

they could earn money outside the household, which was held for them by their masters. This fund was called a peculium, and could be used, eventually, to purchase the slave's freedom.

Peristylium: An open courtyard surrounded by a collonade.

Pietas: The quality of dutifulness toward the gods and, especially, toward one's parents.

Plebeian: All citizens not of patrician status.

Pomerium: The line of the ancient city wall, attributed to Romulus. Actually, the space of vacant ground just within and without the wall, regarded as holy. Within the pomerium it was forbidden to bear arms or bury the dead.

Pontifex: A member of the highest priestly college of Rome. They had superintendence over all sacred observances, state and private, and over the calendar. There were fifteen in the late Republic: seven patrician and eight plebeian. Their chief was the pontifex maximus, a title now held by the Pope.

Popular Assemblies: There were three: the centuriate assembly (comitia centuriata) and the two tribal assemblies: comitia tributa and consilium plebis, q.v.

Populares: The party of the common people.

Praenomen: The given name of a freedman, as Marcus, Sextus, Caius, etc.; i.e., *Caius* Julius Caesar: Caius of the stirps Caesar of gens Julii. Women used a feminine form of their father's nomen, i.e., the daughter of Caius Julius Caesar would be named Julia.

Praetor: Judge and magistrate elected yearly along with the Consuls. In the late Republic there were eight Praetors. Senior was the Praetor Urbanus, who heard civil cases between citizens. The Praetor Peregrinus heard cases involving foreigners. The others presided over criminal courts. Insignia were the toga praetexta and the sella curulis, and Praetors were accompanied by two lictors. The office carried the imperium. After leaving office, the ex-Praetors became propraetors and went to govern propraetorian provinces with full imperium.

Praetorium: A general's headquarters, usually a tent in camp. In the provinces, the official residence of the governor.

Princeps: "First Citizen." An especially distinguished Senator chosen by the Censors. His name was the first called on the roll of the Senate and he was first to speak on any issue. Later the title was usurped by Augustus and is the origin of the word "prince."

Proscription: List of names of public enemies published by Sulla. Anyone could kill a proscribed person and claim a reward, usually a part of the dead man's estate.

Publicans: Those who bid on public contracts, most notably builders and tax farmers. The contracts were usually let by the Censors and therefore had a period of five years.

Pugio: The straight, double-edged dagger of the Roman soldiers.

Quaestor: Lowest of the elected officials, they had charge of the treasury and financial matters such as payments for public works. They also acted as assistants and paymasters to higher magistrates, generals and provincial governors. They were elected yearly by the comitia tributa.

Quirinus: The deified Romulus, patron deity of the city.

Rostra: A monument in the Forum commemorating the sea battle of Antium in 338 B.C., decorated with the rams, "rostra" of enemy ships (sing. rostrum). Its base was used as an orator's platform.

Sagum: The Roman military cloak, made of wool and always dyed red. To put on the sagum signified the changeover to wartime status, as the toga was the garment of peace. When the citizens met in the *comitia centuriata* they wore the sagum in token of its ancient function as the military muster.

Salii: "Dancers." Two colleges of priests dedicated to Mars and Quirinus who held their rites in March and October, respectively. Each college consisted of twelve young patricians whose parents were still living. On their festivals, they dressed in embroidered tunics, a crested bronze helmet and breastplate and each bore one of the twelve sacred shields ("ancilia") and a staff. They processed to the most important altars of Rome and before each performed a war dance. The ritual was so ancient that, by the first century B.C., their songs and prayers were unintelligible.

Saturnalia: Feast of Saturn, December 17–23, a raucous

and jubilant occasion when gifts were exchanged, debts were settled and masters waited on their slaves.

Sella Curulis: A folding camp-chair. It was part of the insignia of the curule magistrates and the Flamen Dialis.

Senate: Rome's chief deliberative body. It consisted of three hundred to six hundred men, all of whom had won elective office at least once. Once the supreme ruling body, by the late Republic the Senate's former legislative and judicial functions had devolved upon the courts and the popular assemblies and its chief authority lay in foreign policy and the nomination of generals. Senators were privileged to wear the tunica laticlava.

Servile War: The slave rebellion led by the Thracian gladiator Spartacus in 73–71 B.C. The rebellion was crushed by Crassus and Pompey.

Sica: A single-edged dagger or short sword of varying size. It was favored by thugs and used by the Thracian gladiators in the arena. It was classified as an infamous rather than an honorable weapon.

Solarium: A rooftop garden and patio.

Spatha: The Roman cavalry sword, longer and narrower than the gladius.

SPQR: "Senatus populusque Romanus." The Senate and People of Rome. The formula embodying the sovereignty of Rome. It was used on official correspondence, documents and public works.

Stirps: A sub-family of a gens. The cognomen gave the name of the stirps, i.e., Caius Julius *Caesar:* Caius of the stirps Caesar of gens Julii.

Strigil: A bronze implement, roughly s-curved, used to scrape sand and oil from the body after bathing. Soap was unknown to the Roman Republic.

Strophium: A cloth band worn by women beneath or over the clothing to support the breasts.

Subligaculum: A loincloth, worn by men and women.

Subura: A neighborhood on the lower slopes of the Viminal and Esquiline, famed for its slums, noisy shops and raucous inhabitants.

Tarpeian Rock: A cliff beneath the Capitol from which traitors were hurled. It was named for the Roman maiden Tarpeia who, according to legend, betrayed the Capitol to the Sabines.

Temple of Jupiter Capitolinus: The most important temple of the state religion. Triumphal processions ended with a sacrifice at this temple.

Temple of Saturn: The state treasury was located in a crypt beneath this temple. It was also the repository for military standards.

Temple of Vesta: Site of the sacred fire tended by the vestal virgins and dedicated to the goddess of the hearth. Documents, especially wills, were deposited there for safekeeping.

Toga: The outer robe of the Roman citizen. It was white for the upper classes, darker for the poor and for people in mourning. The toga praetexta, bordered with a purple stripe, was worn by curule magistrates, by state priests when performing their functions and by boys prior to manhood. The toga picta, purple and embroidered with golden stars, was worn by a general when celebrating a triumph, also by a magistrate when giving public Games.

Tonsores: A slave trained as a barber and hairdresser.

Trans-Tiber: A newer district on the right or western bank of the Tiber. It lay beyond the old city walls.

Tribal Assemblies: There were two: the comitia tributa, an assembly of all citizens by tribes, which elected the lower magistrates—curule aediles, and quaestors, also the military tribunes—and the concilium plebis, consisting only of plebeians, elected the tribunes of the plebs and the plebeian aediles.

Tribe: Originally, the three classes of patricians. Under the Republic, all citizens belonged to tribes of which there were four city tribes and thirty-one country tribes. New citizens were enrolled in an existing tribe.

Tribune: Representative of the plebeians with power to introduce laws and to veto actions of the Senate. Only plebeians could hold the office, which carried no imperium. Military tribunes were elected from among the young men of senatorial or equestrian rank to be assistants to generals. Usually it was the first step of a man's political career.

Triumph: A magnificent ceremony celebrating military

victory. The honor could be granted only by the Senate, and until he received permission, the victorious general had to remain outside the city walls, as his command ceased the instant he crossed the pomerium. The general, called the triumphator, received royal, near-divine honors and became a virtual god for a day. A slave was appointed to stand behind him and remind him periodically of his mortality lest the gods become jealous.

Triumvir: A member of a triumvirate—a board or college of three men. Most famously, the three-man rule of Caesar, Pompey and Crassus. Later, the triumvirate of Antonius, Octavian and Lepidus.

Tunica: A long, loose shirt, sleeveless or short-sleeved, worn by citizens beneath the toga when outdoors and by itself indoors. The tunica laticlava had a broad purple stripe from neck to hem and was worn by Senators and patricians. The tunica angusticlava had a narrow stripe and was worn by the equites. The tunica picta, purple and embroidered with golden palm branches, was worn by a general when he celebrated a triumph.

Usus: The most common form of marriage, in which a man and woman lived together for a year without being separated for three consecutive nights.

Via: A highway. Within the city, viae were streets wide enough for two wagons to pass one another. There were only two viae during the Republic: the Via Sacra, which ran through the Forum and was used for religious processions and triumphs, and the Via Nova, which ran along one side of the Forum.

Vigile: A night watchman. The vigiles had the duty of apprehending felons caught committing crimes, but their main duty was as a fire watch. They were unarmed except for staves and carried fire-buckets.